*My lycanthropic clock struck
the next morning . . .*

The majority of my stretches come when I least
expect them. It begins as a spark in my solar plexus.
During these times, the werewolf legend and the werewolf reality meet. It feels like my insides are shredding.
I'm positive that my heart is torn from its moorings and
my lungs are flayed with each labored breath I take. My
intestines cramp and one of these days I'm certain that
they're going to explode.

The pain makes me howl.

Quantum Moon

QUANTUM MOON

DENISE VITOLA

ACE BOOKS, NEW YORK

This book is an Ace original edition,
and has never been previously published.

QUANTUM MOON

An Ace Book / published by arrangement with
the author

PRINTING HISTORY
Ace edition / August 1996

The Putnam Berkley World Wide Web site address is
http://www.berkley.com

ISBN: 0-441-00357-5

ACE®
Ace Books are published by The Berkley Publishing Group,
200 Madison Avenue, New York, NY 10016.
ACE and the "A" design are trademarks
belonging to Charter Communications, Inc.

PRINTED IN THE UNITED STATES OF AMERICA

10 9 8 7 6 5 4 3 2 1

For Irene Kraas.
Because she keeps believing.

1

MARIA RAYNOR'S HUSBAND, Jack, didn't like to be seen with her in public. He said it didn't look good for the councilman representing District One to have his picture taken with his arm around a three hundred pound woman, especially when so much of the world was starving.

She should have listened to her mother. Mother always harped on the importance of marrying carefully. A nice boy who did honest work like delivering natural gas for appreciative customers right in their own neighborhood had been her idea of a good companion, but Maria hadn't listened. She had wanted wealth and comfort. She had wanted a man who was known and admired. She had wanted a handsome man who wanted a large family unit.

Squeezing in with memories of Mother's old reprimands was the sound of the wind. It was the rainy season, and a big storm was coming up the coast. If she were home in Ward Three right now, she would be helping her younger brother to collect this free water, but here it wasn't necessary to do all that extra work. Instead, she sat alone in her rich house, bingeing on homemade ice cream and admitting to herself that she could have done better in choosing a mate.

Because she was so unhappy, she ate constantly and yes, the pounds did not magically recycle like the daily trash. They'd come on and on, stockpiling in her body until she was full to overflowing with fat.

Her problems all had to do with Jack and his philandering. He acted as if that wasn't his fault, too. The man was trying to drive her away with his constant nagging about the rising waste tax levied on household utilities. He screamed

1

each time the monthly statement showed that they'd exceeded their allotment of electricity and water, but he really lost his temper when he found out that the weekly refuse weighed almost as much as she did. Keep it low, he shouted. Recycle! The less trash they had, the more credit allowances they could earn at the end of the year and then, maybe, he said, not every extra cent of his paycheck would go toward funding her indulgences.

Well, he wasn't perfect, either. He took a hot shower on those mornings when he was home. He played his stereo and then would forget to turn it off while he went out to do errands. He would use three hours' worth of natural gas to bake a roast beef for a business associate he wanted to impress.

Maria sighed and tucked her feet up under her, digging for the vid control buried in a crease of the sofa. When she did, she felt crumbs lining this velour nest. She licked her forefinger and retrieved the droppings, discovering as she did that Jack had been eating chocolate cookies. It made her instantly angry, but it was useless rage, so it disappeared quickly. If she confronted him with this evidence of his own excesses, he would just smack her across the face and call her a fat, selfish bitch.

It wasn't fair. She was trying to lose the weight. Her friend had a great idea that was supposed to work. You could eat anything, he said. Just don't forget to take the pill twice a day. On top of that, she had the other things, too. One of them was bound to start melting the pounds away.

Maria ate the errant cookie morsels before tuning in to the evening broadcast to see the news of the coming storm. The reception was lousy, a sure sign that the government was rationing power again by cutting down on the available electricity feeding the district's only vid station. She stared at the fuzzy screen for a bit and realized that there would be

no weather report tonight. The whole half-hour program
was devoted to pushing the humanitarian party line by
showing scenes of a famine in progress.

This particular horror was in District Four Hundred Ten,
three thousand miles south and a continent away. You would
think they'd have plenty of food, because the climate was so
mild for growing. It was nothing more than pure misman-
agement by local officials, and because of it, the Confederated
government was getting into it, trying to divert resources to
help the unfortunates affected.

One day, the whole world would go down the shit hole
and people like Jack would be out of a job.

The glass in the French doors rattled, causing Maria to
stop pushing the dessert into her mouth. She turned a bit to
glance behind her but saw nothing out of the ordinary. The
blue shimmer of the security net enveloping the house
reflected comfortingly through the windows.

She returned to her snack, using the tip of her tongue to
coax the ice cream from the back of the spoon. The flavors
were so sensual that they had sex with her; chocolate fudge
foreplay and an orgasm of caramel delight. It made her
moan.

Sex. That was something she hadn't had in a while. Jack
was always gone, just like he was this night. With a violent
storm in sight of land, he was out whooping it up with some
hussy. Tomorrow or the next day, he would come home
complaining of hard work and late hours.

The wind banged at the entryway again, and suddenly the
electricity went out right in the middle of her binge. She
sighed, then smiled. What horrible luck! If the power didn't
come on soon, she'd be forced to eat the other tubs of ice
cream stored in the freezer. Her husband couldn't have a
problem with that. Waste was waste. She couldn't let
anything spoil.

She shoveled the dessert for a few more minutes before struggling from the encompassing folds of the couch to stand, stretch, and grope her way into the kitchen in search of a flashlight. Even though the power was out, the shine from the digital counter attached to the freezer door was still maintained by a battery charge. It reflected in bright red numbers how many times she'd opened it this week: six hundred forty-seven. By Friday, the total would exceed a thousand.

What the display measured was beyond her, but Jack often grumbled about the rising cost of refrigerant and how in a recycled world, this chemical was getting hard to come by. When the memory was dumped for taxing purposes, she would be in trouble with him. Maria shrugged off the thought. What was new about that?

The recharge unit for the flashlight was set up on the counter by the stove, but as usual, she'd forgotten to store the lamp, so it was on to the pantry to root out a candle and matches. She found both easily enough, except that Jack had left the matchbox open. All the little sticks spilled out onto the floor.

A genuine sigh gushed from her. Now she would have to scoop them up. Meanwhile, her ice cream was melting and to add to her predicament, she heard the wind beat open the French doors. She felt the chill of a damp November night and started worrying about her silk curtains being torn by flying debris. With a grunt, she leaned down to collect the matches and light the candle. The flame waffled for a moment, but straightened out as she shielded it with her hand. She toddled back toward the living room.

It had started raining, and the wind blew streamers of dirty water onto her white carpet. She hurried to shut the doors, her steps shaking the china pieces displayed in the cabinet as she passed by. The breeze snuffed out her pitiful light before she managed to clamp the doors closed again.

Maria returned to the kitchen, lit another candle, collected her ice cream, and went back to the sofa. She had just put a glob of goodie into her mouth when her eyes finally adjusted to the darkness and she noticed the man standing in the shadows by Jack's favorite chair.

At first she thought it was a trick of her brain, caused from all the sugar she was eating. Mother had often said how too many sweets could bring on hallucinations.

The shadows created too many hard angles for her to be sure, but for a moment, she thought it was her husband sneaking in to check up on her dieting.

The man came toward her, eliminating the idea that he was a figment of her imagination. As he stepped into the glow cast by the candles, she recognized him.

Maria was so startled by his appearance that it took her a second to think about speaking. In that uncertain interim, the intruder came forward to grab her by the hair and shove the spoon down her throat.

2

I DON'T LIKE death threats, especially where environmental tax auditors are concerned, but I have to admit that I considered making one.

When they assigned him to me, I knew Henderson was

going to be trouble. He enjoys our encounters because he always wins. I can't take a belch in the park without him finding out. He's the toughest ETA ever to be born. One of these days, I'm going to choke the SOB so hard that his beady, black eyeballs will pop right out of his head and roll around on the floor. Then, I'm going to stomp on them.

It was Tuesday. I'd been called to the mat at precisely 12:03 P.M. You never know when an audience will be mandated, and as for me, I'd been yanked in four times in the last two quarters to discuss things like why my toilet paper consumption was so high.

Henderson is short, bald, plump, and smells like he rations soap at his house. "You've severely exceeded your electricity allowance, again, Marshall Merrick," he said. "If you keep going like this, by the end of the year you're going to be paying some stiff penalties for flagrant disregard of environmental limits." He paused and then visibly warmed to the subject. "Your Class A designation will be pulled if you can't pay the tax. I know I keep repeating myself on this, but if you don't do something, you'll eventually lose your job and someone else whose proven himself frugal and hardworking will move up into your place." He smiled. "I do expect it to happen. Soon."

I placed my hands on his desk and tried to look menacing. "I have a certificate of disease from the Planetary Health Organization," I growled. "You can't dispute the medical records. I need electricity for light therapy to keep my seizures down. How many times do I have to tell you that?"

His voice grew sharp. "It doesn't matter what your problem is. Your petitions to up your electricity allowance have been denied. Repeatedly. You'd think you'd have gotten the message by now."

I sat back in the chair, flustered, frustrated, and sure of my defeat. Taking a breather while he computed my tax, I glanced around at the line of other desks in his big, gray, windowless room. The place was crowded as usual, and as usual, too quiet for the number of people trying to work through their returns. I wondered, again, how they could do it without shouting. In the next moment, I was reminded why—they didn't have an ETA like Henderson.

"Your claim is ridiculous, Ms. Merrick," he said. "Lycanthropy? No one in the Office of Taxation believes that you have such a disease. The physician who wrote the certificate is no longer at the PHO. I checked. He died in one of our assorted plague situations." He tapped his pencil on the desk pad and then added wearily: "It was a swindle on your part from the start. Don't you realize that there are millions of needy people who would give assorted body parts to have as much electricity allowance as you have for the size of your family unit? We consider your claims for more power to be unsubstantiated and frivolous."

"Don't you mean *you* consider it unsubstantiated and frivolous? My claim is probably lying in the bottom of your in basket."

"You're not endearing yourself to me."

"Look, I support a senior. She has to stay warm, you know."

"Is it my fault that her pension doesn't include a larger portion of electricity credits? She cut the deal with her company when she retired. She should have thought about it then."

There was no talking to this beast, so I stood up to leave. He followed my rise calmly by tilting his chin.

"Where are you going? We're not finished here."

"I am. Call me later with the bad news."

"Don't you want the opportunity to defend your other claims?"

"I really don't care." I took my time zipping up my fake

goose down vest. "You know, Mr. Henderson, since you're so good at giving advice, I'd like to return the favor."

"What, then?"

"Never, under any circumstances, hold one of these interviews with me on a full moon, because if you do and you give me more snotty-assed trouble, I'll take my fist and use it to ram your nose into the back of your head." Smiling sweetly, I winked and then fled the office and building, stepping into an afternoon of cold, stinging rain.

I had just flipped up my hood when my communications node nearly deafened me. I tapped down the volume on the earplug, hearing as I did, my partner's voice summoning me to a crime scene. Before going off-line, he said: "You aren't going to believe this one, Ty."

I tend to be a cynic where unbelievable things are concerned, but I'll admit to being one who can be conned into exploring the possibility of something interesting, so I jumped the subway at Viking Street and came out topside into Ward Two, a neighborhood known as Shanghai Alley.

This section of District One is all rickshaws and bamboo shacks. Electricity and natural gas are things that they have a couple of blocks away, but despite the lack of utilities, this section is, undeniably, a special place. The environmental corporations should take a lesson from here about what good air smells like. It shouldn't be bland, because it's too clean. It needs layers and nuances to excite the nose. When you visit Shanghai Alley, you can savor the odors of stir-frying vegetables, grilling meats, and pickled cabbages that remind you of dirty feet. The people create this glorious flood of olfactory sensation without the obvious amenities of the modern world. From what I know, they literally have one can of Sterno per fifty family units. They've learned to share fire as though it was communal property.

I trudged onward with hands in pockets and head bent

low against the sleet until I came upon the subway entrance at Traveler's Circle. I ducked inside just in time to throw my token at the commuter operator and catch a departing train. The car was packed, but no one spoke; there was no distraction at all, which left me alone with only my irritating internal dialogue to sort through.

I wasn't lying to Henderson. I really am a werewolf, but I prefer to think of myself as a lycanthrope. It lends some medical credence to a condition that seems suspended in the supernatural.

You see, a few years back, I was on a stakeout trying to nab a serial killer. A ward cop and I were assigned to a room across the street from our murderer's apartment. We were trading off surveillance time, and one night I was on duty and freezing my rear end off, so I flipped on the furnace. The next thing I remember was waking up in a health care clinic and finding out that I had been overcome by carbon monoxide. I was lucky the officer returned to bring me some dinner before going home for the evening. He found me unconscious and sliding toward death. He should have let me die, because after I was released from the hospital, I began to have strange seizures, which I refer to as stretches.

They occur throughout the lunar month and their onset is impossible to predict, but I have found that the worse the stress, the more stretches will occur. Sometimes, I'll have upward of ten convulsions; other times, I'll have as few as three. One thing is for certain; these stretches take me into my subtle lycanthropic form. They increase in length and ferocity until the day of the full moon when the transformation becomes complete and for twelve solid hours, I'm suspended in an eerie place where demons dwell.

What happens to me in the course of my transformation is nothing like the stories and vids would have you believe. I've read myths where a person will purposely seek out this disposition by doing such crazy things as wearing a wolf's pelt while drinking the warm blood of a freshly killed animal. According to some of these legends, it's a desirable circumstance in which to be, because it's a chance to control supernatural power akin to that wielded by sorcerers or shamans. Well, if magic sparks fly, I've yet to see them, because my own transformation into a werewolf is not so much a periodic, metaphysical alchemy, but is instead the unsanctioned development of a dark and dangerous psyche.

I, of course, went from doctor to doctor looking for a cure. I kept coming away being labeled as mildly delusional or as having something called a bipolar disorder, which was caused by the accident. Then, one day, I met Dr. Pastore, who said I exhibited all the signs of lycanthropic melancholia. He told me the medical profession didn't know much about this particular madness. They thought of it as an alteration in brain waves, but since little research had been done on the condition since the twentieth century, not much more was known about it.

I have my own theories of lycanthropy, and whether it has to do with the gravitational effects of the moon or the increased hormonal activity of my monthly cycle, it has become a regular part of my life rhythm. Dr. Pastore recommended light therapy to alter my erratic delta brain waves. For the last several months, the stretches have seemed milder, even though it just might be my fancy on the matter.

After several subway stops, I finally jumped off at Ward Eight, the comfortable neighborhood of district officials, professionals, and advisors. Unlike the rest of the locality, there are no power blackouts here and the water comes into the houses via copper pipes and spigots. Whole family units could live on the contents of just one of their trash cans. Still, they weren't immune to bad weather and the rain came down just as hard in this upper-class section, so I kicked into a jog toward my destination. Five blocks later, I found the home surrounded by emergency vehicles. I wound my way through curious residents, stepped over the crime scene cordon, and identified myself as a district marshal to the uniformed ward cop posted at the entrance.

He checked my badge and let me squish on inside. I paused in the foyer to toss back my hood and drip on the Oriental carpet.

We're talking *house* here. There were cathedral ceilings so high that they must have had a heating bill from hell. The place was polished teak wood, expensive silk, and sparkling crystal. It was conspicuous consumption at its best, and I was immediately so envious that my mood tripped downward a notch. Compared to this joint, I lived inside a turkey carcass.

My partner, Andy LaRue, ducked around a corner to greet me, and when I saw him, I couldn't help a smile. He's a handsome fellow underneath it all, but he always looks like he's just gotten in from a day spent bin diving. He has curly, waist-length, dark brown hair that usually needs combing, and it's a good thing that his standard issue cammies are black, because he wears a variety of stains upon them. He totes a fifty caliber Magnum Death Piece, which he will gladly show you, just so he can talk about the craftsmanship of the hand-tooled shoulder holster, and from there, he'll go on to explain how this is a dying art form. If you don't interrupt, you'll soon be caught in a noose of useless information.

"How'd it go with the tax man?" he asked.

"About like I expected, Andy. What do we have?"

I could tell by the way he stared at me that he didn't want to turn the subject, but after a moment, he did. "Her name is Maria Raynor. She was the wife of Councilman Jack

Raynor. Remember him; the guy who shoved through the district bill on the rotating power program so that all PHO facilities would have electricity on a constant basis?"

"Oh, yeah. He's in charge of public health policy, right?"

LaRue nodded. "I see from your look, you're wondering the same thing I am: Why would someone kill his wife instead of him?"

"He would make a great target, that's for sure. A whole lot of people are going to go cold this winter because of him."

"Jack claims that he was out of the district this week and he just got home this evening. According to the forensic tech, she appears to have been dead for almost two days."

We strolled deeper into a plush living room where we were met with antiques, electronic equipment, and house plants that you couldn't eat. Hanging over the stone fireplace was a six-foot, flat-screened vid. The response team on the case was large and there were folks working all over, except for a few who stood in the middle of the crime scene glued to a broadcast of an interdistrict soccer tournament. Mrs. Raynor was lying dead on the couch right beside them.

A good, hearty stink blended with the sweet odor of cadaver de toilette, a spray disinfectant. Ever since my accident, I've not appreciated this smell though I encounter it in some form nearly every day. Death, alone, is bad enough, but when you mix it with perfume, you have serious air pollution problem.

I hunkered down beside a photographer who was taking some close-ups of this enormous woman. He muttered something about needing a wide-angle lense to get her whole body in the picture.

The victim lay on her stomach and her dark hair was flung forward to cover a portion of her face. She was naked, except for a pair of white socks and a large, brightly colored, woven bag hanging about her neck. Her left hand was draped over the side of the couch and looked as though she had tried to reach a plastic tub half full of melted ice cream.

Not only was she dead, her body had been mutilated, as well. Long, vertical panels of skin and muscle located on her butt and thighs had been sliced away with what appeared to be surgical precision.

"I take it Councilman Jack is being sedated and such?" I asked.

"Health Care Facility Twenty," LaRue answered. "He was pretty shaken up."

"From what I've seen and heard of the man, I can't imagine that."

"I'd say you're right, but his act was convincing."

Mrs. Raynor had died the way she had fallen. The rolls of fat eclipsing her torso were purple with lividity, the postmortem circumstance where the blood pools at the lowest point of the body. Rigor mortis looked as though it had come and gone.

"Cause of death," LaRue announced, "was suffocation. Without disturbing the body, it appears that she has a rather large spoon lodged in her throat. From what we can tell, this artwork on her backside was done shortly after she died. At this point, we can't find any detectable signs of struggle."

I nodded, disconnecting from my review to admire the beauty of the wood on the French doors. "Was the security system knocked out or just turned off?"

"Hard to tell. The house's computer processor was down when we got here. The electrical field fizzled at some point. We're canvasing the neighborhood for anyone who might have seen something going on over here, but I don't expect much."

"Have you had a chance to have a good look around?"

"Oh, yes. You may find the kitchen interesting." He led me down a short hall decorated with family photos and handmade flower wreathes. We were met by several investigators lurking over spills and bread crumbs.

I was amazed. The galley was huge and the appliances were state of the art. There wasn't an ice cooler or propane burner in sight, but there was a restaurant-size refrigerator and stove, a dishwasher, rubbish compactor, and more consumption gauges than I'd ever seen in one place in my whole life. The meters were all fully functional, keeping a register of the number of times the fridge was cracked and the amount of natural gas used when the oven was heated. There was even a counter on the sink to measure the water flowing down the drain. I wondered briefly what we'd find in the bathroom.

Now, being the kind of person who does what she can to scam the system, I found all these indicators to be a little excessive, even for a wealthy family unit who could easily afford the waste taxes. I guess I must have stared with an open mouth, because LaRue laughed.

"Bizarre, isn't it?" he said.

"Do you actually think this guy lives under all the restrictions he votes in?"

"It looks like it. Maybe it's a political thing. You know, he doesn't want the ethics board to get the idea that he's on the take."

Two ward cops grubbed through the trash can. I wiggled by them to check out the pantry. "Were the cupboards razed?"

"I doesn't appear so."

He came over to lean against the wall, shielding me from the officers with his bulk. I yanked open the closet door to see what provisions might be inside.

It was a wonderland of food, stocked to the hilt: instant

dinners and cans of soup, packets of freeze-dried vegetables and bottles of carbonated soda.

A voodoo bottle hung from a brass hook just inside the door. These containers are filled with dirt from a graveyard, a bit of dried grass, old buttons and paper clips, and then lined with a special magical incantation to ensure that a thief couldn't come along and steal food, because if he did, he would grow sick in the belly and die. It's pure bullshit, but it did make me wonder what was inside that charm Maria had around her neck.

"Would you look at this stuff?" I whispered.

"Fantastic, huh?" He turned toward the investigators. "Take it in the other room, gentlemen. I want to talk to the district marshal in private for a moment."

They all shook their heads knowingly and did as they were ordered, slamming the kitchen door behind them. LaRue swiveled his attention to me once more as I unzipped my jacket and held it open so he could help me load up the oversized pockets sewn inside.

3

LaRue collects Soviet Communism. Get him started, and he can tell you all about Russia and the Bolshevik Revolution, the overthrow of the party, the years under Stalin, Yeltsin, Petrovsky, Lobrogov, and the eventual UN interference that led to the trouble we have now. He can tutor you in the best way to make borscht, brown bread, and potato pancakes. He knows all the old writers and musical composers, and he insists that a bottle of vodka needs to be blended with a bulb of crushed garlic to give it some taste. On top of this, he drives an antique, East German Trabant, replete with Victorian chintz upholstery, a silver cross dangling from the rearview mirror, and on the back dash, a spring-necked plastic statue of Lenin that, with each bump, bobs its head and squeaks, "Comrade! Comrade!"

I'm not sure what this says about a man who is of French-Canadian extraction on both sides of his family unit. What I am sure about is this: Even though LaRue gets extra gas credits because he uses his own vehicle in service to the District Marshals Office, he still drives like crap.

He gave me a ride from the crime scene to my flat in Ward Thirteen. The rainstorms hadn't done much for the conditions of the roads and this didn't help LaRue's marginal steering abilities, so by the time we reached the boundaries of the neighborhood, I was more than ready to climb from his little Baltic box on wheels.

I live in a three-room apartment in a low-rent neighborhood. My tenement building shares the street with the district's paper recycling plant and glass cooking factory. It's a gritty, industrial stretch along the Black River, which intersects the entire locality. I'll tell you a fact, too, about that flow of water: It didn't get its name for nothing.

Before LaRue had a chance to stop completely, I bolted from the car and charged toward the building's stairs. I expected him to follow me, but he paused to check his alignment with the curb, finding, as usual, that his parallel parking stank. I heard him call the car a Communist bitch and then he rushed inside behind me.

My flat is five floors up, chiseled in the space just under the tenement's eaves. My roommate, Baba, and I are

cramped, but at least we don't have to share a toilet at the
end of the hall like the other residents do. The walls, though,
have long since turned the colors of a bloody egg yolk, and
years ago someone decided that black trim would accent the
small windows and bore-ridden molding. We hid the stains
and the chipped paint with Baba's rubbish rugs, weavings
made from rags, bits of thread, yarns, used plastic wrap, and
sliced-up cardboard.

LaRue and I pushed into the apartment and shook down.
Baba watched us silently by the light of a propane lantern as
she sat before her loom where she worked on her latest
masterpiece. The place was freezing.

"Baba, we can afford heat," I said.

"Oh, I know, dear, but I'm really quite warm. I've got my
thermals on. And these." She poked out her leg and wiggled
her feet to show us a slipper made from assorted pieces of
malleable garbage. "Do you believe that someone actually
threw away a perfectly good chair? I was out on one of my
forays the other day and found it on the curb. I got to it
before anyone else had a chance, but I wasn't greedy about
it. I took the stuffing and the fabric and left the wood and
springs." She threw in a cackle. "Don't you think I did a
good job? Pretty, aren't they?"

"Very nice, Baba," LaRue said. "But if you're not cold,
are you hungry?"

"Yes, that I am."

I walked over to the rickety kitchen table and began
unloading my pockets. "We have treats tonight. Things
you've only dreamed about." I pulled out a package of dried
cherries and held it up for her to see. "When was the last
time you had fruit?"

She stopped weaving and rose to join us. "It's been at
least six months. I take it that it went well with the tax man.
Are we celebrating?"

It was a moment before I answered because my attention fell immediately upon the three banks of light tubes necessary for my therapy. They were the focal point of the room and had taken me nearly a year of scrounging to find. The setup would be a hard thing to avoid. "No, we're not celebrating," I finally replied. "In fact, we have to cut back on the electricity." As I said it, I rebelled by flipping on the space heater.

"That gentleman, Mr. Henderson, has it in for you, my dear," she said. "You must do what I told you: coax him into a back alley and bludgeon the bastard to death."

LaRue tried to contain a laugh, but he couldn't. "I suppose you've done that, huh, Baba?"

"Yes, I have, Andy. Back in forty-four, I got stuck with an ETA just as slimy as Ty's. He wanted to have sex with me, but I wouldn't do it. Surprising as it seems, I was a charming young thing in those days."

"You still are," he said. "What happened?"

"This particular ETA was determined to have me lose my Class A designation over at the water treatment plant. I tell you, he wanted to see me on the street. Me, with two brat kids and a worthless husband."

"So what did you do?"

"I told him he could have sex with me. I led him to a house where my brother was waiting for him. Thomas beat the ever loving hell out of him." Her face split into a toothy grin. "And then he died."

I could tell LaRue only half believed her. "Your problem was solved, then."

"Yes, right up until the day I went into the seniors program and came to live here. When that happened, I discovered to my displeasure that my ETA has been reincarnated as Henderson."

He glanced at me. "You could request a change in auditors."

"Killing him would be easier," I answered. "I've tried to get him switched, and like everything else with that office, it came back denied." I tossed a jar of pickled lemons to LaRue, who opened it along with a tin of fish and placed both on the table.

We sat down, but before I could take the first bite of dinner, Baba began filling us in on the local news. "Mrs. Chumley came by today. She said she heard on the radio that the district is being forced by the government to rotate water service again. It's a good thing we've had all this rain. By my count, we have thirty-one jars filled up now. We might have to do a little trading, but we'll be all right."

I sighed and what little appetite I had disappeared. It was all so tiring, the business of survival.

LaRue, the good cop he is, noticed me playing with my food. He knew exactly where my thoughts were. "You need to find the right government health program," he said. "There must be a study you can volunteer for. You might be able to find one that will jibe with your needs and let you get the extra electricity allowance."

"That's a good idea. I'll check into it." But I didn't have much hope.

Baba started in again, this time explaining her new idea for recycling garbage, and I began to get a case of indigestion when, thankfully, my communications node beeped and Frank Wilson's voice came through. He was one of the district's medical examiners, probably the best one we had. In his message he complained about being pulled away from a dinner that included a portion of fresh beef, but he had done the autopsy scan of Maria Raynor, despite putting his chow on hold. I excused myself from the others and flopped down on the lumpy old chair sitting by the phone.

I dialed up the ME. He answered after only one ring.

"I have some interesting results from the autopsy scan, Ty," he said.

"Give me the rundown."

"There were several bruises on the lady's body, but according to my little robotic assistant here, they're old ones. She did have a large gash on her left breast and one on her face, but again they proved to be a few weeks old, too. She either has a balance problem or someone likes to bat her around."

"Were there any signs of recent struggle?"

"No. Nothing evident from the condition of the body. The murder weapon was a large soup spoon lodged in her throat. Her larynx was crushed. In my expert opinion, this lady didn't have a chance to fight. She was dead before she knew what hit her."

"What about the surgery?"

"Done after the fact. It looks like the killer used some sort of laser scalpel. The incisions were just about perfect and neatly cauterized." He inserted a pause for drama and then said, quietly, "There's something else."

"What?"

"According to the scan, Mrs. Raynor had a high chromium level in her blood."

"What does that mean, Frank?"

"I'm not really sure, Ty. Chromium is required in minute amounts by the body. It's considered essential for life, but as far as I know, there's never been a reported case of chromium deficiency. That's how little you need. In Mrs. Raynor, though, it was at a toxic level."

4

BECAUSE OF THE factories in my neighborhood, the mist that settles in from the Black River is occasionally caustic. It burns your nostrils and makes your eyes water, and on the bad days, I swear it can bleach the color right out of your hair. The district, of course, swears that the plants meet clean air standards, but that's a load of rubbish, if you'll pardon the pun.

The air was particularly bad the next morning as I jogged through St. Ophelia's Memorial Park and with each deep breath I took, I worried that I was going to catch a case of emphysema or something.

Baba had started clicking on her loom early, so I was off before dawn. I often come to this cemetery for my morning exercise. It's a quiet place of wrought iron fences, dead trees, decaying tombstones, and perpetual fog. Just the kind of place lycanthropes love, because here we can find our brethren of myth: vampires, ghosts, and zombies.

Rounding the Turner family plot, I wheezed on by Mr. Khiam's fancy mausoleum. According to the date chiseled on the side, he was laid to rest just after Vivian Duvalier became the world's dictator. People in those days were still embalmed with chemicals and given grand funerals. Now, only the rich were buried. Take, for instance, Mrs. Raynor. She would be properly entombed by being plasticized into her eternal mummified form.

Our humanitarian system is unfair right down to death. Everyone else gets toasted in the furnace of some factory or utility plant, and then their family unit is sent a letter from

21

the government thanking them for having shared the resources to the last.

I was trotting past Mrs. Gilby's headstone and trying to figure out how best to approach my problem with the Office of Environmental Taxation when a leg cramp seized me. I yelped and went down, rolling on the cracked pavement while I tried to stretch the searing calf muscle.

When one of those babies pull, it's agony. Thankfully, most of the pain is over in a minute or two. Take that minute and multiply it into twelve hours and that's what my whole body feels like during a full-moon lycanthropic phase.

I lay on the cold ground until my huffing and puffing was interrupted by a message from LaRue. His voice thundered through my earplug. By the way the sound seemed to pierce my eyeballs, I could tell he wasn't a happy man.

"Merrick, are you turned on? Please respond."

I crooked my finger under the string around my neck and pulled the microphone from beneath my shirt. "Go ahead, Andy."

The district's communication array layered static into his reply. "Can you meet me at the office? We're expecting Clyde Smith."

"Not again."

"Yeah. I'm getting real tired of seeing this guy, too."

"Was he right the last time he came by? I can't remember."

"He's always right, according to him, even if he isn't. When can you get here?"

"I'm over at St. Ophelia's cemetery. I'll be there in about forty minutes."

I came to a stand and hopped about before putting my full weight on my leg. From there, I hobbled to the graveyard's biggest maple, but I had to stop again because of the muscle tremor. I took a second to glance up at the washed-out tatters

of prayer banners fluttering from the tree branches, and
then, with a deep gulp of carcinogenic air, I bucked my way
up the street. It took me an hour and twenty minutes to reach
the District Marshals Office.

The first voice I heard when I entered the homicide pen
belonged to Smith. He was standing in our cubicle talking to
LaRue. Actually, he was roaring at LaRue. The man only
had one volume and it was always set to shout.

Since technology and humanitarianism took over our
lives, we've had to make the spaces in between palatable, so
as a society, we've moved toward mysticism and magic. A
long time ago, the District Marshals Office started using
psychic investigators who were good at getting images of a
crime as it happened. I've found that some of the people
are genuine, though I wouldn't go so far as to say they
operate in paranormal circumstances. And then there are
those like Smith who are conceited, smelly, stupid, and who
do nothing more than use their consultant agreements to
plague and hinder rather than to actually help.

"Ah, Frenchy," he said to LaRue as he saw me, "the
she-wolf has arrived."

I bared my teeth and hissed at him. "Get the hell out of
my chair."

He took his time getting up because he was busy giving
me his usual lecherous perusal. "Eat anyone lately, Merrick?"

I leaned over and propped my hand against his shoulder.
"One of these days, I hope you go into a trance and can't
find your way out."

He grunted as he came to a stand. "Is she always this
bitchy?" he asked LaRue.

My partner ignored him, turning instead toward his desk
and pointing to the Lucite evidence tray sitting there. He
plucked out the woven bag found on the victim. "Here, do

some work for your fee. See if you can get anything off of it."

Smith grabbed the pouch, grumbling about ingratitude, and took it to the empty chair with him. I leaned against my desk to watch him perform. A moment later, he let his eyes slip back into his head. I nodded toward him. "He looks better like that. Maybe he'll get stuck that way."

LaRue grinned but didn't comment. He gathered my attention to the tray. "Check this out."

There were several tiny pieces of rolled paper stacked neatly inside. They were rainbow colors and each was anchored into its tube shape by a sparkling thread.

"Forensics was busy last night," he said. "They did a scan on this stuff and came up with the following facts." He paused to punch up the database on his computer terminal. "The paper is recycled, sixteen pound weight, dyed using an aniline derivative tint. Probably made by the same factory in District Seventy-one. The analyzer found several smudged fingerprints but nothing useable. There's writing on the inside of each scroll done with an indelible marker. The threads tying them closed actually have silver filaments running through them."

Smith interrupted him to throw in some theatrics by abruptly sitting forward. Off came the ski cap to expose his tarnished field of corkscrew curls. He ran his hand through this rigid mane before squeezing the bag with fingers edged by filthy, chipped nails. "Big guy," he muttered.

I glanced at LaRue while the consultant played with the evidence. "Anything else discovered from the crime scene?"

"Scuff prints leading from the set of French doors to the living room. The killer got in and got out. He apparently didn't bother to explore the house."

I pointed to the scrolls. "He did sign his work, though."

"Maybe. We'll see when we open them. As much as I doubt it, they might have belonged to Maria Raynor."

"And then we're really nowhere."

Smith popped into the conversation with a groan. We both looked his way to see his histrionics continue. This time he was sweating. The perspiration flowed over the ridges of his face like the Black River flows over the rocks down by the hydroelectric dam. LaRue has often called him a "sickic" instead of a psychic. It was a good fit.

"What, already?" I growled.

"Big guy," he murmured. "Muscular. Good looking. Dark hair."

"How enlightening," I answered. "That fits about half the population, I'd say."

He abruptly stopped his show to glare at me. "Do you want my help or not?"

"I don't have any use for your kind of help. You're so full of shit, Smith, I don't know how you keep it in your britches."

"At least I don't rip my clothes off and howl at the moon."

"Well, at least I don't smell like a refrigerator project while I'm doing it."

LaRue stepped into the argument when Smith jumped up. We had started gathering an audience, so he tried to send me off with a tender shove. "Ty, take a break. Let him finish."

I lingered a moment to deepen my scowl before slowly stalking from the cubicle. I'd only gotten a couple of steps when I heard Smith say: "Damn! I'll bet you come out scratched to hell after you have a night in the sack with her, huh, Frenchy?"

I turned around, ready to pounce, but my partner saved me the effort. He savagely clipped Smith by the collar, running him against the waist-high partition enclosing our nook. The fight brought instant silence to the room. Even the suspects, enjoying interviews regarding other crimes, knew not to utter a sound as the attack unfolded. The tone in LaRue's voice was enough to scare dirt out of water. "If you were any kind of mind reader, you would have realized how inappropriate that question is."

Smith reacted by shaking free. He straightened his ragged jacket, aware of the quiet surrounding him. Then, as though it was an afterthought, he tossed the bag back into the tray. "I know one thing for sure," he said. "You're both going down on this one." He hurried out of the pen, chased by launched paper wads.

After he left, the place settled back into the semiefficient homicide squad that we were. LaRue went on to spend the morning coaxing open the paper packets as I tried to get through to the Planetary Health Organization for an evaluation appointment on my lycanthropic condition. My partner had more success than I did. I kept getting lost in the computer scheduling system and it didn't do much for my mood. Following the fourth time of slamming down the phone receiver, he said something.

"I'm hungry. What about you?"

"No. I'm aggravated."

"I couldn't tell." He stretched in his chair and considered me with his very gentlest look. For him, it amounted to a small smile offset by a strange squint, but I appreciated it nonetheless.

"I'll grab us some lunch from the cafeteria," he said. "Why don't you slide over here while I'm gone? See what you think." He abandoned his seat without a backward glance.

LaRue may always look like a rumpled mess, but when it comes to his work, he's a fastidious man. While I was fighting the robots over at the PHO, he had neatly unrolled and laid out the scrolls in a straight line on his desk. There were eighteen in all, presented in sets of three and further organized by the pastel hues of the papers: red, orange, yellow, green, blue, and violet. Precise script printed in miniature labeled each swatch and when taken by group, the writing was then arranged according to language. I aimed LaRue's magnifying glass on each page.

I was to the point of wondering if the bag and its contents might have belonged to the killer when my phone extension buzzed. It was the watch commander.

"We've got to hold up the interview with Councilman Raynor," she told me.

"Still sedated?"

"No. He's waiting for a special government counsel to accompany him." She dropped in a pause, then added: "Don't harass him, either. We'll bring him in for questioning. I assure you."

"It looks like we could have the makings of a multiple murder case, Julie," I said.

"Recommendation noted. Oh, and Merrick, next time you and LaRue abuse a criminal consultant, do it someplace else. I don't like Mr. Barkley coming in here with his office reports." She hung up.

LaRue returned, bearing the nutritional fare offered to those of us participating in the food allowance program. This month it was oatmeal. Someone in the procurement section had gotten a good deal on mush.

He broke out a jar of hot sauce blended by his father and we both smothered the slop before dipping our spoons into it. I almost choked when the snap of chili peppers collided with the back of my tongue.

"Your pop put together a good batch this time," I finally managed.

"My sister-in-law found the ingredients down near the

Verrazano somewhere. Hottest peppers I've tasted in a long while." Sweat began to bead on his forehead, but unlike Smith's, it was real. He wiped at it with his sleeve as he nodded toward the unrolled papers. "What do you make of those?"

"Written in Chinese, Greek, and Cyrillic. I'm not sure about the last three sets."

He jabbed a finger at the violet group. "That one's Latin. I don't know the others, either."

I sucked down the rest of my gruel, feeling the hot sauce burn a groove in my esophagus. "I suppose asking the university for help is out of the question?"

"Have they been nice to us before?"

"Not in recent memory."

I tossed my cup into the recycling bin and picked up the woven bag. Baba would have been charmed by the colorful detail of its slender threads. Small glass beads were sewn near the opening and the tie was carefully braided with black and gold yarns. I pulled it open, discovering with a small sniff that it had not always held the scrolls.

To confirm the odor, I checked the computer and the forensic report before glancing at LaRue. "I think we need to have a conversation with Madame Janetta."

"I agree." He checked his wristwatch. "If we hurry, we can get there by two o'clock tea."

I stood to pull on my jacket, stuffing the killer's woven bag into the front pocket as I did.

Madame Janetta's Class A designation listed her as a music tutor, but for those who regularly shopped the bargains on the back door market, she was an entrepreneur who spent her free time gathering a variety of controlled substances and hand-rolling them into cigarettes.

5

SEEING MADAME JANETTA at the two o'clock tea meant that her best violin student would be playing a Chirelli concerto in the next room, while she would be busy serving up cups of black darjeeling and tiny sample rolls of Havana tobacco. For all this ambience, she only charged three credits per person. As usual, I had to borrow money from LaRue.

Madame Janetta is a self-proclaimed middle-aged Gypsy who swears she's been granted seven interdistrict visas. She often tells people that she's just returned from her most recent trip to the farthest locality, where she's discovered a bright new musical talent so good that the government would be foolish not to include him or her in the Arts and Humanities Program. Unfortunately, her eccentricity makes her a liar, because she rarely leaves her neighborhood and none of her students has ever been selected to receive a district scholarship to attend the university, though the ones I've heard certainly could qualify if they had wealthy family units to back them up.

The sale of tobacco is big business on the back door market, but it still doesn't make it any more legal than the other drugs available. Its illegality has nothing to do with the fact that it's habit forming and unhealthful. Tobacco falls under the Emissions Control Act. As district marshals, it isn't our place to seize and arrest anyone breaking these regulations; that's up to the ETA and fellows who are vicious clones of Henderson.

Madame Janetta's parlor was decorated in red and gold flocked wallpaper and several hard-backed chairs that she claimed were Shaker antiques. Old, faded family photographs strategically placed about the room lent a coziness to the atmosphere. Janetta admitted that she had bought the pictures several years before from a woman who had needed money, and during the passing decades had developed a strange kinship to these nameless people by giving them histories and personalities. She mentioned one of these purloined ancestors as she served up the cups and smokes.

"See that handsome gentleman standing by the car? That was Great Uncle Walter. He was one of the first people to import the blend you're sampling right now." She paused to admire her own cigarette before continuing. "Wonderful, flavor, huh? There hasn't been this kind of Cubano seed around since Castro's time. And you'll notice, please, that it's cocooned in the finest dark Maduro wrapper. I even added a splash of rum before rolling them. I have an extra box of nippers if you're interested."

"Maybe," Andy said. A smile twisted the corners of his eyes, but moved no farther down his face as he dragged on his cigarette.

She tilted her head toward the music room. "Good student; don't you agree?"

"Absolutely," I answered.

"Good student, but still, she's a little prima donna. I offer these young people my worldly guidance, extend to each the comforts of my home, and for that they have not one bit of gratitude. This one here called me an old witch the other day. Do you believe it?" She ran a baubled hand through her long black hair. "They're foul creatures, these musical geniuses."

Andy suddenly choked and coughed, interrupting her.

"Don't try to suck up the whole thing in a single breath," she scolded. "You want to savor it. What you're doing only burns your sinuses and wastes the tobacco."

I tossed him a haughty grin as I attempted to inhale

correctly, but a fireball built up in my lungs and I had to release the pressure with a snort.

She laughed at me. "Obviously you don't need any of my products. What, then?"

I dug into my coat pocket to produce the woven bag. "We found this pouch on a recent murder victim. Residue samples taken from the inside lining indicate that it once held a popper of tobacco and quantum."

When I mentioned quantum, her expression fell like one of Baba's chocolate cakes. Possession of the drug could net a person a ten-year stint on the rock pile.

Quantum is a designer favorite among people, because it expands the ego, and at the same time it induces a greater sense of creativity. Those who use this drug experience elevated confidence and a rash of enlightening ideas that lead to works of literature, art, and invention, but following continued experimentation, the insidious aftereffects become apparent. While quantum sparks the brain to achieve creative feats, it slowly starts to destroy the synaptic connections responsible for logic.

For those who can afford it, tobacco is blended with powdered quantum, oil, wine, and herbs and then formed into a ball, called a popper. Small chunks are pulled from the glob and chewed.

"I don't deal in the stuff," she said.

"But you sell the tobacco to folks who do," I said. What about Axion Howard? Where has he pitched his tent this month?"

She hesitated, taking the bag, but keeping her gaze upon me. Then she changed the subject. "Do you still suffer from moon madness?"

"Yes. Why?"

"I have a blend that might interest you. Good-grade cherry tobacco with assorted ingredients. This concoction keeps away insanity, night tremors, and depression. You're not allergic to petroleum jelly or curry powder, are you?"

It was an old game she played. "No. How much do you want for the pack?"

"What do you have?"

The District Marshals Office recognizes the existence of the back door market and provides us with a bimonthly credit voucher so we can buy trade items. The trick is to trade for better and more, so the detective can stretch out the allotment, but you do have to be strong about not becoming attached to the bargaining items. There's no regulation about taking the junk home for personal use, but if you consume the goods, you might not have enough left to do your job.

A week before, I had bargained for a dark blue hand-knit cap. I pointed to it, and said, "Does wool make your head itch?"

"It messes up my hair." She ran her eyes over me. "This blend is powerful stuff. Not cheap. You chew it and it will help to relax you when the time comes." She pointed toward my earring. "I like the hoop. It is real gold, I assume?"

Taking a swig from my tea, I pretended to think about it, finally saying, "It cost me three days' pay, but you can have it if you give us the information and throw in the box of nippers, too."

She considered it for a moment. "Agreed." With that, she ran her thumb into the pouch's opening and made a space to bury her nose. She sniffed, surfacing quickly, and then dove once more before coming up for air a final time. "I smell China Blue. Fine, gentle flavor. One of my favorite tobaccos, but not easy to find. They grow it in selected places in the Sino districts and nowhere else."

She sucked on her cigarette and beat on the wall when the

violinist stopped playing. After a minute, she said, "I sold a kilo of China Blue to Axion Howard a few months ago. And I'll be honest. Whoever made this popper up, put some money into it."

6

WHILE WE VISITED Madame Janetta, the PHO's computerized scheduling system called the office to inform me I had an appointment at 6 P.M. at the clinic in my ward.

It was a surprise, because the opening came so quickly, when normally the PHO would take several days to process a nonemergency request. I suppose I should have become suspicious of it, but LaRue started talking about how the universal energy saw my need and set everything up to answer my call. Usually, I ignore these particular discourses of his, but whether it was PMS, anger at my situation with Henderson, or the influences of the moon, I grasped at the metaphysical straws he offered and took it as a good sign.

He dropped me off at the clinic, and as usual, I was afraid to touch anything. To open the entrance door, I cuffed the knob with my sleeve. I brought my own pen to sign in with, and I used my elbow to balance the clipboard while I did. Once in the chair, I avoided the slimy handles and the magazines on the table. I tried not to breathe when someone coughed, and I made sure that I didn't pick my nose or rub my eyes, just in case I'd touched something unawares.

I know these precautions must seem rather extraordinary. I just don't want anyone else's illness. I don't want sinusitis, a heart attack, or irritable bowel syndrome. I already have madness, and that's enough.

While I was fairly certain that I remained reasonably germ free, I wasn't quite sure about the doctor.

His name was Lane Gibson. He was a tight-assed man about thirty years old, with long, sandy-blond hair that was yanked back in a leather thong. He had a few pockmarks on his face, but rather than detracting from his looks, they added texture to his angular features. His pants could have been cleaner and his hands were so dirty, he could have grown mushrooms on his knuckles.

The nurse showed me into the examining room just as he entered from a side door. He stared at me before sitting down at the computer terminal set up in the corner. His back was to me. "Let's get the prelims done," he said as a greeting.

"Nice meeting you, too, Doc," I answered, climbing up on the smudgy table.

"Eye color?" he asked.

When I didn't answer, his neck spring loaded around so he could scowl at me. "What color are your eyes, Marshal Merrick?"

"Brown."

He snorted and squinted at me. "They're green."

I looked surprised. "Now, when did that happen?"

He muttered something and then turned back to his flickering monitor to type in the answer.

"Hair?"

"Oh, about four billion. I would guess."

He swiveled on me again. "I beg your pardon?"

I smiled innocently. "Hair. I figure I have about four billion strands." When he didn't respond, I added, "Four billion. Seems like a lot, doesn't it? But I'm pretty sure that's what I have. Usually."

His sneer turned into a slow grin and he wheeled the chair around completely. It squealed, but now he was at least facing me. "Have you ever had cholera?" he asked.

"Yes."

"Diptheria?"

"Yes."

"Tuberculosis, Type B?"

"Yes, indeed. That one, especially."

"Worms?"

"A fluke worm. Came from drinking bad water channeled off the roof of my apartment building. My roommate thinks that it came from outer space, because she can't figure how a sewer monster got up there. Doesn't matter. We merged bodily functions for a while."

He shook his head. "I have to test your body's fat content."

"Why?"

"District survey." He flicked a pair of plastic calipers from his shirt pocket. "Please remove your side arm and change into the examining gown. I need to take several measurements." To give me time to undress, he turned back to the computer and concentrated on entering data from a paper file.

I did as instructed, realizing when undressed, how chilly the room was. Gibson took his time with the exam, doing a little more touching than I thought was necessary. Fifteen minutes later, he was done checking my arms, torso, thighs, calves, and butt. He sat again before his computer.

I was just hooking my holster on when he spoke. "These figures indicate that you carry only thirteen percent body fat."

It's true. I'm all straps and sinew. "What's wrong with that?"

"You're a female of childbearing age. You should have more fat."

"Why would it matter? I don't have any children."

He veered his comments again. "You fall into the lower percentile in the district survey. You need to fill out their questionnaire. Remember to see the nurse on the way out and she'll give you a copy."

"Well, what about the reason I came to see you? I need an upline referral."

He spun the chair toward me again, propped his ankle on his knee, and bought his hand up to cup his chin. "I've got news for you, Merrick. This clinic is as far as you're going. You won't get that referral. I'm the only doctor you're going to see regarding your lycanthropy."

It was obviously my week for government threats. "What are you talking about?"

"You've been placed in my specific care. My specialty is neurology. I study the brain and its physical chemistry. Your friend, Henderson, told me all about you months ago when your electric consumption started creeping upward."

"Bastard. So much for confidentiality."

"Think of him as doing you a favor. No one else is going to give you the consideration you deserve like I will."

"Why?"

"I've been studying your case, Merrick. I'm here to tell you, that quack, Pastore, didn't do you any favors prescribing his so-called light therapy."

"It works."

"Does it? Then, let me read you Pastore's signed comments in your medical file." He cleared his throat. "It is my opinion that the patient suffers from a form of dementia precipitated by a change in her neurological chemical balance. She proves resistant to the various drugs commonly used in cases displaying schizophrenic symptoms and so to alleviate her discomfort, I've managed to convince her that she can control her seizures through delta wave light therapy. Although there are no scientific conclusions based on this treatment, the mere suggestion of a treatment was enough to calm the patient to the point that she can function in society." He glanced at me and added, "He put a bandage on you, Merrick. That's it. And that's what the other doctors did, too. It's all right here. I'll open up the confidential logs for you to read, if you don't believe me."

I tried to answer him, but my words were stuck to the back of my throat. Gibson saw my difficulty and continued. "I think your lycanthropy is a purely physical manifestation. From this point of view, you're not crazy, you're curable. I want to try to make this happen for you."

When I still didn't say anything, he was forced to fill in the silence. "You're not the only werewolf I've come across. I've worked with one other."

His statement still wasn't enough to make my tongue work.

"We were getting somewhere," he said. "Unfortunately, he died in an accident that wasn't related to his illness. I want to share what I found out with you."

"Why?" I managed in a husky voice. "What's in it for you?"

"To be honest? A grant that will get me off the clinic rotation duty and into a research institute."

He picked up a prescription pad lying beside the computer. Scribbling a page, he tore it off and handed it to me. "Take this to the hospital before tomorrow evening. It's a chit for a baseline brain scan." When I just stared at him, he threw in the final threat. "I suggest that you don't balk at this association, Merrick. Your class designation hangs in the balance. A good report from me and you get to keep your job."

7

MADAME JANETTA SAID she thought Axion Howard was filling quantum orders right under the noses of his bosses at the Black River Fish Hatchery, so the next morning, we went to find him. Factory whistles echoed across the district signaling the release of night shift workers. Howard came out of the gate with a crowd, but lingered beside the installation's twelve-foot-high wooden fence; ready, I'm sure, to meet with a customer. When he saw us approach, he scowled and tried to hurry away, but I had some speed on him. In the end, though, I was forced to use the weight of my body to shove him against the fence.

LaRue said that he smelled like rotting caviar. Whatever it was, his odor was so intense, it made me back away. That small movement was just enough to make him think that he wasn't going to be arrested immediately. He relaxed a little but stiffened again as LaRue leaned on the fence and propped open his jacket to show off his Magnum.

"What?" Howard whined. "I got no info on murder and nothing to say to youse."

Hearing the "youse" brought on a chuckle from LaRue.

He said, "We'uns are looking to know who's been buying your merchandise."

"I don't sell no more. I'm on probation."

"And I'm sure youse would like to stay that way."

He blinked and brought a hand up slowly to scrape his fingers across a five o'clock shadow as he considered the validity of the threat. He finally decided it was better to spill. "What do youse want to know?"

"We want to know who bought poppers from you made of China Blue tobacco."

He delivered his reply with a grimace. "Ah, Janetta, that old bitch. Ratting on me like that."

"Who?" I demanded.

"Well, I don't exactly keep a list. Let me think."

"Let us help," I said, in a clenched voice. "How about Jack Raynor?"

"The councilman? Are you a joke or what?"

"You've never sold to him?"

He shook his head and his stink wafted around us like an invisible curtain. "I sell to lots of richies, but he ain't one. Maybe I sold to some folks he knows, though."

"Who?"

"Youse are going to let me go if I say, right?"

I thought about lying, but didn't. "Yeah. You're as good as gone. Just give us what we need to know."

"His brother, Max."

"This is getting interesting, now. Anyone else?"

"Some friend of his. A guy called Orson."

"Is that a first name?"

"I suppose. I don't ask for no district ID."

"How do you know he was a friend of Jack's?" I asked.

"I don't. Max and this guy were slinging the councilman's name around like it was going to net them a better deal or something. Fat chance on that. Discounts are out."

"What did they say, exactly? Do you remember anything specific?"

"Naw." He went into his consideration mode again, before blurting, "I think they were talking about a party that they were going to together." A pause, then, "Yeah, that was it. A party. They were supposed to meet Jack, I think."

"What kind of party was it? Any idea?"

"What do you think? I sold him all the hors d'oeuvres."

"Have these gentlemen been back to see you since?"

"Orson bought from me a couple times. Just for little stuff."

"What kind of little stuff?"

"Oh, squeezes and dribbles. Nothing more than a gram a shot."

"How long ago did you last see him?"

"Has to be at least two weeks."

"We want a description," LaRue said. "Come down to the office so you can talk to the police artist."

"No can do." He explained quickly to stall his arrest. "About the description, I mean. I got bad eyesight. I need glasses, but don't got any. You can ask for my yearly exam if youse don't believe me. These characters always meet me at night in a back alley on Brimmer Street. I gotta squint just to get things to clear up good in the bright sunshine."

"You sure noticed us fast," I said.

He snorted. "Youse sort of stand out."

"How's that?"

"Youse both walk like cops."

"What do you mean by that?"

He held his hands up as we edged away from the fence. "No offense, but youse both look like you can't wait to bugger somebody with a billy stick."

8

LIFE IN OUR society demands a certain flexibility, even when it comes to finding a killer. If you want your share of the goods that the district provides, then you have to take time from your work to stand on line to get them. It was propane delivery day in the ward and I didn't want to miss the truck running the afternoon schedule, so LaRue dropped me off at home on his way back to the office.

Our flat was cold and dark. Baba was at her loom, squinting by the feeble light of a wax candle.

"Didn't think you were going to make it for the refill, my dear," she said.

"I got held up with a client." I rifled my jacket pocket and found the small woven bag I'd smuggled from the evidence tray. Letting it dangle by the string, I showed it to her. "What do you make of this, Baba?"

She snatched it up to study it. "Nice work," she said. "It's my guess it was done on a hand loom by someone with good dexterity. The weft is even and the materials are delicate." She glanced at me. "I take it this is an artifact from your latest investigation?"

"You take right. Any idea who might be selling these?"

"Any one of your botanical shops on the back door. Terrin Foy down on Severin Street has been known to dabble in these expensive purses. Or, at least, he knows who does."

"Expensive? How much would you guess this one's worth?"

"I can't really say, my dear, but probably for the intricacy of the work, I'd guess upwards of three hundred credits."

"Three hundred credits?" No one but LaRue knew I had

the evidence on my person, and for a moment I thought about not returning it to the investigation, but my sense of honor outweighed my natural pilfering proclivities. It might be needed to convict the killer. Still, hocking it would have helped out with my bills.

I packed the bag with a sigh and began gathering the four gas bottles we owned. As usual, the head on the stove unit stuck, forcing me to use a pair of rusty channel locks to pry it loose. After a few seconds of tugging, it came apart, and I was able to separate the container and stow it in the carrier Baba had weaved for me.

These large rucksacks were a fashion statement among the lower classes, used for hauling fuel and supplies from the district distribution points, as well as everyday shopping and trash foraging. Baba had created my bag with extra pockets sewn along the straps so I could store small trade items. Digging my hand into the pouches, I found them already full. She had seen to the chore while I was at work.

By the time I hit the street again, the day had turned to slate. It grayed my mood considerably, especially when the propane truck rumbled by, making me realize that I was later than I'd thought.

There were fifty weary folks ahead of me when I finally stepped into line. Many were elderly and like pack animals, they stooped beneath the weight of their own harnesses.

Old Man Stravinksi, Ward Thirteen's only butcher, was in front of me. He smiled and held his hand up in greeting.

"Ah, Ty, how are you?" he asked.

"I'm fine, sir, and you?"

A frigid wind peeled down the street. He shivered before answering. "It's already a hard winter, wouldn't you say? Too cold for ancients like me." He squinted, allowing no more time for social formalities before opening a parley

with me. "I have a quarter slab of bacon. No end pieces and
cured with honest-to-god rock salt. Interested?"

"Bacon gives me indigestion and Baba claims it dries her
skin. Do you have barley perchance?"

He nodded. "A small bag. Two ounces, but it cost me a
whole government-inspected beef blade."

I pulled out a glass jar. It was the container that Mrs.
Raynor's pickled lemons had come in. "I have this and three
disposable butane lighters."

"Not enough."

"What do you need, then?"

"Name some things."

"Thread?"

"Do you have needles?"

"Yes. A new packet."

"What about iodine?"

"Full bottle. Throw in something else. Do you have
beans?"

"Yes. Dried whites."

"How much?

"A pint's worth. Seal the deal?"

I smiled and shook his hand, then searched my pockets
for the goods. After we made the exchange, Mr. Stravinski
turned away from me and no more was said between us.

I used the time to engage in one of my favorite hobbies:
the art of eavesdropping on the people around me. By
cocking my ear just right into the breeze, I can pick up
conversations for several yards. So, as we edged forward, I
collected the gossip from those lining up behind me.

There was plenty of talk about the water rationing and
about how the District Manager's Office was screwing up
the disbursement of pension dividends. Mrs. Kincaid was
irritated about being placed in a hold status where her food
stamp credits were concerned, saying that the government

claimed she'd been overpaid the last time she'd received them. A lady farther down talked about how the latest government regulations regarding poultry standards had made chicken prices soar out of reach of the common man. Someone else moaned about having his transportation chits stolen while riding the subway. These complaints went on and on.

An hour into my eavesdropping, I had made it to second place. Mr. Stravinski turned his back to present his cannisters to the guy handling the propane filler hose. I heard the hiss of ejecting gas as he rammed the quick-connect into the bottle's nozzle. It's impolite to stare at the person being served, so I angled away and hunted down the line for some tidbit to gnaw on. I got one, too.

A woman dressed in a blue trench coat and ragged denim trousers was holding a low-toned conversation with her male companion.

"I'm telling you the truth, Thaxter," she said. "I've seen this chair. We should try it. What's to lose?"

"Nothing but time and forty credits," he answered. "We just don't have that kind of money for silly superstition."

"Hush, or you'll curse us further! You're exactly the reason why we have no children. I've spent three years doing it your scientific way. It's time we tried something else. Now, you can either come with me or not, but I'm going to sit in the chair."

"I won't allow it. You're being foolish."

"No, I'm not. I've known three women who've conceived immediately after sitting in it. It's a miracle seat, and it doesn't just make a person pregnant."

"Oh, and what else is it supposed to do?" he asked.

"It'll chase away migraines and cure the flu better and faster than an antibiotic agent. I've even heard that it'll make fat people thin."

9

THE GOVERNMENT ALLOWS some measure of free enterprise, so long as the local officials receive regular kickbacks and the owners of all these small businesses put in thirty hours of community service a month instead of the required fifteen. Because there are so many bribes and boondoggles, though, the cost of operating a legitimate storefront keeps most people active in the back door market where things can be bought and sold without value-added tax attached.

There are many entrances to access this hidden economy and one of them leads to a whole range of services devoted to the occult. To the folks who deal here regularly, this layer is known as the bazaar. With the types of things sold, it should rightly be called the bizarre.

I've seen everything from shrunken heads to magical beads to love potions. Being a lycanthrope, you would think that I would be comfortable in this mystical midregion where superstitions and miracles come with a price tag. At one point early in my exploration to find a cure for my disease, I hit this marketplace only to come away half poisoned by concoctions of castor oil, turpentine, and old prayers that are no longer dedicated to St. Ophelia.

Here, there are a few people who are masters at selling what I like to call invisible magic. These folks are the ones who take ordinary things and promote them as having an unseen power. The most popular objects just happen to be chairs.

I went back home to drop off the propane tanks. Baba was gone, probably out coaxing the coat off of a beggar, so I didn't wait around. Hearing the young couple's discussion

45

while standing in line made me think to have a chat with Edward Polinato.

Edward Polinato's invisible magic scam is the most ingenious one I've heard. He claims that Leonardo da Vinci crafted his chair about the same time he was busy diddling around with the *Mona Lisa*. The Renaissance genius had intended to give it to one of the Medicis, but the nobleman he had entrusted to deliver the chair apparently saw it as the work of the devil, so instead, he took it to the pope. His Magnificence was threatened by its technological innovation, but he also realized what the nobleman had not—that the eccentric inventor was offering blatant contempt toward the ruling class. Leonardo could be cranky on occasion and would not hesitate in his efforts to defy the church and state with his creativity. He'd boasted about everything from cataloging the human body to designing submarines and helicopters, and it was the upper class who had supported him. There's was no way the pope could let the chair get through. He pronounced it as being evil and hid it away in a Vatican treasure room.

Several years after Duvalier pasted together the world economies, this so-called throne was found, and Polinato was in the right place when it was put up for auction. He had originally intended to use it at home, but a short time later discovered that it had been blessed with remarkable invisible magic. If a person who sat in it believed in its power, then his wish would be answered.

Polinato contends that he has a ninety-nine percent wish completion rate and the price he asks is minimal, considering that he's willing to share all this invisible magic with the world. He keeps the true lines of the seat hidden with a fancy throw cover embroidered with stars, saturns, and crescent moons, but if you pull off this rug, you will discover that the DaVinci Chair is nothing more than an old, beat-up, portable potty. I don't know about other people, but I have a problem believing in the power of a miracle crapper.

I took the subway and hopped the cross-district train, coming out an hour later in a neighborhood known as Spaghetti Downs.

Contrary to its strange name, it's a dynamic ward, the home of many artisans who offer their talents on the government-funded historical restoration projects. Stone-cutters, painters, architects, and Class B engineers share this space with some of the best chefs in the locality.

Polinato was one of those folks fortunate enough to be recognized by the district to operate a food distribution business. He was not licensed for the chair, and it didn't officially exist.

The moment I walked into The Macaroni Hut, my salivary glands started up. The thick smells of garlic and pesto absorbed my senses and forced me to consider the scrawly hand-painted menu spilling over on several chalk-boards propped behind the counter. I got in line.

The place was filthy. A layer of grease washed the unpainted, Sheetrock walls, reminding me of the sepia shades of old Chinese parchment paintings. A heater hanging in the far corner managed to push out a warm breeze despite the dusty fur that blanketed the grate. Beneath it, a dented metal recycling bin overflowed onto the floor. A gray cat sat close by, licking the remains of some juicy meal from a crumbled paper plate.

People bellied up to the serving bar, many of them leaning into the steam coming off the pans. A constant barrage of orders busied four chefs who tended a long, oily stove, and a harried young woman did her best to chop mushrooms and onions while pushing her red hair out of her eyes.

I had just enough credits with me to buy a bowl of

dumplings decked with vodka and butter sauce, and when my turn came, I told the woman my selection and asked if Polinato was in. The word went down the cooks' line until it reached the end, whereby the last fellow screamed for him. Polinato appeared from the back just as I paid the cashier.

"Marshal Merrick," he said, coming around the counter to shake my hand. "I haven't seen you in months. Got a craving for the best food in the district?"

"I always have a craving for your cuisine." To demonstrate, I dipped a cracked plastic spoon into the sauce and layered it onto my tongue, appreciating the flavor with a small sigh. "Can we talk for a few minutes?"

He nodded, hiked up his baggy pants higher around his saplinglike torso, and led me through a set of swinging doors into his healing room. This was the place where Polinato bullshitted his customers into believing that the Da Vinci Chair had an awesome power that would change their beleaguered lives.

The alcove housing this mystical marvel was the room's focal point. The walls were painted a deep red, just the proper hue to excite the molecular properties of miracle manifestation. An empty ceramic incense burner dangled from a rusty nail pounded crookedly into the wall, and as usual, the potty was covered with the blanket.

I used a chest of drawers as a table and dipped up a dumpling as I fished into my coat pocket for a photo of Maria Raynor. "Have you ever seen this woman?"

He frowned at it. "That's a terrible picture."

"What do you want from me?" I said, stabbing another noodle. "It was taken off her interdistrict passport. Artistic and technical presentation are not hallmarks of that particular office."

"I'll say. As much as one of those things costs I'm

surprised they don't do better." He glanced at me. "I've never crossed a checkpoint, have you?"

"A few times." I curbed his stalling by cutting him with one of my hard-edged stares. "Listen, Ed, this lady weighed about three hundred pounds. She may have sought a holistic cure through you or someone else in the chair business. Any ideas?"

He blew a hard breath that snapped his ropelike frame. "What's her name?"

"Maria Raynor. She was the wife of Councilman Jack Raynor."

His expression beefed a little, and I suddenly sensed a rise in his interest. "She was murdered. I heard about that. The killer cut her up pretty bad. Isn't that right?"

I nodded. "There's a bounty on her murderer. Information leading to a conviction pays a thousand credits."

"I haven't met anyone who's helped the marshals and walked away with the money."

"Some have. Anyway, it's her husband paying this time, and he has the cash. Being that he's already a controversial politician, he can't afford to have a thick layer of shit smeared on his public image. He'll come across with the funds when it's time."

Polinato pursed his flabby lips and ran his fingers through his greasy black hair. The action made me think of the olive oil in which my dumplings swam. I winced before I could dismiss the image.

"Let's face it, Marshal, there aren't many chair owners who would let a person that heavy have a sit down. She didn't try here; that's a fact."

"All right. What about her husband, Jack? Did he ever stop by to use the chair?"

His expression grew hooded and he glanced out the swinging doors as he said, "I would have remembered that."

10

I HURRIED TO get my brain scan after visiting Ed Polinato and then I called LaRue to ask him to meet me at Terrin Foy's Mystical Botanical Shop. When we arrived, we found the proprietor busy helping a customer put together a charm guaranteed to correct a hair lip on an infant. It was complete with dried herbs and strong spices, fake gold nuggets, and a smear of cream depilatory to set the magic. He included a handwritten prescription for its use and then charged the woman ten credits.

LaRue and I wandered around the store while the shopkeeper handled the transaction. It was a place of heavily scented incense, gaudily painted plaster effigies of St. Ophelia, bottles of herbal essences, baskets of used rosaries, and colorful jars filled with dried chicken feet, frog lips, and the occasional testicle of an albino bull. The owner was also having a half-price sale on a variety of werewolf protection charms.

I wasn't really surprised to see the sign that announced the discount. Despite the fact that many doctors at the PHO denied the existence of lycanthropy, it was considered a reality to the average man, as were banshees, vampires, and the occasional boogey man.

I studied the rack, running my fingers over the items. There were nickle-plated bullets that passed for silver, tiny bottles suspended from leather thongs that on closer inspection were filled with crushed garlic and cracked pepper, and my favorite, a bright blue brooch of fake feathers, which was to be pinned over the heart during a full moon. I lingered over these gems until the customer left.

Terrin Foy turned his attention to us and bowed slightly. He was squatty in build and completely bald, with ears that looked like they'd been borrowed from a cow. His hands were a series of knots, calluses, and bruised fingernails, and tattooed around both wrists were the symbols of his profession: bracelets of bright red roses and green thorns.

"What can I do for you folks today?"

We showed him our IDs and he lost his pleasant smile. I produced the pilfered evidence. "Do you carry any of these charm bags?"

He took the purse and studied it. I noticed that a rough spot on his forefinger pilled one of the threads. "Yes. I carry these, but nothing so finely made. My merchandise is more reasonably priced. My customers can't afford the ticket price on something like this, and frankly, I don't think they need it for the magic to be effective."

"Do you ever get certain requests?" I asked. "Perhaps from people who have plenty of money to burn and don't mind spending on the craftsmanship?"

He considered me for several seconds before answering. "Suppose you tell me who bought this particular item and I might be able to help you figure out who made it. Fair enough?"

I nodded, but LaRue spoke. "Councilman Jack Raynor," he said.

"That bastard who's in charge of public health policy?"

"One and the same."

"He's trying to run botanicals straight out of business by making our services illegal. Says we treat people for illness when they should be going to the PHO. As if the PHO is going to make immediate appointments for them. Have you tried to get through the system, lately?"

I nodded, but LaRue spoke.

"I'll admit, he's a flaming prick," he said.

"I heard that his wife came up murdered. Is he a suspect?"

"Yes, sir."

Foy smiled. "I hope the SOB did it and you run him up a flagpole. Impaling him on it would be even better."

I couldn't contain a grin but managed to gently bring him back to the charm bag. "That's precisely why we need to know who made this sack. Can you help at all?"

"You should try up district; that's my best suggestion."

"Do you have any names?"

"From the look of the work, I'd say this was made by an artist who calls herself Topaz. Her real name is Jolene Nebraska. I seem to remember hearing that she'd had a run-in with some councilman. Might be your man." He dusted the counter with the blade of his hand. "So, can I interest you folks in supplies for a talisman or perhaps materials for"—he looked directly at me—"an elixir to ward off the vapors?"

11

I DECLINED TERRIN Foy's vapors cure, but LaRue ended up buying a silver vial, a bottle of rose water, and a package of toenail clippings taken from a recent bride. He intended to make an old Russian love charm for himself. In fact, my partner tried to convince me of its potency the whole way back to the office. When we got there, I tried to tune him out by reading the clinic questionnaire Gibson had given me.

It was a ten-page affair and demanded detailed answers to such questions as: How much food did you eat as a child? What kind? How often? When?

It went on from there to discuss favorite foods and details concerning any family unit members who had ever died from starvation.

My family unit was all dead, victims of an earthquake that broke off a huge chunk of District Fourteen when I was just a kid. I don't know how I survived, but the story goes that a member of the Citizenry Guard found me sleeping inside a recycling bin. The first thing I remember after the world shook was waking up in an orphanage and having to learn to kick and bite if I wanted to be first in line and guaranteed some food.

"Did the doctor give you that?"

LaRue's voice punched me clear of my reverie. I was so absorbed that I hadn't heard him come up behind me. He sat down at his desk and logged onto his computer with a couple of energetic taps at the keyboard.

"It's another district survey," I said. "What do you figure they do with these things? I had six of them to complete just last week."

He divided his concentration between the keyboard, the screen, and me. "I had closer to eleven to fill out, myself. I think there's a glut of recycled paper or something. They come from everywhere." He frowned at the screen, then said, "What's this new one about?"

"Nutrition."

"So give us a question," he said, as he typed.

"Let's see. Here's one: What is your favorite beverage?"

"That's easy. Coffee liquor."

I penned in the answer. "When was the last time you had this beverage?"

LaRue squinted at the computer and didn't respond.

"Four years ago," I said, while I scratched at the form. "If answer is over six months, please explain why."

"The revenuers have destroyed all the stills," he murmured. Then louder, "Did you get an upline referral?"

"No."

He jockeyed his full attention onto me. "What do you mean?"

"I've been made a research project, Andy. I go no farther than Dr. Lane Gibson, and if I don't cooperate, I'll lose my Class A designation."

"That's the shittiest thing I've ever heard. How can they threaten you like that?"

"I suppose the government is tired of hearing me whine about my illness."

"Is this guy just going to study you or is he genuinely interested in helping you?"

I shrugged. "Who knows? Now, I have to spend time trying to worm around him; though he tells me it's impossible." I knocked a knuckle against the paper. "Maybe I can join the nutrition club here and score some extra electricity allowances."

"When's your follow-up appointment?"

"It's at his discretion. I had to get a brain scan this afternoon. I suppose as soon as the results are in, he'll call me, and we can take this crap a little farther." I paused and then added, "He said the light therapy was a scam on Pastore's part. He read to me from the signed medical log."

For once, he didn't have a comment ready, just a comforting frown of concern. I guided the subject back to the survey form before LaRue could ask more questions. "All right, what's my favorite food?"

He kept his eyes level on me for a couple of heartbeats before turning toward his monitor. "Fresh water trout. Deep-fried."

"Favorite dessert?"

"Strawberry shortcake."

The survey took over an hour for us to answer. As we came to the final page, the questions began to dig at things like weight-loss programs and eating disorders. I clacked off the names of diets like beads on an abacus. "Low salt, low fat, high fiber, no sugar, no dairy, all vegetable, all liquid, all fruit, all meat, all grain." Then, "Have you ever participated in any PHO weight-loss therapy programs where vitamins and minerals such as iron, zinc, phosphorous, or chelated chromium were used as part of the treatments? If so, name them."

That's where we stopped. LaRue stared at me and I stared back. After a moment of exchanging squints and telepathic thoughts, I decided to call Gibson to see if he would fax us a copy of any nutrition surveys Maria Raynor may have filled out for the neighborhood clinic.

12

IT WAS NINE fifteen when Dr. Gibson made a house call. I was going over my case notes, Baba clacked away on her loom, and Craia, a friend from downstairs, sat close by, sorting through a cardboard box of stolen goods. The only light we used came from five citronella candles placed strategically about the cold room. The old women half listened to incidents on the police scanner provided to me by the office.

The radio was supposed to be used to monitor emergency situations, but during those odd moments when the district was quiet, the government fed worldwide bulletins into the array. Tonight, the news was about another crisis somewhere in the Sino districts. It was turned up loud because Craia was hard of hearing.

Gibson wore a dark green suede jacket and toted a large, bulging, blue canvas sack. His hair was no longer restrained by the leather thong and flowed off his shoulders. He had shaved since our last encounter.

"So, did you look me up in the district database yet?" he said.

In fact, I had. He had a good lineage, traceable back to an ancestor who had licked Duvalier's ass. All of which meant that Gibson had wealth, land rights, and pull. I ignored his question by throwing him one of my own. "Did you find a district nutrition survey filled out by Maria Raynor?"

He set his sack on the table and took a swing around the room, stopping finally to study the bank of lights on the far wall. His reply was slow to come. "I found the same questionnaire you're to fill out, and a few surveys on PHO weight-loss programs, but there wasn't anything on the chromium therapy that you asked about." He dropped the subject to introduce himself to Baba and Craia. He then moved back to open the sack.

"Is there a cure for lycanthropy in that bag?" I asked.

"No, but there are a few benefits for being in the research project."

"Oh? Do you have any electricity in there?"

He snorted and swung the pack onto a chair. The furniture creaked under the weight, but he seemed not to notice while he pulled out a three-pound cannister of propane. "This will have to do for now." He went on to withdraw a carton of preserved milk and an unmarked jar holding chocolate-colored liquid.

"What's this?" I asked, pointing to it.

"The makings for a caffeine cow. Coffee liquor is your favorite beverage, isn't it?"

"How do you know that? I haven't turned in my nutrition survey yet."

He didn't answer, but instead coaxed a loaf of brown bread from this big wallet. He tore away the waxed paper, revealing a package of fresh-baked wonder. The fragrance almost defeated my curiosity, but not quite.

"My partner came to see you," I said. "Didn't he?"

He nodded. "He expressed his desire that this research project should remain on a professional level. He also said that you tried all day to get through to PHO scheduling to attempt to shoot around me. Forget it. You're wasting your time. I would have thought you would have realized that after you ran the background check on me. I have, pardon the wolfish expression, my fangs in you."

More food followed the bread: a half wheel of cheddar cheese, dried chicken fillets, canned asparagus, an onion, and a bunch of carrots. I thought Baba was going to swoon when she saw this bounty.

"Sweet St. Ophelia!" she sang. "My dear, I can't believe you're a friend of that no-good sonofabitch, Henderson."

He laughed. "I never said I was his friend."

"Well, bless your generosity, anyway." She rose from her loom and scraped the food off toward the counter by the sink. Craia joined her and they began making stew and chattering in loud whispers about how handsome the doctor was.

He stepped deeper into the room so he could study the bank of lights better. His eyes roamed across the entire setup as he absently removed his jacket. Baba felt compelled to explain.

"We scrounged half the district for those bulbs," she announced. "It took us practically forever to collect everything we needed and another four months just to find the right lucky charms to decorate them with."

He nodded but turned to me with a sad smile and a sympathetic sigh. Then, "Who stays with you during the full moon? LaRue?"

"Sometimes."

"Where do you go? Do you stay here?"

"It depends."

"On what?"

"On what I decide to do when it's time."

I tried to change the subject. "You said you worked with another lycanthrope. What did he do when the full moon came?"

He shrugged. "The normal things. He would rip off his clothes, howl, and be convinced that he had actually turned into a werewolf." He left the lights to stand a few inches away from me. "I have a feeling that your seizures are very different."

When I didn't comment one way or the other, he hung his coat across a chair and sat down. "All right, we'll save the hard questions for later. Let's start with something simple to gain each other's trust. How about that?"

"Better," I answered, sitting down.

"Have you eaten today?"

"What does that have to do with anything?"

"Diet, Merrick. In any illness with a physical base, what you eat affects your overall health and behavior. Now, did you have food today?"

"No," Baba said, without turning from her chores.

The onset of a snotty mood forced a nasty snarl to work

into my response. "Why don't you interview my roommate? She seems to know more than I do."

He touched my arm and that's when I saw that his hands were clean and his fingernails manicured. "Relax, will you? This project doesn't have to be painful." Sitting back, he pointed to the milk. "Why don't you serve up the drinks?"

The minute he suggested it, Craia appeared with four of our best chipped mugs and a spoon. I undertook the task of preparing the cups while trying to think of something to say that would juggle loose his intense scrutiny of me. He saved me the trouble. "Your brain scan looks fairly normal, aside from a few red spots, which suggest increased areas of activity. We'll take another scan in a few days to see if things change."

He said no more as he watched me stir the drinks slowly. It was only after I was done that he spoke. "You have no signs of palsy," he said. "That's good."

I scowled, and he clarified his point. "Tremors, jerks, and twitches can indicate neurological dysfunction in various parts of the brain."

"That's nice to know."

Baba swung into place again. "Do you come from this district, Doctor? I've never seen you in this neighborhood before."

"No, ma'am. I come from a district to the north, but I've been working in Ward Seventeen for several weeks. I was asked to head the free clinic in your neighborhood just recently. The services there haven't been up to published guidelines, so I'm trying to turn it around."

"It's a dump," I said.

"Yes. More than you know. I had to get down with a hammer and saw this past week because the floor in my office area was starting to cave in."

I didn't answer, intent on savoring the taste of the liquor, so he glanced at the papers spread across the table, took his own slug, and mentioned them. "Are you working on a case?"

"Yes. The murder of Maria Raynor."

"I just finished reading an article about that. Pretty gruesome stuff. The tabloids said something about her body being disfigured by the killer."

"We're not sure if it was the murderer who mutilated the body."

"Who, then? Her husband?"

I shrugged, sampling my drink again.

"He seems to be a jerk," Gibson said.

I suddenly liked the man. We actually saw eye to eye on something, and so I thought I'd use it.

I pointed to the enlarged copies I'd made of the scrolls. "Several pieces of paper were found on the victim each containing paragraphs written in languages other than the standard Barrier language. LaRue and I have been trying to get some translations on the damned things, but of course, the university won't talk to us. We think part of it refers to medical terms or medicine, but we can't check it out because we can't get a pass to the government library to find out." I handed him the pages written in Latin. "If it belonged to Mrs. Raynor, then that would suggest she might have intended these slips to be part of some form of traditional healing. Perhaps a cleansing ritual of some kind." Scooting the pages toward him, I said, "You're the doctor. See if you can read these, Hippocrates."

He studied them, like he had studied me when we first met. His reply came abruptly once he finished swishing a swig of his drink around in his mouth. "I have a friend who can tell us what it says all the way through. If you loan me this copy, I'll have him look it over." He pointed to the one written in Greek. "Give me that one and I'll see if he can translate that, too." Then, he narrowed his look and I knew what was coming.

"What do you want in return?" I asked.

"Your company on the full moon."

13

FAT TAKES ON a pearly luster after it's been plasticized. I hadn't seen too many dead people who'd been pumped full of recyclable liquid Styrofoam, so when LaRue and I arrived the next morning at Maria Raynor's viewing and wake, I was amazed at the results.

You would have never known that she'd had a soup spoon forced down her throat. The bruises and tearing around her mouth were gone, expertly glued together so nothing of the trauma was visible. The mortician had a real flare for makeup and had decorated the corpse with blue eye shadow, thick mascara, delicate pink blush, and ruby red lips. Her pallor had none of the sallow color that comes with traditional formaldehyde embalming. She was dressed in a tent-sized beige suit. Fake nails had been applied and painted, each one artistically airbrushed with a yellow rose pattern.

At least a hundred people showed up for the burial held at the district's only recognized mortuary, but among all these attenders, Jack was conspicuously absent. According to the funeral director, his parents had shown up early to pass on their respects. The mother had confined her condolences to Maria's parents; the father had merely mumbled something along with a perfunctory handshake, and then the two begged off, giving some excuse of a prior engagement.

We tried our best to blend in with the guests, but most were dressed to the nines and were obviously there to do more than stare at Maria in her coffin. As we wove our way through the crowd toward a long buffet table heaped with food, I tuned into conversations that had to do with money and government projects rather than death and eulogy.

As we helped ourselves to cream cheese canapés and greasy little sausages, we managed to meet Maria's sister, Mrs. Arlene Debney, a woman who was just as enormous as her dead sibling. She concerned herself with the snacks, holding a paper plate loaded with goodies under her chin. We introduced ourselves, and between bites, she chattered.

"Such a tragedy, isn't it?" she trilled just before stuffing her mouth with a triangle of shrimp toast. After swallowing, she said, "My poor, dear Maria. And that bastard she was married to. I hope his dick falls off." Then, realizing what she'd said, she apologized. "Sometimes my mouth gets the better of me. That's why I usually have it filled with food." She giggled. "Maria used to say that it was the best thing I could do."

"You were close to your sister?" I asked.

"Oh, extremely close. I had visited her on the very day she died. She was planning another one of her fabulous parties."

"Parties?" LaRue asked, around a soda cracker heaped with salmon. "What kind?"

"Dinner parties," she answered. "My sister was a creative genius. It's so sad that Jack never saw it. Well, maybe he did; he just didn't appreciate it."

"What was so special about her dinner parties?" I said, as my hand hovered over a tray of chicken wings.

"She made them adventures. Maria had a wonderful imagination and she read and watched vid disks, and then she invented theme parties. Just two weeks ago, she gave an African safari."

"She gave an African safari?" I said. "What kind of things did that party include?"

"It was marvelous. She decorated the house in animal prints, played tribal recordings, and even found crockery dishes that were made in Little Morocco." She swallowed another glob of food before going on. "And the cuisine! Oh, it was out of this world. Couscous that was oily with real butter and studded with raisins; a fragrant lamb stew made with sweet onions, potatoes, and fresh parsley; rice delicately flavored with saffron and cardamom. And the dessert! She called it, Mt. Kilimanjaro. A chocolate fudge ice cream mountain topped with shaved coconut and caramel sauce. It was heaven, I tell you."

"You explained that just like a food critic might," I said.

She smiled thinly. "I am. I write a column for the *District Observer*." Then with a haughty expression: "The society page, of course."

"Oh, sure; now I know who you are," I said, when I really didn't. "Tell me, did Mrs. Raynor cook all these foods?"

She considered me a moment. "I'll be honest with you. No, she didn't." She leaned toward me and I smelled garlic on her breath. "She had them catered."

"A legit catering company?"

"Are you serious? Of course not. Those places are lucky if they can produce a decently cooked hot dog. Not one of them is acceptable, as far as I'm concerned."

"So she used a back door operation?"

She nodded. "Jack fixed it to make it look legal. He

started inviting his business associates over and impressing them. Maria said the ungrateful bastard never, never thanked her."

"Do you know who catered these parties?"

"At first, she used different people, but toward the end she was relying on just one. I suppose it was easier for Jack to slide it through the system."

"Which one was it?"

She shrugged. "I haven't the vaguest idea. I do know, though, that whoever created those dishes was a master."

We took some more steps down the food line and were coming close to the end when someone announced that they would be taking death portraits with the immediate family unit. Mrs. Debney fled the table for this photo opportunity, leaving LaRue and me to continue gathering canapé provisions. I finished my plate off and looked down to see what comprised the next square foot of the banquet board. It was then that I noticed the bowl of dumplings swimming in vodka and butter sauce.

14

UPON DISCOVERING THIS minor connection to Edward Polinato, we had him brought in for a visit to the Marshals Office. We all three sat in the interrogation room. I concerned myself with picking at a piece of pork lodged between my teeth; LaRue used the harsh light of the bare bulb to pour his toenail clipping mixture into his new charm vial; and our illegal caterer nervously ran his fingers through his greasy hair. Each time he laid his hands on the table, he left oil smudges on the already slick suface. Finally, I worked the thread of meat clear by using the corner of an envelope and began the interview.

"Ed, I thought you were a law-abiding citizen," I said.

"I am," he answered, shrilly.

"Are you? Do you know that we discovered that you haven't put in any community service hours for over a year and a half?"

"That's not true. I've been doing my part. Ask my ward's project leader. He'll tell you. I've been helping down at the district soup kitchen."

"Your project leader died two months ago, Ed. He had a heavy caseload and his replacement hasn't had a chance to contact you about your delinquency."

He rubbed his hand through his hair again but said nothing, so I continued. "I suppose you've been busy with The Macaroni Hut and just thought you went down to the soup kitchen."

He sighed, but he knew it was a small trap. "All right, I'll make retribution. I'll pay the civic fines. What else can I do?"

"You can tell us about Maria Raynor."

His expression wilted. "I never met her. I told you that."

"But you were catering her dinner parties. How did all that come about?"

"One day she called me. She said she'd heard all about me from a friend."

"What was the name of the friend?"

He glanced away. "I don't know. I didn't ask."

"Now, I find that strange, Ed. Why not? Don't you think it's important to find out which customer is recommending your services so you can continue to increase your sales volume?"

"I just didn't think about it. Her call took me by surprise."

LaRue grunted as he spilled a couple of clippings onto the table.

"What did you say to Mrs. Raynor?" I asked.

"I told her that I wasn't licensed by the district to do catering, only carry out. Well, she insisted and explained to me that her husband could fix it so I could do it legit."

"And, of course, he did."

"I don't know who did it. I called for a labor update the next day and it was listed on my docket. That's the honest truth, Marshals."

"Is it?" I said. "I looked over your employee declaration, and I didn't see one person assigned to the task of catering foods. How do you explain that?"

He winced, and it made his face look like it belonged on a dried apple doll. "Well, you know." When I remained silent, he dragged his sentences along. "The fix for the catering operation didn't include an addendum for my employees' class designations. If I'd waited for the paperwork to go through, I would have missed the boat on this one. My assistant chef handled the catering business and hired under the table most of the time. Besides, Mrs. Raynor supplied most of her own serving help."

"She did? Do you remember any names?"

He shook his head. "Like I said, I never met Mrs. Raynor face to face. I do remember, though, that one of her workers acted up during a dinner party and got fired on the spot."

"Your assistant told you this?"

"Yeah."

"Why was she fired?"

He hesitated and tried to hide it. "I don't know, but it was apparently a bad scene. My guy thought they might have been illegal interdistrict immigrants."

"We'd like to talk to your assistant chef. What's his name?"

He shook his head. "It won't do any good. He was killed in a train accident a couple of weeks ago."

15

AFTER WE MADE sure Edward Polinato pledged to pay his civic fines, we let him get back to his business and we visited the artist, Topaz. I had expected someone with such a professional moniker to be young, gorgeous, and wealthy. What we found was a woman who fit her given name much better.

Jolene Nebraska was a thin, white-haired lady who looked like she hailed from good Puritan stock. Her words were clipped, suggesting years of living in one of the northern districts. Her apartment was on the top floor of a walk-up located in a quiet section of the locality, and while it wasn't a rich ward, it was far enough removed from the general squalor to be appealing. She met us at the door with a dour expression, which when we showed her our IDs, changed to one of surprise.

She invited us into a space crammed with artist's canvases each in a different stage of painting. Dull sunlight dappled the room as it streamed in through scratched skylights to heighten the hues of splattered acrylic that had dried onto a drop cloth rug.

"Is there something wrong, Marshals?" she asked.

"No ma'am, not where you're concerned," LaRue answered. "We're investigating the death Maria Raynor. We were given your name as someone who does special art commissions for private individuals."

That familiar look of having been found out by the feds tailored her features and erased the severe expression she wore. LaRue jumped into the silence that these accusations always brought. "We're not here to bother you about your unreported income, Ms. Nebraska. We're only concerned with finding a killer. You might be able to help us."

She sat down in a wooden rocking chair and pointed to the overstuffed couch before answering. "Whatever I can do."

I pulled the bag from my pocket and dangled it by the string to show her. "Did you create this charm bag, Ms. Nebraska?"

When she saw the sack, she pursed her lips, then flattened them. Finally, she said, "Yes. That's one that I made."

"For Councilman Raynor?"

It took a moment more before her words surfaced. "Yes. And he never paid me for it."

"What happened?"

"Legitimately, I work for the Public Art League—painting, sculpting, whatever the assignment might be. Privately, I do something called aura art; that being art inspired by a person's metaphysical energy."

We must have looked confused because she dolloped in a sigh before explaining this cryptic concept. "The aura is like an electromagnetic halo that surrounds every living being. I have the ability to pick up these subtle vibrations and make artwork that is individually attuned."

I nodded to myself. It seemed that Topaz had an invisible magic scam going of her own.

"Councilman Raynor said he wanted a special birthday present for his wife. She'd specifically asked for one of my handwoven charm bags. He didn't ask the price and I didn't volunteer it. He just stopped by for a few minutes, told me what he wanted, and flew out the door like he was late for an appointment. So I started by doing an aura reading on his wife."

"Did you meet with her?"

"No. It's not necessary. I can do it from a remote location."

LaRue saved me from making a smart remark. "What did you find out?"

"Her aura was a mess. Full of holes and evaporating energy. I also tuned into an intense sadness, and when I meditated on it and reviewed the pickup from her energy field, I got the idea that the woman's spirit was trapped inside a tiny bag, as though her universe was a very closed place.

"Well, I'm an honest person when it comes to aura interpretation. I fashioned that beautiful charm pouch for her." Her expression narrowed as she added, "And the materials weren't cheap."

"What happened then?"

"Councilman Raynor returned, and when I told him my fee, he lost all control and told me in no uncertain terms that he would never pay that kind of money for a—how did he put it? A stinking voodoo bag."

"We found this in the possession of Mrs. Raynor. Do you have any idea how it got there?"

She shook her head and I thought for a minute she was going to say no, but she fooled me. "I can't tell you for certain, understand, but the next night, when I came home from work, I found my apartment ransacked and several art pieces missing." She pointed to the purse. "That bag was one of them."

16

―――■―――

WHEN WE RETURNED to the office, we found that Maria Raynor's father, Hale Conroy, had come in for a visit. Sitting there patiently waiting in the interrogation room, he looked just like Duvalier's vice chamberlain, Amish Qua: a big, burly man, with a face etched with a constellation of burst capillaries. We both offered our condolences as we joined him at the table. He accepted our uncomfortable mutterings with a sad smile.

"My wife is beside herself," he said, in a low voice. "She would have come, but the doctors have her tranquilized. She has high blood pressure and can't take the stress."

"We understand, Mr. Conroy," LaRue answered. "Is there something you would like to discuss with us?"

He nodded. "I want to discuss my son-in-law, Jack Raynor."

"What about him?"

"You may not believe me, but he was capable of killing my daughter."

"Why do you say that?"

"Because he physically abused her. A lot."

"Domestic violence doesn't necessarily translate into murder, sir," I offered.

"What about when that person threatens to kill you?"

"Did you hear Jack express a desire to kill Maria?"

"Not exactly. One night we were attending a dinner party at their home. From what my wife tells me, Maria confided that she had new cuts and bruises from where he'd beaten her. She told her mother that he'd said: "You're so damned fat, you should be put out of your misery." Now, if you ask me, that statement makes this man capable of murder."

"Had your daughter ever mentioned this type of thing before?"

"She may have, but not to me. She always talked to her mother about the abuse and right now my wife is in a state of hysteria. I haven't been able to get much out of her."

"When did this particular incident happen?"

"Just a couple of weeks ago."

"Why didn't your daughter leave him?" I asked. "Proven physical abuse would have gotten her a legal divorce."

"She said she loved him and couldn't leave." Two tears spilled down his cheeks, but he ignored them. "My daughter had an inferiority complex that no number of psychiatrists could cure. She was afraid to take the chance because she thought that she was not good enough to find someone who would truly love her. Maybe I see it as a father would, but Maria had a heart, a big heart. She never treated anyone badly."

LaRue pushed some more buttons. "I understand why your daughter may have been hesitant to leave this relationship, but what's Jack's excuse? There have been media rumors flying about him for several months linking him with various women from the better neighborhoods."

"I know. Those rumors are true, too. It makes me sick to think of it." He finally wiped at his tears. "Theirs was an arranged marriage. Jack's father was once my best friend, and not so long ago, my daughter was very thin and very beautiful. It was supposed to be a union blessed by St. Ophelia. Instead, it grew into something demonic." He paused again to press his nostrils shut with his forefinger and thumb. "The terms of the dowry contract specified that if Maria died, then Jack and their heirs would receive a trust fund of 200,000 credits, but if they divorced, then the money would revert to my family unit." He looked apologetic. "I wanted assurances that my daughter's children would be taken care of should the marriage fail. Well, it failed, but the money was enough to overpower the breakup."

LaRue dragged the subject father. "What did Maria say about Jack's philandering?"

"She hated it, of course, but didn't do anything to stop it. So, instead of having the comfort of the man she loved, she settled for the comfort of food that she loved. I suppose it was the one thing she figured she could control."

"What about all the environmental meters in the house?" I asked. "Why so many?"

"Guilt. Jack had them installed a few months ago to make Maria feel bad about how much she consumed. He screamed at her in front of me one time about how the entire trust fund was going to go to pay the taxes if she didn't stop wasting energy."

"What did she say to that?"

He shook his head. "Nothing."

"Your daughter was a quiet woman," I said.

"I believe the term is *whipped*." He ladled in a sigh. "She was gentle, and she never raised her voice to a living person."

"What about her domestic help? Her maid, for instance? How did she treat her?"

"What maid? Jack was too cheap to actually hire a maid. The domestics were all illegals."

"Did Maria tell you that?"

"Yes. They came in through Jack."

"What does that mean?"

"He had contacts with other districts. He was shimmying visas and bringing in no-names. He was indenturing them for the cost of the transportation and papers. Once here, he rented them to rich friends so they could get their housework done and their gardens weeded without having to pay employee benefits. To answer your original question, my poor Maria always felt that people didn't deserve to be treated like slaves. I suppose it's safe to say that she identified with their plight."

"Do you think Jack is capable of such a brutal murder?"

"To gain the trust fund? I certainly do."

"Excuse my abruptness, but what about the mutilation? Why would he do such a thing?"

"To cast away suspicion, of course. But I know better. He's capable of it. Maria once told me a story about his viciousness."

"What happened?"

"He and his younger brother had a disagreement when they were children. Jack cut off his right hand with an ax."

17

THAT EVENING, BABA went to bed early and I found myself sitting alone in my lumpy chair trying to enjoy the one indulgence I give myself: watching a rented movie on my portable vid system. It's a small setup with a small screen, but then I don't need anything fancy to engage my attention. Though the disk was one of my favorites, I kept straying from the film's story line to stare at the bank of lights.

Lycanthropy is a series of emotional changes as well as subtle physical alterations. At least, that's what I blame my violent tendencies upon, and sitting there, I wanted nothing better than to smash every bulb to shards. The only thing that stopped me was the fact that I'd have to clean up all the glass, so rather than taking out my anger in an immature manner, I resigned myself to nibbling on a piece of cheese and considering the charms decorating the lights. It seemed that Baba had added several more in the past few days, despite the fact that I wasn't using them for my delta wave therapy.

Since I came down with lycanthropy, I've been relegated to the land of superstition. Even those I'm closest to can't fathom how I perceive the world now. LaRue's mother is afraid that if I bite her son during one of my full moon episodes, he'll end up with the same affliction, so she makes him wear amulets and charms. The closer it gets to the turn, the more junk he has dangling around his neck. He tells me he wears it to please her, but I've wondered how deeply he believes in the power of the magic.

The decorations on the bank of lights were supposed to bring an assortment of invisible energy to bear; things such as good luck and good health, as well as keeping away generic demons and low-flying UFOs. On one side, Baba had strung a rope of miscellaneous buttons found in a garbage heap. When I asked what significance they held, she had told me that they helped close any openings in the interdimensional fabric that separated the human realms from the ghostly planes. To increase the overall potency of the outfit, she'd draped a woven trash banner across the top and fitted it with rusty safety pins, from which dangled such magic grabbers as crow feathers, plastic beads, and sacks of smooth stones fished out of the Black River. Traveling down the other side were a series of clangers: dented tin can lids, bent silverware, and broken crockery pieces, all objects that made noise and kept evil spirits at bay.

After staring at the objects for over an hour, I couldn't seem to recover my interest in the vid, so I flicked it off and rose to get ready for bed. It was then that I noticed an unfamiliar charm hanging near the bottom of the lights. It was one of Baba's famous woven trash baggies. I plucked it from the hinge and opened the flap. Inside, I found seven tiny scrolls.

As you can imagine, I had a hard time believing my eyes. I dumped the contents onto the table and started unwrapping the papers. They were handwritten miniatures, similar to those we'd found in Maria Raynor's charm sack. I took the scrolls into the bedroom to ask Baba where she'd gotten them.

One of the things that Gibson had brought with him the night he made his house call was a small bottle of apple brandy. My roommate had made short work of it during the day and now she snored heavily. She also didn't move when I set the propane lantern on the rickety nightstand. I even turned up the lamp and still received no response.

I shook her gently. "Baba? Can you hear me, Baba?"

Her snoring ceased and she smacked her lips, but she still didn't open her eyes. I put a little more urgency into my rousing technique. "Baba, wake up. I need to talk to you. Come on you old drunk, let's go."

It took a moment before she groaned and came to life. Her arm went up immediately to shield her eyes from the lantern's bright glow. "Oh, my head. Is there a fire?"

I smiled. "No, there isn't a fire." I showed her one of the scrolls. "Where did you get these?"

She squinted at them and tried to wet her lips again. "I don't know. What are they?"

"It's part of a charm I found hanging on the lights. They're little bits of paper with miniature handwriting on them."

She looked as though she searched through fog trying to find some useful bit of information that would shut me up. "I don't remember, my dear. Try Virgil Cree. I do know he was the one who put the luck on the bag. I just don't know if I bought the whole charm from him, or if I scrounged it some other way. He might be able to tell you."

"Where can I find Virgil?"

She yawned. "At the junk bazaar next to St. Ophelia's Cathedral. Now, can I go back to sleep?"

I nodded. Baba closed her eyes, and in a moment she was snoring again.

18

As I SAID , the majority of my stretches come on when I least expect them and, of course, my lycanthropic clock struck the next morning as LaRue and I made our way to the Trabi, which was parked in the muddy lot serving the Marshal's Office. To make it all the more embarrassing, Gibson just happened to be pulling in as I fell against the hood of my partner's car.

The stretch begins as a spark in my solar plexus and during these times, the werewolf legend and the werewolf reality meet. It feels like my insides are shredding. I'm positive that my heart is torn from its mooring and my lungs are flayed with each labored breath I take. My intestines cramp and one of these days I'm certain that they're going to explode.

The pain made me howl. When LaRue reached me, I was already deeply absorbed in my agony. I slid to the ground, falling helplessly into a rain puddle. I rolled around, slinging greasy water against him as he tried to control my flailing by grabbing my arms and sitting on my legs.

"You're all right, Ty," he whispered, hoarsely. "Just relax. It's a short one. You're almost through it."

I tried to nod, but a wave of nausea kept me from speaking. My body kept reacting to this lycanthropic pump and it was a few more minutes before I could respond to his efforts to help me sit up. The water seeped through my cammies and I shivered as a frigid wind cranked up around us. Gibson hunkered down beside me to take my hand and check my pulse, the whole time studying me with a concerned expression.

"She'll be fine in a couple of minutes," LaRue said.

"That was part of it, wasn't it?" Gibson asked.

"Yes."

Turning a glare on me, Gibson lost his bedside manner. "There's no mention in any of your records about violently recurring seizures and you didn't bother to tell me the other night. I assume you weren't going to say anything, either. Am I right?"

LaRue answered for me.

"Ty tried to explain to the first doctor about the seizures. He wanted to cut out some of her brain. Would you go on with it at that point?"

He scowled and worked his lips until some words finally came out. "Let's go to the clinic. I want to take some tests."

I tried to protest, but was dragged off, anyway. Gibson shoved me into his pickup truck, ignoring the mud I brought in with me. LaRue left in the Trabi to continue on with the day's work, thankful, I'm sure, that he wouldn't have my mess in his car. The doctor said nothing until we arrived and I was sitting on an examining table.

He immediately checked my blood pressure, frowned at me disapprovingly, and then tried his stethoscope. He slid it up the back of my shirt and curtly told me to take a deep breath. Satisfied that my heart was still there, he checked my pupils, pronounced them dilated, and stood back to study me.

"If I had known this, we could have prepared for it."

"You think so? Why don't you hand me one of your culture slides, there, Doc."

His frown deepened, but he did as I asked, unwrapping the glass from its tissue paper container. Holding it by the edges, he passed it to me.

"How does the brain control growth during a person's

lifetime?" I asked, while I rolled my forefinger print across the slide.

He watched me, answering slowly. "It controls the metabolism and the secretion of certain hormonal chemicals that stimulate the organs and skeletal system."

I nodded and gave him the sample. "Sorry about the mud," I added.

He took it to the computer, pushing it into an electronic cavity. Seconds later, a beautifully elongated fingerprint appeared on the screen.

I heard him hiss and then he said, flatly, "This is impossible." He turned from the analyzer to take my hands.

At some point during the seizure, I actually undergo a physical stretch. My skeleton grows, giving me a more sleek design; and while my lycanthropy is measured in inches and millimeters, it's enough of a difference to make my regular uniforms too short in the crotch.

I held my arm out straight and pointed to the cuff of my jumpsuit. "Do you see how the bottom of the sleeve hits me an inch above the wrist?"

"Yes."

"Well, it should be an inch below."

For just a moment, he dropped the intensity in his gaze, but after blinking at me, allowed it to return along with a theory. "There must be a portion of the brain that controls spontaneous growth in a human, something that neuroscience hasn't discovered. This is incredible."

"It was impossible a minute ago," I said. "Would you go so far as to say that this undiscovered part of my brain also controls the lycanthropic transformation process?"

"I don't know. It might be a symptom and nothing more." He headed toward the telephone. "I'm going to arrange for several neurological tests." He held up a silencing finger when I started to talk. "I'm curious to see whether your brain has increased in mass."

I had never considered that my brain might actually grow along with my bones. "What would that mean?" I asked cautiously.

"Swelling might suggest a splaying of brain tissue, which can give us a clue to specific neurological changes. Increasing pressure against the skull could be the reason for your ultimate full moon episodes."

I shivered involuntarily against the thought. "Then, after that final seizure, my brain might shrink again?"

He held his hands out. "Some schools of science believe that the moon not only controls the tides, but because humans are composed mostly of water, we, too, are affected. Along with the swelling, there might be an increase in cerebrospinal fluid." He reached over to gently touch my forehead. "Things might get pretty tight in there."

19

I SPENT THE rest of the morning at the hospital being scanned, swabbed, and stuck. After the final review, I bolted from the building, anxious to put my problems aside for a little while. I called LaRue immediately and suggested we go over to see Virgil Cree.

The area known as the junk bazaar was a collection of huts, tents, shacks, and booths whose owners officially catered to the tourists visiting the nearby cathedral. It was a bustling place, filled with purse snatchers, part-time beggars, and assorted con artists who worried shoppers away from the legally designated stores into various back door scams.

Virgil Cree officially ran a small souvenir shop set up inside a huge, rotting, stripped-down, walk-in freezer. You might think that you could buy all manner of cheap mementos in there, but the most to be found were a few raggedy postcards strewn across a crooked wooden table.

The thing that Virgil Cree really sold was invisible magic, and he peddled it by telling people that he was a man born lucky. For the right price, he could transfer some of this energy onto the customer. Depending on the need, he could do as little as wave his hand across the person while whispering benign words, or as much as pricking his finger for a drop of blood to include in a charm sack. According to Baba, he swore he had never failed to provide quality luck, but still there was a disclaimer in the form of a faded sign over the broken cash register announcing that all sales were final.

When we introduced ourselves as district marshals, Cree nervously tucked at a loose flap of his dirty linen turban. He motioned to a car bench seat and invited us to sit down. As we did, he paused to stoke a small coal burner standing in the corner of the freezer, most likely using the interim to come up with a denial regarding his back door operations. It was the first thing out of his mouth.

"If you're looking for souveniers, you're a little late. The tourists came through and bought my entire stock just this morning."

LaRue smiled and answered for us. "We're here to buy some good luck. We understand you fill such prescriptions on a regular basis."

He hesitated again, considering us with an appraising stare. Finally, he decided that we weren't there to arrest him and so he relaxed by sliding onto a broken secretarial chair. "What kind of luck do you need?"

"I'd like a lucky break on my next quarterly tax audit," I said jokingly.

"That's easy. Is there more?"

LaRue jumped in again. "We need some help in a murder investigation. Can you do that for us, too?"

"Yes, of course, but for that, you'll have to be specific."

It was what my partner waited for. He fished out the enlarged copies made from the scrolls and handed them to Cree. "Specifically, we need a little good fortune in finding out who wrote these. The originals are miniatures and we found them stored inside a charm bag similar to one you lucked up for Marshal Merrick's roommate."

He shook his head and the turban wobbled. "There are a lot of street scribes who could have written these."

"Any ideas who might have done this?"

"You might try a lady named Brown Hilda. She pushes a cart in the ritzier part of the district, and I understand she has a large clientele of folks who wish to have things written in miniature for healing spells and love hexes." He carefully studied each page before passing them back to LaRue. "That's the best I can come up with on that, but since the kind of luck you're seeking on this investigation serves the welfare of the public, I'll throw it in for free. It couldn't hurt, anyway." Turning to me, he said, "But yours, you must understand, is personal, and will cost a credit and a half."

I glanced at LaRue with an accusing look. He grinned and produced the appropriate cash.

When Cree had the money safely in his possession, he had us stand in the center of his junkyard shop. He then walked several circles around us while flicking a butane lighter on and off. A singsong incantation added a little drama. Just as I was starting to wonder how long it was going to take to transfer the luck, he finished. "The required good fortune for a speedy and successful end to this investigation is in place."

With that, he concentrated on laying on my tax break. First, he produced a bit of dried sage from his suit pocket, which he placed in a pile before my feet. He then borrowed a book of matches from LaRue and set it ablaze. The smoke smudging from the herb began to clog my sinuses and burn my eyes, but before I could move away, he stomped on the fire and started to sing another incantation. Once that was done, he then spit into the palm of his hand, and with a few more nonsense words, he dipped his fingertip into the mucus and dabbed the juice onto the center of my forehead.

20

THAT AFTERNOON, WHILE ordering pita pockets stuffed with scrambled eggs and cumin-spiced sausage from Nick's Sandwich Stand, word filtered down over the array that Jack Raynor was in governmental protection pending the outcome of the investigation. You would have thought that the message from the dispatcher had given LaRue a blood clot in the brain by the way he yanked out his earplug.

He paid the counter help and led me back to the Trabi before saying, "I did some checking on Jack last night."

"Did you find anything interesting?"

"A couple of things. It seems Jack was a juvenile delinquent. He had three assault actions filed against him before he turned eighteen. One of those was filed by his brother over the ax incident."

"Did he do time on any of them?"

"No. Not even community service."

We stopped the discussion long enough to spread our lunches on the trunk of the car.

"Do we know where his brother is now?" I asked.

LaRue paused to rip open a package of ketchup with his teeth. He answered me while squeezing the contents onto his sandwich filling. "Max Raynor was, until recently, held in the district lockup undergoing rehabilitation for quantum abuse. And before that? He worked as a courier for—you guessed it—Councilman Jack. I suppose he was feeling badly about cutting off his brother's hand and offered him a job."

"I take it Max has fallen off the edge of the earth, too."

"So far. But with his apparent drug problem, I don't think it will be long before he surfaces again. I've got feelers out. We should hear something shortly." With that he wrapped the burrito together and stuffed half the sandwich in his mouth. After he chewed it down, he continued. "Jack started getting his act together when he did his mandatory humanitarian service."

"Where was he assigned?"

"District Twenty-one. To a veterinary corps, of all things. According to the available information, he spent a year touring the agro regions and giving farm animals hormone shots. He got some outstanding commendations from the unit commander, and then he went on to the university where he received a degree in public health administration. Following that, he worked as a civil servant for various programs at the PHO before winning the number-one spot as a councilman."

"So someone is carrying him," I said. "It's not unheard of."

He smiled around his sandwich. "I agree, but why? As things go, he's not that high on the totem pole. All he does is set health policies and make people's lives a little more miserable. So, what does he know?"

I shrugged and settled into my meal, but my thoughts jumped around too much to come up with a logical take on the situation. I wondered more if it hadn't been Maria who knew something she shouldn't have.

Just as we finished up, my com node beeped and the dispatcher came through with a location on Brown Hilda, so we cleaned away the crumbs, fired up the Trabi, and went up district to visit her.

We found the street scribe pushing a rusty shopping cart down one of the more exclusive avenues in the district. Perched atop this conveyance was an old stop sign, which carried an antique, manual typewriter, a cardboard box filled with damp, curling paper, a cup of felt-tip pens, and a large magnifying glass held to this makeshift desk with a pair of vise clamps.

Brown Hilda specialized in writing in miniature. A strange business, yes, but important to those who believed in the power of charms, because most magical envelopes contained spells that were several pages long. The smaller the prescriptions, the better.

When we reached the corner of Winchester and Divine, we found the woman writing up something for the ward cop who had responded to our APB on the itinerant. She refused to acknowledge us until she had collected a half credit from the patrolman and sent him on his way. Then, pulling back the hood of her coat, she gave us a stern look.

"What can I do for you?" she asked in a crackly voice.

We showed her our IDs, but before LaRue could begin his pitch, she said, "Oh, you want a protection spell. That will be six credits. Up front."

"Maybe some other time," I answered, as I showed her the scroll copies. "We want to know if you or one of your colleagues may have written these for a charm recently."

She cackled. "Colleagues. That's funny. Like we really exist with a class designation and all that. Good one."

"Do you remember writing down these paragraphs for someone?" LaRue probed.

She spread the paper on her makeshift desk. "I wrote that," she said, proudly. "Some of my best work, too."

"What do the pages say?"

She shrugged. "I don't speak any other language but what you hear me talking right now. I would have copied something like that."

"From what?"

"From whatever the person wanted copied, of course. I can't remember where these came from."

LaRue flipped a five credit piece at her. "Does this help your memory?"

"Afraid not. I've got a touch of forgetfulness."

He tossed in another fiver and it fell with a clink against the stop sign.

"Now I recall," she said, brightly. "They were already written up in a notebook."

"What kind of notebook?"

"A red, three-ring binder. It was a journal or something. It had lots of diagrams in it. He wanted certain pages copied in miniature and he wanted them on my best paper."

"Do you remember who brought this notebook to you?"

She studied the pages before venturing an answer. "It seems to me he was a big guy with dark hair."

LaRue glanced at me and I knew he was hearing an echo of the psychic, Clyde Smith's words.

Hilda thought a moment more before adding, "His face is a blur, but one thing I can tell you about him for sure."

"What?" LaRue said.

"His right hand was missing."

21

TULLEE JONES WAS a citizens' project leader in my ward, the man who advised family units on birth control options and the humanitarian party line. For years, he had taken the word throughout the whole district, working as a chiropractor for the government and riding along with the university bookmobile. While folks waited to be given new propaganda to read, Tullee would crack their backs for a fee and counsel them on how best to serve the community. He also lived in my apartment building and could read and write Chinese.

That evening I found him sharing the building's front stoop with a couple of other old men who were fast approaching the fall down drunk stage from a bottle of home brewed whiskey that was being passed between them. Each had a large plastic bag filled with aluminum cans ready for pickup and payment, if the recycling truck rolled through the ward. Unfortunately, it had been three months since we'd last seen it and the residents of the building had enough tin to build a car.

Tullee had that Kung Fu master look about him, even dressed in baggy jeans and a wrinkled blue shirt. He was openly smoking a cigarette as he smiled at a neighbor known to work for the Pollution Control Board, a watchdog organization that did its part to victimize the citizenry. He turned the smile onto me when I climbed the steps and sat at his feet.

"Tulee, I need your help."

His smile turned into a ragged-toothed grin. "Do you need your back cracked? I still have the strength in my hands. Retirement hasn't changed that, you know."

I shook my head and his grin evaporated. "I need your help on a murder investigation."

His friends moaned and reminded him of his civic obligations in loud voices spiced with sharp remarks and laughter.

"How can I help?" he asked, ignoring their input.

"We have a series of scrolls found on the murder victim. They're written in several different languages and one of them is Chinese. I need a translation."

His friends passed the bottle between themselves and leaned in to look over his shoulder. I handed Tullee the paper, and he quietly read the contents, going back for a second run-through before glancing up at me.

"When Duvalier instituted the Barrier language, he destroyed the Babylon Factor. Don't you think?"

I had no idea what he was talking about, so I stared at him stupidly until he continued. "The distillation of the world's unique languages has placed most of us at a disadvantage. We can no longer read the untainted works of the great masters who wrote in pure dialects." He squeezed the paper between thumb and forefinger. "This is beautifully written."

"But what does it say?" I asked with a little more impatience than I meant.

His friends helped by pressing him on with slurred words.

He adjusted his Ben Franklin glasses and scanned the sheet using the slide of his nose as a scope. He read: "'Sun Ye Sung carried the soul of Leonardo da Vinci. In her time, world peace had been established and technology had made it possible for people to live comfortably into old age. Unfortunately, the population had increased to the point where the resources no longer served the people, but the social beliefs precluded euthanasia, abortion, and even the death sentence for criminals. Something had to be done so that the strong had a chance to survive.

"'Being concerned for the overall good of humanity and a brilliant scientist, Sun Ye Sung decided to do what she could to save the world. She invented the genetic isotope.'"

He paused to take a swig from the offered liquor bottle before continuing. "This is interesting. Maybe it's an excerpt from a book or paper, although I've never heard of the author. At the bottom of the page, it says: *The Moral Question of Saving the World*. Dr. Philip Ligotti.'"

22

AT 7 P.M., we hauled in Ms. Emily Church, Jack Raynor's ex-girlfriend. She was a gorgeous thing and she knew it. Buxom, raven-haired, impeccably dressed, she paused to brush at the seat of the chair before sitting down at the interrogation room table. I glanced at LaRue who was in

danger of tripping over his tongue. I let him salivate while
I took the interview.

"How long have you known Jack Raynor, Ms. Church?"

She had slow sex in her voice and she tried to use it. "I've
known Jack practically all my life, Marshal. He came to
work for my daddy when I was just out of secondary
school."

"Your daddy is Cecil M. Church. Is that correct?"

"Yes, of course."

"What did he do for Mr. Church?" I said.

"He developed an immunization program for the PHO
Bureau of Social Welfare. He started out as a junior
administrator and before the whole thing was over, he was
running the project. It practically made his career."

"Did this program have anything to do with something
called a genetic isotope?"

She frowned, and the expression started lengthening into
a scowl before she spoke. "You would have to ask Jack. I
don't know."

"What about your father? Could he tell us?"

"Daddy suffers from Alzheimer's disease," she said
quickly. "You can verify this fact if you want. He won't be
any help, the poor dear."

LaRue stepped in with a hard edge to his voice. "Let's
talk about something different. Was Jack a superstitious
man?"

She pursed her perfect lips. "No. I mean he didn't avoid
crossing the paths of black cats or anything." Then, looking
right at me, "And he didn't believe in ghosts or werewolves."

I took a deep breath and tried to shake off her comment.
LaRue continued.

"What about charms?"

"Maria was the one who loved charms and witch magic,

but Jack had a very scientific head. He was always trying to dissuade his wife from buying that junk."

"Do you know where she would buy it?"

"From all over, I suppose. She was always trying some spell or the other to get rid of her fat. I do recall Jack being particularly angry one night about how she had spent four hundred credits on a voodoo bottle. He was livid, the poor darling. Worse than that, she bought it from a supposed friend of his."

"Who?"

"I can't tell you. He never mentioned any names."

I trod back into the conversation. "How long were you and Jack lovers?"

"Oh, just a little over a year. We're great friends; we just can't get along on an everyday basis."

"Why did you break up?"

"Maria wouldn't grant him a divorce. There was no point in going on, you see. His wife gave him permission for his philandering and he started straying, even from me."

"Did you and Maria ever have occasion to talk?"

"At her dinner parties, of course."

"Did she ever speak with you privately?"

"One time. To be truthful, I think she was drunk."

"Why?"

"We were alone in her kitchen during one of the gatherings. She kept going on about how she was losing all this weight. Frankly, I couldn't see it. She was taking some sort of therapy that was changing her whole metabolism."

"Would that therapy be chelated chromium?"

She frowned and I got the sense that she wanted to hesitate but thought better of it. "No, no, that wasn't it. I can't remember. I was just dismissing her as she ranted. The woman was enormous. Well, you know that."

"When was the last time you saw Jack?" LaRue asked.

"About two months ago. I've been out of the district."

"Doing what?"

"I was hunting down antiques and art objects for a friend."

The squad secretary interrupted us just then. "You have a call, Merrick. It's a Dr. Gibson. He says not to blow him off."

I snorted and LaRue chuckled. Ms. Church sat there fidgeting.

I excused myself and took my time getting back to the cubicle. Gibson was his usual intense self. I could sense it in his voice.

"Your neurological scans are in."

I almost didn't want to know. "And did my brain grow?"

"There's a two percent decrease in your frontal lobe and an adjacent increase in your temporal lobe."

I shuddered involuntarily as I created the image. "Which means?" I whispered.

"The frontal lobe controls your reasoning, your emotions, and your cognitive abilities. The temporal lobe processes your ability to learn, to comprehend language, and is the place where some scientists believe they have discovered the storehouse for primal memories."

"What are they as opposed to the regular kind?"

"Well, there's a big controversy over it right now in the medical community, but the theory is that every human brain is genetically fitted with memories that have survived from the birth of our species. These memories may have something to do with survival, procreation, and territorial instincts. They may also trigger the fight or flight response commonly attributed to a portion of the brain known as the hypothalmus."

"So, what you're saying is that my temporal lobe just might be the place where the wolf lives?"

"That's right."

I suddenly realized that I had unknowingly depended upon a supernatural status and now, being presented with the medical truth, I wasn't quite sure what I had become. For years, I had labored to make sense of my lycanthropy. I had taken the mythological assumptions and blended them with the physical changes, because there was nothing else on which to draw a conclusion about how it all worked. Gibson's revelations were more than just a bit disconcerting.

When I didn't speak, his voice changed from intensity to concern. "Merrick, are you all right with this?"

"I'm not sure," I murmured. Then, "What you're saying is even stranger than the legends themselves."

There were no words of comfort following my answer. Instead, he said, "You have an appointment at the PHO compound at 10:30 P.M., tonight. Wear comfortable clothing, and don't be late."

"What is this for?"

"To satisfy my curiosity."

23

GIBSON MET ME at the front gate of the PHO District Medical Compound. From looking at the twenty-foot-high fence with its concertina wire valance, it was hard to believe that the converted maximum-security prison was a thing of the past. The ugly, pockmarked building still had bars covering the windows and the grounds were decorated with square redbrick huts known as ovens. These cramped spaces held malcontents at one time and now were used as ready-built examining and therapy rooms by doctors and research scientists.

I could tell Gibson was mentally rubbing his hands together in anticipation of the upcoming experiment. His excitement gushed out as he explained what would occur in oven number thirty-three.

"I want to see what happens when you sleep. The computer in this hut has special software that can measure the activation levels of your brain neurons during the dream state."

I stopped walking. "You're going to have to explain that."

He dragged to a stop, shucking the knapsack he carried on his back. It was an impatient gesture that didn't do much for my mood. "Your brain has neurons," he explained. "These particles are part of what makes it work. You have about one hundred billion of them, and each one can be activated on ten different levels to produce ten different patterns in response to stimuli. I think that when your brain was damaged from the carbon monoxide, the activation levels changed. They started firing in new directions." He nodded for me to follow him before continuing. "With this increase in temporal lobe density, it may suggest that your normal neuron activation reverts to a firing sequence more consistent to that which occurred in early man."

"Accessing the primal memories you mentioned."

"Yes. Of course, I could be way off base. We just don't know that much about how the physical brain and mental mind work together. Scientists discover new things every day. Then, it's usually another decade before the mainstream medical community accepts the hypothesis."

"Supposing you're right. How do you change the neuron patterns so I don't have the seizures?"

He glanced at the ground as he answered. "I don't know. I'm hoping what we do here tonight will give me some clue. If nothing else, I'll be amassing information that we could use later on when we compare your hospital scans."

We reached oven thirty-three. Gibson fought the rusted lock for a couple of minutes and then led me into the unit. It was cold inside and there wasn't any form of heating to change that. A small metal bunk was hitched to the wall next to a dirty toilet, a cabinet, and a plain wooden table that supported a variety of electronic instruments. I glanced up to see that the ceiling was covered in of all things, scribbled prescription notes. I pulled one down and found that the tag was used like grafitti—to announce the names and dates of those who had come before. The piece of paper I'd selected had been taped up when I was ten years old.

"Have a seat on the bed," Gibson said.

I did as he ordered. "I'm not taking off my coat," I warned. "It's colder than my flat in here."

He shrugged while he pumped up the computer. Moving to the cabinet, he collected a variety of electrodes, a dingy white towel, and a tube of gel. He tossed them next to me. "I'm hooking you up to the monitor this evening. All you have to do is get a few hours of sleep. I'll be able to have a better look at any delta wave fluctuations. We'll go through a couple of REM periods." He popped open the glue and began applying the leads to my forehead. "In the twentieth century, scientists did a lot of work with sleep disorders. They realized that brain waves could be measured during REM sleep and dream patterns could be isolated. They also discovered predictable activity in certain parts of the brain. I want to see what happens with you."

"So, you'll be studying my dreams, then?"

"I will definitely want to know what you dreamed about. The images might help localize the fluctuating segments of neuron bursts." He paused in setting a drop of gel against one of the sensor pads to squint at me. "That makes you uncomfortable. Why?"

I tried to figure out what it was in my expression that had betrayed my feelings. "No," I said, bravely. "I'm all right."

"I'll bet you get some humdingers," he murmured, as he finished applying the lead. When he was done, he produced a thermos from his pack and poured me a cup of steaming liquid.

I sniffed the offering and glanced at him. "What is it?"

"Russian tea. It's cold as shit in here. Drink it." When I didn't move, he added, "It's not drugged. I'd be up front with you about that." To prove it, he took the cup from me and swigged down two good gulps. "I have sandwiches, too. Here, I'll split one with you."

We shared the food in silence for a few minutes. I'd barely finished my last bite when he demanded that I stretch out on the cot. Once done, he proceeded to cover me with a dirty blanket brought from the cabinet and then bid me a good nap as he took a seat before the computer.

The meal lay heavy in my stomach and the blanket warmed me. I had all the right conditions to slip into sleep, but instead, I started thinking about Maria Raynor again. I couldn't help wondering if she was as frustrated with her inability to lose weight as I was about my inability to control the wolf in me. I could understand her steps toward possible recovery, even the charms and spells. She was grasping at straws to have a normal life as defined by society. I felt sad for her, but if the truth were known, I felt more pity for myself.

"Gibson," I said, abruptly, "do you know anything about chromium therapy?"

"You're supposed to be asleep, Merrick."

"Well, I'm not. Do you?"

"Yes. Now go to sleep."

"Tell me a bedtime story, Doc."

He harumfed. "I assume you're referring to chelated chromium."

"That's the one."

He sighed. "People used to take capsules of chelated chromium because it was supposed to affect the metabolism's burn rate. Chelation is a chemical coating process that allows the chromium to be absorbed by the body."

"Did it work?" I asked.

"Who knows? Chromium therapy included a lot of things. A low-fat diet, exercise, and antioxidant supplements. You do all that and you're bound to lose weight and feel better, but relying on just chromium? I don't think so. As far as I know, reduction of calories is about the only way to shed pounds. Now, will you go to sleep? We are supposed to be concentrating on your problem, remember?"

"This investigation is my problem."

He blew another loud sigh through his nose. "Will you please relax and forget about murder and mayhem just for a little while?"

I smiled to myself. "I'll try." Waiting about ten seconds, I asked, "How much is it costing you to rent this box, anyway?"

"Plenty, and I want to get my money's worth. Why don't you think of something pleasant to help you sleep?"

"Like what?"

He moaned.

"You didn't answer me."

"Oh, all right. Do you like music?"

"Sure."

"Do you want me to sing to you?"

I cocked an eye his way and found him grinning.

"Do you have a nice voice?"

"True, it's been a number of years since I sang with the St. Ophelia Boys' Choir, but I can probably still hold a tune. If you'll shut up, I'll try."

A grin played at my lips, but I was determined not to let it escape. "OK. Serenade me."

Gibson came up with an old Irish tune, which he sang in a soothing baritone. I closed my eyes to appreciate the song and the next thing I knew, I was in the middle of the razor blade dream.

This episode played like an old movie. The colors softened to shades of sepia and the air was dense and hot. I found myself in a bare room with no door or windows. My hands and feet were chained to a large wire rack that ran from floor to ceiling in the center of the space. I knew that I was naked, except for my gun and shoulder holster. I was certain that my body was covered with a downy gray fur and while I knew my face hadn't changed into that of a wolf's, I could feel the points of emerged canine teeth pricking my bottom lip. I tasted blood and realized a male figure was standing before me slowly shoving pieces of a shattered razor blade into my mouth. I tried to protest even as I tried not to swallow.

So here I was, caught in sleep, but lucid enough to know that I was in an oven with Gibson. My mouth was filling up fast with steel as my sluggish brain cast around the ether, looking for a way to escape the nightmare.

The pieces sticking to the back of my tongue felt as though they were sliding into my throat and my gag reflex threatened to undo me. Tears of frustration bedeviled me and turned the dream juicy, making it even harder to concentrate on the forming face of this amorphous torturer. I managed to see a pair of ice blue eyes, but his features remained distorted and runny. I tried not to think about my discomfort by studying the man, but suddenly I was yanked from the dream and left gasping for air.

I came awake with a jolt and found that Gibson was holding me in his arms. There was that moment of disorientation when I thought I was with an old lover. I lingered for a few seconds to work off the shakes, but soon enough, I pulled away.

The carbon monoxide poisoning triggered so many things in me. After that night, I've suffered from some form of sleep apnea. My respiratory muscles have become paralyzed; I can't force air to pass into my lungs; and my imagination translates it into the razor blades adhering to my tongue. Without sounding too philosophical, I think that I literally start holding my breath before the occurrence of a full moon.

"Well, you've managed to keep that problem a secret," Gibson said. "It's not in any of your medical records, either."

"Is there more tea?" I husked. "My throat is on fire."

He nodded and fetched me a drink, silently watching me as I gulped it.

I tilted my head toward the computer. "What did you find out?"

"Your brain experiences an unusual explosion of activity when you hit the REM state and a lot of the flare-up is confined to the temporal lobe. What were you dreaming about, anyway?"

I was ready to give him the whole thing, when my answer was stalled by the realization that the man filling my mouth with razor blades had no right hand.

24

CATIE BENNET WAS Jack Raynor's administrative assistant and she looked like Duvalier's third wife, Maralaxa Vaughn: tall, chunky, and wearing a badly fitted black wig. With a flare for the dramatic, she met us the next morning in the lobby of the District Council Building, spearheading a small army of flunkies who strode through a throng of angry citizens demanding fair labor practices and an impartial hearing by the mediation board regarding public health. LaRue and I stood on the periphery of this demonstration, watching Catie dispatch her bureaucrats to occupy the masses by drawing them into small committees of two and three. These followers dropped off like fishing net weights being thrown from a cruising boat.

Ms. Bennet arrived at our position with just one servant left in tow. He was a stereotypical government employee dressed in black leather britches and a white shirt trimmed with lace. When they stopped to greet us, he cut LaRue a fierce look that was magnified by his thick glasses.

"This is Mr. Wainwright," Ms. Bennet said. "He's my chief of operations for Councilman Raynor's office." She didn't wait for the courtesy of a handshake, but instead marched by us, throwing her next statement over her shoulder as she did. "I'm sorry our conversation must be on the run, but I've got to cover this engagement, and I'm late."

"That's all right," I said. "We don't mind walking while we talk."

She grunted and pulled out ahead as we started to follow.

"What's the engagement all about?" I asked.

Mr. Wainwright answered. "Ms. Bennet is scheduled to

100

speak before a gathering of the District Shriners. Mr. Raynor was supposed to do it, but the poor man is devastated and unable to appear."

"Has he contacted your office?"

Ms. Bennet boomed in. "No, he hasn't, and grief-stricken or not, I don't enjoy making public excuses for him."

I glanced at LaRue who stayed stoney-faced as he asked, "Why is that so unpleasant a duty? Don't you like him and feel for his pain right now?"

She shook her head and stomped her conservative high heels against the cracked sidewalk pavement. Mr. Wainwright once more took the con.

"It's no secret that Ms. Bennet disapproves of the councilman's lifestyle," he said. "We all do. The employees, I mean."

"That's not it at all," she thundered, stopping in her tracks to face us. "It's the subject I'll be speaking on today. I don't agree with his stance."

"Oh?" I said. "What's it about?"

"I have to deny allegations that the district is running a children's sweatshop over in Ward Nineteen. Apparently, there was an outbreak of Legionnaires' disease and twelve people died. We inspected that installation and it was clean. This has nothing to do with public health. It has to do with labor practices. Period."

"Is there one?"

She looked at me like I had just grown a mustache before her eyes. "One what? A sweat factory? Of course, there is." Then, spinning, she clopped away, explaining her dilemma in hisses and snorts. "Tell me, Marshal. Weren't you required to join a District Youth Challenge Group?"

"Yes."

"What kind of work did they have you do?"

"I worked on a recycling truck."

"Did you work more than four hours a day?"

"Sure. It was more like twelve hours day."

She stopped again to make her point. "And now, look at you. A model citizen protecting the innocent. By your position, I know you didn't dodge the mandatory humanitarian service or evade your birth control designation. So you tell me, did all of these things hurt you or make you better? You see, I simply have a hard time worrying about something that's been going on for decades to the benefit of the community. It's ridiculous."

"But Jack Raynor feels differently?"

"He doesn't want to cause a commotion. For some reason, he's trying to appease the masses instead of dealing with the resistance. The government is changing, I tell you. People don't know their places. Like that gathering in the District Council Building. That wouldn't have taken place ten years ago; I can tell you that for sure. The populace simply has too much time on its hands."

"How does Councilman Raynor feel about this so-called sweatshop?"

"Who knows? He hasn't had time for this since he started—" She stopped and I could tell that she tacked on a different ending from the one she intended. "Since he started his flagrant womanizing. Especially all that philandering with Emily Church. His poor wife, may she rest in peace."

With that, she doubled her speed and shouted a dismissal, leaving us standing on the corner with Mr. Wainwright. I turned to the man. "She doesn't much care for Ms. Church, it seems."

He shook his head and gave me a toadish look. "Catie and Maria were good friends."

"They were?"

"Yes. They met for the first time at one of Maria's dinner parties."

"We've heard about these dinner parties. What were they all about?"

He smiled sadly. "They were marvelous. Maria was so talented at creating special fantasy themes. Whenever Jack wanted to entertain important people, he had Maria think up a party. At first, Catie was helping her, but when Jack lost interest in his job, Catie had to take over much of the workload, so I started helping her."

"What would you do?" LaRue asked. "Cook?"

"Of course not. The affairs were catered. Jack and one of his friends arranged that angle." Then, donning his conspiratorial voice again, "He got around having to use legit businesses because this friend of his knew about a guy who would do it cheap and do it good."

"So, what did you do to bring off these affairs?" LaRue pressed.

"I organized the particulars. Maria came up with the ideas and I would see that the arrangements were made. You know, things like ordering the proper linens or decorations. I sent out invitations and made sure that no one had a negative reaction to the planned dinner theme."

"You sent out invitations?" I said.

"Yes. Someone had to do it. Jack certainly wouldn't."

"Did you keep guest lists?"

He flattened his lips and gave me a scornful look. "Of course I did."

With that, LaRue charged the man and turned him back in the direction of the District Council Building. "We want copies of everything you've kept for these parties. Can you do that for us?"

"Since Jack isn't around to deny access, I'll do you the

favor, but I want my nose left out of it if this thing sees him in court. I was just doing my job, you understand."

"We understand," LaRue answered, as he steered the man down the street.

When we got there, we found that we had to wait. Wainwright was called to attend to a matter immediately, leaving us to cool it in his private cubicle while he went off to accomplish some bureaucratic feat.

He had a comfortable little cubbyhole with a door, so LaRue and I squeezed inside to wait for him. I sat behind his desk and studied his personal photos, which showed a handsome, mildly overweight family unit. There was also the conciliatory picture of Wainwright shaking hands with the boss while Catie looked on. After getting fingerprints all over the glass as I studied the shot, I rifled his desk drawers where I found several manila files that meant absolutely nothing and a large purple lunch sack, complete with two roast beef sandwiches, a piece of pineapple upside-down cake, and a baggie of sliced carrots. I tossed LaRue a share and dipped my thumb into a small plastic container of horseradish.

We wolfed the man's food and I had just stowed the wrappers back in the colorful pouch when Wainwright returned, carrying several computer disks.

"I hope you'll excuse me, Marshal Merrick, but I'd like to have my seat," he said.

I rose, and he literally jumped into the chair, dropping the plastic disks on the desk with a clatter. He brushed at bread crumbs, but didn't seem to realize that they had come from his lunch. I didn't give him a chance to, either. "Tell us about Maria's choice of party themes."

"She would design whole parties around a historical event or recreate ethnic celebrations. One of my favorites was a party to observe Bastille Day."

That got my partner's interest up. "What did she do for that party?" he asked.

Wainwright smiled. "She and Jack dressed in period costumes. Jack was having a great time that night imitating Napoleon."

"Maria was Josephine, no doubt?"

"Yes. And she served some wonderful French cuisine. It's too bad that one of the servers sent over by the caterer had a fight with Maria's maid. Jack was forced to fire the girl."

"What was her name?" I asked.

He thought a moment. "Her name was Sun Ye Sung."

25

∎

CYCLOPS SAM HAD one eye and no conscience. Yet, with that good eye, he saw everything that went on around the District Council Building and because he had no conscience, he also had no trouble being a productive mole for the Marshals Office.

We found Sam, as usual, trying to fix the escalator system that served the main lobby. He approached his maintenance chore from this underground room, a place, he decided, also served well as a rent-free retreat.

LaRue muttered something about just having his coat cleaned as we took the stairs that led to the trapdoor of the subbasement. I could hear water rushing through the sewage system as it vented off the overflow from the rain-swollen

Black River, which ran along the back side of the complex. Mixed with this noise, my hearing picked up the peep of rats and the occasional metallic echo of machinery.

We followed the track of overhead steam pipes and the few emergency lights that still burned, finding Sam standing idly by the gear-driven innards of the broken escalator. He aimed a flashlight at the motor while he smoked an illegal cigarette. When we came around the corner, he jumped.

"St. Ophelia, Merrick. Why do you got to scare me like that?" He readjusted his eye patch, and I noticed that the swatch of cloth was sewn to resemble the district flag.

I pointed to it. "Showing your patriotism, Sam?"

He shrugged and ran a hand over the greasy braid he wore. "My ex-wife made it for me. Birthday present. I suppose it don't hurt or nothing to wear it around this joint."

Sam never talked directly to LaRue. He once told me that my partner reminded him of mad Rasputin without the beard. "How's business?" I asked.

"Stinks. I been down in the muck and the heat trying to fix this piece of shit for a week now. God-awful mess. You don't got a few cervo-rotors on you by any chance? I'll look good here if I can get this contraption to work."

"Sorry, I left my equipment in my other jacket."

"Yeah. That's the same thing that the guy in the district parts warehouse says." He shook his head, took a final puff, and crushed the butt with the toe of his boot. He then pulled off his T-shirt to display his sweat-soaked chest. I almost laughed out loud because piercing each nipple were two golden rings decorated with dangling beads and miniature charms. I didn't dare look at LaRue because I knew what his expression would do to my composure.

It took me a moment to force down a chuckle. "You called and said you might have some skinny on Councilman Raynor."

"How come it took you so damned long to get here? I put the word out a day after his wife came up dead." Then, leaning toward me, he said in a conspiratorial voice, "You know his admin assistant hates his guts, don't you?"

"We talked with her and her displeasure with him came across loud and clear."

"She called him a womanizing turd one night and he never did deny it. I think she wanted him for herself, but he already had one dog at home. As far as I could tell, he never did give her a toss."

"You've been watching these folks for a long while, haven't you, Sam?"

"Hey, I'm the best mole the Marshals Office has. I home in on these political soap operas like you guys home in on murderers, and I been filing reports for six months. Ain't nobody reads them, though. You guys over there ought to pay more attention to me."

"Duly noted," I said. "So, what's the latest?"

"It was just after one of these arguments with his admin that a broad named Emily Church showed up to talk to Raynor."

"When was this?"

"A couple of weeks ago. Like I said, I called, but who am I? Just some wart who tries to repair moving stairs and boiler units. My snitch status apparently doesn't count for much."

I let him go, and after he was finished, I did manage that glance at LaRue. "She said she hadn't seen Jack for quite a while, didn't she?"

"That's right."

Turning back to Sam, I prodded him for more information. "Tell us what was said."

"It was after midnight and I just happened to be checking out the air-conditioning duct leading into his office. You know, you can overhear a lot of stuff hiding in those things. Course, it's hell on your knees and elbows, and backing out of a juncture is damned hard sometimes."

"What was the conversation, Sam?" I asked, trying to keep the exasperation out of my voice.

"She was concerned about some guy named Orson."

"Orson?"

"Yeah, Orson. I'm sure of the name. Apparently, he was endangering some project. From the sounds of it, they were both working on this program, but I got the idea it was something secret. She kept referring to it as the F-Project."

"What was Orson doing to endanger the project?"

"It sounded like he was convincing some of the players that they were being used and abused. She demanded that he speak to the man. From the sound of her voice, I'd say she was frantic over it."

"Did she say anything else? What about a last name on this guy?"

He paused to adjust a string of beads that had snarled around his titty ring before answering. "Sorry. She did say that someone named Sun Ye had come to her with misgivings about the whole project and it was only a matter of time until others started protesting. She was sure that Orson had something to do with it and she wanted him off the program."

26

LaRue was going on about Emily Church and talking about Cyclops Sam's titty rings all in the same sentence when we walked into our cubicle to find Gibson waiting for us. He sat in my chair, hunching over the desk, while he studied the crime scene photos.

"Pretty gruesome stuff," he said. "For all that cutting, I'm surprised there wasn't blood everywhere. The killer must have used an LMP."

That brought LaRue's attention around. "LMP? What's that?"

"It's a microlaser. Surgeons use it in the field."

"How powerful are these cutters?"

"Do you mean could they slice fat from buttocks?" LaRue grinned. "Yes."

"It would take a while. The lasers are used for small wounds. It cuts and cauterizes at the same time, but they're slow."

"Are there any other kinds of lasers out there that could do the job faster?"

"Sure, but your killer would have needed a hand truck to carry them. The ones used in the operating room have a heavy, bulky power source. The LMP is about the size of paperback book. The laser pen is the size of a pencil."

"Who has access to this kind of equipment?" LaRue asked.

"Like I said, field surgeons. New, they're expensive. Reconditioned, still expensive. The PHO hasn't sold too many to private citizens, you can bet."

"What about the veterinary units? Could they have access to this kind of thing?"

"Yes. They use LMPs in agro districts."

I sat on the edge of my desk, crossed my arms, and stared at him. He stared back with a look that traced down along my neck and breasts. "What are you doing here, anyway?" I asked.

"I have the translations you wanted. Did you forget?"

To be honest, I had. "No. What do they say?"

He plucked the papers from his shirt pocket and squinted at the page. "Your Greek scroll is a list of symptoms concerning some unidentified illness. It reads: 'I have found that the onset of the disease caused by the injection of the hormone is signaled by an excessive weight loss. Following this, the victim suffers from a general malaise that is remarkably similar to a chronic fatigue disorder. He then begins to experience an ever-present hunger that cannot be satisfied. In later stages, the person suffers from rectal bleeding, blood in the sputum, hair loss, cankerous growths, and migraines. Death follows a few months after these initial symptoms are identified.'

"The Latin text says: 'I have learned through government informants that some compounds seem to stall the advance of the illness, but unfortunately, do not halt it. Eating foods rich in iron and chromium help to strengthen the body, as well as the spirit, and while no cure was forthcoming from this therapy, it proved that nothing, not even the injection of this insidious killer, can totally overcome the resiliency of the human species.'"

LaRue ran both hands through his hair and blew a sigh through his lips. "Do you have any idea what illness these symptoms might identify?"

Gibson shook his head. "It's hard to say. If I were to go on this description alone and discount the sentences talking about injections, I'd have to say they indicate various stages of starvation."

"Have you ever heard of a scientist named Sun Ye Sung?"

He thought a moment. "The name's not familiar. At least, not in the neurology field. Who is it?"

"According to the Chinese scroll we have, she invented something called a genetic isotope," I said. "Any idea what that might be?"

"I can truly tell you that I have no idea. I've never come across the term before."

I glanced at the paper on which he'd written the translations. It was done in a scrawly script, sterotypically belonging to a doctor. There were a few words hanging loose at the bottom of one of the pages. "What's this?" I asked, pointing with my pinky finger.

"It says: *'Toward Human Extinction.* Dr. Philip Ligotti.'" He shuffled the pages. "The Greek text had something similar. Here it is: *'The Genius of the People.* Dr. Philip Ligotti.'"

We each exchanged looks and confused expressions. "That's the second time we've found that name attached to the scrolls," LaRue said. "Just who is Dr. Philip Ligotti?"

Gibson shrugged. "I checked for the name in the *Register of Practicing Physicians*. It doesn't appear anywhere."

I nodded. Dr. Philip Ligotti wasn't listed in any of the district databases, either.

27

SUN YE SUNG had the biggest family unit I have ever encountered, and they were all stuffed into a large, single-room flat located on the lower east side down by the Black River Hydroelectric Dam. They were so close to it, in fact, that I could hear the thunder of water through the tightly latched windows.

The only furniture in the room was a small vid setup and a vanity table that served as an altar to dead ancestors. Photographs of selected family members were taped upon the mirror and incense sticks had been propped inside canning jars, the smoke from which stank up the whole apartment.

Pointing to a chewed-up rush mat, Mrs. Sung apologized for the accommodations. I sat down and LaRue leaned against the front door.

According to our records, Sun Ye's mother was only fifty-eight years old, but she looked closer to seventy. Her long hair was completely white and she was obviously suffering from malnutrition. She sat on the floor peeling a mound of potatoes while she screamed at a group of children who were fighting over a toy.

My partner's attention was off around the room, so I took the interview. "Mrs. Sung, you reported your daughter as a missing person several weeks ago. We're working an investigation that may be related. Could you please tell us the circumstances surrounding her disappearance?"

She stared at me with a confused look.

"What happened to her, Mrs. Sung?"

"We don't know," she answered, in a voice made thick by having more gums than teeth. "One day, she was gone."

"Was it a workday for her?"

"Everyday is a workday."

"I mean, did she go to Mrs. Raynor's house that day?"

"Yes. She went always. She had no time off."

"What kinds of things did she do for Mrs. Raynor?"

"Clean and cook." She stopped to reach over and smack a young boy as he tried to bite a little girl. Her explanation didn't stall. "Laundry. Errands. Always buying stuff for her."

"On the back door market?"

"Yes. Where else?"

"What kinds of things would she buy?"

"Food. Clothes."

"Did she ever buy her charms?"

"Yes. Luckies. Toward the end she was shopping for all kinds of things. Some man was helping Mrs. Raynor. I don't know his name."

"Was he making a charm for her?"

"Yes. It was supposed to make her thin." She clipped off a "Ha!" and turned to pop the kid again, yelling at his mother to watch him. The younger woman rose from her place in the corner, tossed LaRue a shy look, and then proceeded to give the child a Dutch rub. By the time she finished whacking his head, he was quiet and from the looks of him, almost unconscious. I continued with the interview, satisfied that the brat wouldn't interrupt again.

"What were some of the things he needed to make the charm?"

"Usual things." She squinted and dropped her peeled potato into a pot of scummy water. "Well, there was one thing strange."

"What?"

"Sun Ye told me that Mrs. Raynor had to take a white powder many times during the day. She said it was what gave energy to the charm. I've never heard where a lucky would need energy. It's supposed to have it already."

"Where would she get this white powder?"

She shrugged and the action caused water beads to fly from the potato. "The man was selling them to her. He was making money, I suppose. The husband found out and they had a big fight."

"We understand that your daughter was fired after hitting another employee during a dinner party."

"Yes. It was because the husband was having an affair with her."

"With Sun Ye?"

"No. The other one. The serving girl. Sun Ye told me all about it." She sighed as she fished around in the bowl for another potato. "My daughter went back the next day to get her wages. She didn't come home."

"Do you think Mr. Raynor had anything to do with her disappearance?"

She shrugged, but her expression gave away her true feelings. Then, "Well, at least we now have Qi Pak with us."

LaRue tore his attention away from two old men who used the convenient design of the floor tile to play a game of backgammon. "Who's Qi Pak?"

"My nephew. He's from our home district. His visa was granted after five years. We were all happy about that."

28

ARMED WITH A bit more information, we invited Catie Bennet in for another talk. She came into the homicide pen armed with a nasty attitude, complaining about not having time to answer more questions. LaRue guided her into the interrogation room where she copied Emily Church by brushing at the seat of the chair before flopping heavily into it.

"This shouldn't take too long, Ms. Bennet," LaRue said.

"It better not. I have three meetings this evening and the first one is with my upline chief."

"It's hard work not having Jack Raynor around, huh?"

"No harder than it was before. Just more of it."

"Then we won't keep you any longer than necessary. We were wondering if you could tell us about a few people."

"I'll try."

"Good. Mr. Wainwright was gracious enough to turn over his files regarding Maria Raynor's dinner parties. Pretty impressive affairs, wouldn't you say?"

"Maria had talent and imagination. Her efforts helped to push Jack's career along. God knows he didn't do much for it himself."

"Why do you say that?"

"He delegated everything. When it came to actually doing the work, someone else had to show for that. And usually, it was me."

"According to the guest lists, you were invited to every party."

"That's right. I couldn't go to every dinner, unfortunately. I was usually covering Jack's ass on something."

"But you attended enough to get to know the people. Is that right?"

"As far as a party atmosphere allows."

"Is that where you first met Emily Church?"

"No. Her father and she came to see Jack just after he was promoted to councilman."

"Her father? We understand he has Alzheimer's disease."

"He does. He was in the beginning stages of it, then, from what she indicated."

"Why did they come to see Jack?"

"I don't know. I wasn't asked to sit in on their meeting. It was right after that, though, when Jack started his affair with Emily. They were blatant about it, too. She showed up practically every day there for a while."

"Did you overhear them discussing any special programs, perhaps one called the F-Project?"

She deliberately glanced down at her hands. "What about it?"

"What is it?" LaRue said.

She looked up, and her voice grew quiet. "I'm not sure. All I have are my suspicions."

"We'll take those," I said. "What gave you concern?"

"I think the project deals with drugs. You know, quantum."

"Why do you say that?"

"I managed to overhear Jack and Emily discussing the cost of importing research material. I'm positive they were discussing drugs. Then I met one of their so-called associates—a man named Blackburn."

"That name appeared frequently on the guest lists, but there's no first name mentioned. Marshal LaRue called Mr. Wainwright who explained that some close friends didn't receive written invitations. Apparently, he was a close friend. Do you have any idea who Blackburn is?"

"I'm not sure who he is, really, except that Jack and he worked together at one time. I'm afraid that I don't recall anyone using a first name where he was concerned." She frowned. "I can tell you one thing, though. He was always flying on quantum."

"How do you know that?"

"I've dealt with Jack's brother enough to know when someone is blitzed on the stuff. This bastard would make it a point to follow me around when he and I were attending the same party and he always insisted on sitting beside me at the dinner table. He was a boisterous, obnoxious fool. Someone whom I could see might be a close, personal friend of Jack's." When we didn't jump after the last statement, she qualified it by adding, "Jack likes to party loudly, especially when he's been drinking."

"Did Blackburn ever mention the F-Project or anything about it?" I asked.

"He said that it was up to him to save the world, because the F-Project was going to get away from the scientists and destroy us all."

I glanced at LaRue, whose face squeezed into a scowl. "Do you think it was the quantum talking?"

"Probably. Still there was something going on. Jack practically dove for his throat when he came up with that line. It wasn't long after that he was shown the door."

29

ALEXANDROV VUSILI NUMALONOF was LaRue's one true Russian friend. He was a young man who had fled the Moscow District after being pegged as a back door distributor of stolen antique religious icons. Through a series of acquaintances in the government, Alex managed to escape with a new identity and a new labor designation. He still sold hot art, but now he did it when he finished his shift at the local foundry. We found him that evening in his two-room apartment, surrounded by his latest treasures.

Alex's size and his green plaid flannel shirt reminded me of Paul Bunyan. He wore his red hair short, but his beard full and long. If he had carried an ax and dragged around a blue ox, he could have entertained the kids over at PS-31 during story week.

LaRue gave him a quick hug in greeting, and I did my customary wave as he pushed us into the room. He walked delicately as he led us through the maze of art objects toward a heavy mahogany table.

"You're a hard man to reach anymore," LaRue said, sitting down beside an open bottle of tequila. He reached over and took a swig, screwing up his face at the cut of the alcohol down his throat. He offered me a nip, but I declined, seeing that he couldn't talk past the sting.

Alex took his turn at the bottle before answering. "I've been busy. The back door market is starting to support people who have credits. Economy is getting good, so I have to take advantage of this upswing." He glanced at me. "So, how is it with you? Still howling mad?"

I nodded. "I suppose I always will be."

He took another sip. "There are many werewolves in the Russian districts, but I've told you those stories."

And he had. Told over glasses of homemade wine, his stories of the dying Soviet Union during the last decade of the twentieth century weaved witches, vampires, and wirin together. According to one tale, the prima ballerina of the Bolshoi Ballet was a lycanthrope. She hid her affliction well until that fateful full moon when she was forced to perform *Duvalier's Dream* for the then-reigning dictator. Right in the middle of a pirouette, she lost her wits and started biting her male counterpart in the groin.

Sitting back, Alex studied me. After a moment, he said, "I have something for you." Rising, he went to an old crate and dug around, his words rolling off into the trunk as he spoke. "I found this painting. It's from the district where Old Leningrad once existed. It's beautiful! Acrylic on the thinnest slice of tempered steel. Ah, here it is."

He came back with a cloth-covered square. He set it on the table and pulled away the rag to reveal an explosion of bright colors. In the center of the painting was the face of a woman. Her features were overlaid with that of a wolf, but done so expertly that it looked like she was both things at once. I was immediately entranced by it.

"I thought of you when I saw it, and have been saving it to give to you."

"Give to me?"

"Yes. It's yours."

The portrait caught the power and the agony of a full moon stretch. Transfixed, I could have sworn it had been painted with me in mind. "Does the artist have lycan-thropy?"

"It came to me from a friend of a friend, but the story is that she is indeed a werewolf." He sat back down. "Enjoy it in health."

"Thank you, Alex. This is very special."

He flapped his hand at me and said, "So, what can I do for you, my good friends?"

"We need a translation," LaRue said, while I stared at the painting. Picking through his jacket pocket, he pulled out one of the scroll sets and smoothed the copies on the tabletop. "You can read Cryllic, can't you?"

"Is the Duvalier dead? Of course. Let me see it."

He traced his finger slowly along the lines of the paragraph and his lips moved silently as he read them. When he was done, he stared at us both. He then took another tap from the bottle and sighed. "This came from one of your murder investigations?"

"Yes," LaRue answered. "What does it say?"

"It's frightening, if it's real, Andy." Another drink, then, "It reads: 'I discovered that the isotope was distributed to the population of District Twenty-one after the people were convinced that it was a simple immunization against smallpox. It eventually killed all those who received it, except for selected family units who showed a strong natural immunity.

"'The government began using Sun Ye Sung's genetic isotope for controlled genocide on those communities considered unproductive and not contributing to the common good. This practice has been carried on for years and is the true reason why the borders of the famine districts are closed to traffic.'" Pausing to clear his throat, Alex added, "'*Government Intervention and Reasons for Today's Trend Toward Selective Breeding.* Dr. Philip Ligotti.'"

Neither of us spoke until LaRue reached for the bottle. His words followed quietly. "What the hell is going on here?"

"The person who wrote this is insane," I answered.

"And we don't even know if it was Maria making up the

story," LaRue said. "She might have been planning to hand them out as party favors."

"Do you think it might be true?" I asked.

"I hope not, but with the way the world is going these days, it could be. We may have stumbled upon something that we shouldn't have."

Alex pushed the papers back to us. "Well, nothing is to be done about death, but to die. Until then, I'll try to live like my fatalist ancestors did before me. Always expect the worst and then be thankful if it comes in just on the underside of shitty."

30

ABOUT 6 P.M., we found Qi Pak practicing a little invisible magic of his own. He was casing for ghosts at a house over in Ward Sixteen, a neighborhood where many of the midlevel government officials live. The bugaboo removal just happened to take place at the home of an ETA and that in itself made the trip a little more interesting.

Qi Pak was about twenty-five, muscular, and good looking. When we entered the spacious flat of the absent host, he was just about ready to send out a snake.

He had the serpent in a brown linen bag, and he had himself in a matching robe with a frayed gold lamé collar. His hair was tied back with a bright green ribbon that sported red feathers, cockle shells, and a dried human ear.

The man stared right at me as we crossed the threshold, hissed, and then backed away.

"You have an attitude, Mr. Pak," I growled. "We just want to ask you some questions."

"And you are a card-carrying demon," he spit. "I've been around your kind before. You're an abomination. I will have nothing to do with you."

"Now, is that nice?" LaRue said, flatly.

I'm surprised at those times when people can see my lycanthropy clearly. I have yet to figure out what I do to give away my disposition, but it does happen occasionally. LaRue maintains it's a telepathic connection of some kind. Whatever it might be, I don't like it, and it puts me off balance. This time, I was fortunate that I had stepped into a room that was filled with interesting objects. I stepped away and pretended to study the decorations.

My partner pointed to the snake sack. "What are you carrying, Mr. Pak, a cobra?"

"A cottonmouth. It's the only thing to use when flushing out ghosts and evil spirits." He popped another look at me as I quickly turned away to admire a collection of abstract paintings done by someone named, Siltrese.

LaRue played with him a little more. "A cottonmouth, huh? Why wouldn't any other snake do?"

"They just wouldn't. They don't have the proper vibrations to urge a ghost from the premises."

"And you're an expert about this. Am I right?"

"I know enough to tell you that your companion is very dangerous. She should be nullified."

I snorted to myself. Everyone wanted that, including me.

"I like my partner dangerous, Mr. Pak," LaRue said, as he tucked at the wrinkled pocket of his uniform. "We understand you're just in from District Twenty-one. Any interesting news from there?"

"No."

"People going about their business. Living and dying."

I didn't even have to look at Pak to know that his head bobbed like LaRue's dash ornament, but I pulled my attention from a fake Monet just to see his expression. He effectively hid it by bending over the bag and working the knot on the drawstring.

LaRue cast a glance around the room. "So, what kind of spooks are we talking about here?"

"Those who can reach through the boundaries of the dimensions to alter the flow of nighttime energy."

"Mr. ETA has bad dreams, huh?"

"As you say. I'll cure the problem, though."

LaRue took a couple of turns for emphasis before zeroing in on the fright flayer. "What kind of ghosts do they have in your district, Mr. Pak?"

At the question, Qi Pak stood up straight, leaving the knot partially unworked. He stared at LaRue and then glanced at me with a renewed scowl. "It doesn't help to have a demon in the house. The ghosts will cling to her, and I won't be able to exorcise them. You should both leave."

Now, I'll admit I don't believe in shades and haunts, but when someone says something like that, it makes your skin feel like a thousand butterflies are fluttering against it. I shivered, despite myself.

"Sir, we can take this down to the District Marshals Office, if you don't want to cooperate," LaRue said in a low, threatening voice. Then, brighter, "If that happens, I would worry about my snake. Someone is liable to see it, kill it, cook it, and eat it. You see, officers of the law don't make a whole lot of money, and that cottonmouth just might taste like chicken."

The man blinked at him. "You're not serious."

"Very much. At the least, you'll be detained for engaging

in an illegal activity. Keeping poisonous serpents as pets is against district regulations. Want to talk now and avoid all the commotion that one little cottonmouth is going to cause?"

He sighed and nodded. "What do you want to know?"

"Your home locality is an island, isn't it? And right now the borders are closed due to a famine."

"So?"

"So, how did you get permission to leave? It's been sealed for several years."

He fiddled with the snake sack again, and LaRue had to press him. "Don't stall me, Mr. Pak."

When he finally answered, there was a tremor in his voice that sounded like BBs rolling down a metal groove. "I can't tell you anything about why I was allowed to come here."

"Is that because someone has threatened your family unit?"

It took him a moment to nod.

"Who? The government?"

He made another curt nod.

"Is Councilman Jack Raynor connected to all this?"

"I don't know."

"Did he get you out of District Twenty-one?"

"I don't know. My visa was approved. I didn't ask who authorized it."

"Do you know what happened to your cousin, Sun Ye?"

"No."

LaRue stalked Pak with a stare and then, placing his hands idly on his hips, he took a few steps across the room before turning on him once more. "You saw her die, didn't you?"

The man backed away from LaRue like he'd just turned into one of those ghosts he was trying to scare off. My partner smiled.

"How did you know that?" Pak said.

"The same way you know my partner is a demon," he said. "What did they do to her?"

A single hard swallow preceded his confession. "They shot her."

"Who?"

"A couple of ward cops. She had just returned and decided to visit my grandmother. She explained that her visa had been revoked for reasons she didn't understand. I was there preparing to leave the district. The two cops came into the house and shot her in front of the old woman. It was horrible."

"They just shot her? Did they leave you with a warning?"

"Yes. They told me it's what happens to people who defy the government, and I should take heed so the same thing wouldn't happen to me."

"What had she done?"

"I don't know, and I don't care." With that, he let the snake loose.

31

ACCORDING TO GIBSON, there had been some serious studies waged on fat in the late twentieth century. Researchers discovered the existence of an enzyme that controls a person's eating habits. The enzyme signals the brain to let it know that enough fat has been taken in by the body. At this point, the feeling of satiation should take over, but in people considered obese, it was thought that this messaging system didn't work.

Maria Raynor's overweight condition was caused by a faulty brain just as my lycanthropic changes were. The more this murder case wore on, the more I started understanding my own problems better. Everything had to do with the three pounds of gray matter packed between my ears.

From what the good doctor maintained, my illness was no different than having epilepsy or Parkinson's disease. Becoming a werewolf was a rare biological state.

It was after 9 P.M. by the time I arrived at Gibson's apartment to have dinner. From the address, I expected luxury accommodations complete with brass and glass and expensive carpeting, but the focal point of the main living room was a ratty brown couch. It was hard to notice it sitting among the many boxes, crates, and barrels. Gibson didn't have a flat; he had a supply warehouse.

He answered the door dressed in jeans and a red plaid robe that I think he purposely left open to show off his chest. As impressive as his pecs were, I was more fascinated by the paraphernalia he'd collected. He smiled, but said nothing as he let me inside. He then retreated into a kitchenette that was not much more than a stove and a counter. In a moment, I heard a sizzling noise and smelled onions frying. I moved off to study the place.

"I take it you're packing for the end of the world," I said.

He glanced at me from the galley. "It's tight, but tax deductible. How about a glass of ale?"

I took a step toward him. "Don't tell me. You brew your own beer."

He pointed toward a door with a dripping spatula. "This is the storage room. That one is the lab." He lowered his attention to the saucepan to scrape the vegetables around. "So, do you want a drink?"

"Yes." I returned to my inspection of his apartment. "Why the date tonight? What new experiment do you want to talk me into?"

"Just dinner." A pause, and then, "I've been thinking about your case."

"The lycanthropy or the murder?"

"Both, actually. One might help the other."

"Explain away."

"During the 1990s, there was a study program that centered on selected members of a particular Native American population. These people could survive for months in the harshest conditions because they could store fat easily and use it readily. Unfortunately, modern life with all its sedentary gifts also gave them diabetes, kidney disease, cardiac problems, and the occasional stroke. Their metabolism burned like it should—slowly. The problem came when they didn't have a need for the extra energy." He paused to open a small fridge and bring out the pitcher of beer. Pouring it into a glass, he continued. "You, for instance, would be one of the first to die in a famine. Your metabolism sucks. It's like a superconvector."

"Before I came down with lycanthropy, I was heavier by twenty pounds. Do you think it's because my brain cells were rerouted?"

"I've come to believe that metabolism plays a big part in your lycanthropy. As far as I can tell, you're the only one ever on record to show signs of spontaneous growth. It might be that when your firing patterns alter, something in the system signals a change in metabolism. It's my guess that your caloric burn rate steadily increases the closer you get to a full moon." He paused. "Do you like potato salad?"

"With real eggs and real mayonnaise?"

"Will homemade mayo do?"

"In from the lab, huh?"

"Everything comes from the lab."

"Then where the hell did you get the eggs? Synthesize them?"

"Oh. I got those from the balcony."

I walked to the dingy glass doors and pulled back the heavy, soot-colored drape. Stacked neatly along the edge, right up to the top of the railing, were pens of chickens and rabbits. There was also a plastic cistern as tall as I was. He had channeled water into it by placing a PCV pipe at one corner of the upper balcony. Next to this contraption were several bins full of animal feed. Wedged near the entryway was a solar panel and several batteries. This guy could survive a siege.

"I see that scavenging is your hobby."

"Looks that way, doesn't it?"

"Why would you need to scrounge? You come from a wealthy family unit."

"That doesn't mean I have that much personally. My father sent me to school to become a doctor. After that, I was on my own." He left it at that, and in a moment, I heard a new sizzle coming from the kitchenette. "Tell me, in the days just before that last stretch, do you get hungry?"

"Sometimes it gets so bad that I could eat the upholstery out of LaRue's car."

"Well, you'd get a lot of fiber that way."

I laughed. "But not a lot of taste." I sipped the ale. "This is good. Can I buy a bottle or two from you? LaRue and Baba would enjoy a sample."

He plowed ahead with his usual vigor, ignoring my question. "Can you always get enough to eat?"

I thought about lying, but for some odd reason, I didn't.

"To be honest, Gibson, I haven't had enough to eat in years. Why all the questions about food, anyway?"

"Eating affects the glucose level in the brain. Glucose is a natural sugar and the only energy the brain can use. Those very same scientists studying fat also studied it in regard to improving brain function."

"And does it?"

"Yes. There was work involving something called a ketogenic diet that included a phase of fasting alternated with a phase of eating high-fat foods. In many cases, it helped victims of epilepsy. They had far fewer seizures, though the basic reason for it is still a mystery. The supposition is that the enhanced glucose levels affected the firing of the neurons and kept the brain from leaping off into erratic activity."

"Gunked up those little critters, huh?"

He ignored my quip. "Can you tell the differences in your seizures when you don't eat before an episode?"

I hesitated. I do crave food and drink the day before and the day of the full moon. Unfortunately, both are denied me, because when I try to swallow something more than my spit, I choke. LaRue thinks this is a sign of the temporary onset of supernatural rabies. As uncomfortable as it is, I can find nothing supernatural about these symptoms.

When I didn't answer, he peeked around the door of the kitchenette. "Merrick?"

"Yes?"

"What's wrong?"

Another moment went by before I told him. "I can't be sure if there are any differences in the seizures. I can't swallow well enough to take in any food or water."

He considered me with his critical, squinty-eyed gaze. "Does your throat close up?"

"I can breathe, if that's what you mean."

"Fever?"

"Slight."

"Intense thirst?"

"Yes."

"When do these symptoms first occur?"

"About eighteen to twenty hours before blastoff."

A moment more of consideration and he said, "It sounds like your lycanthropy has a built-in fail-safe. Being able to eat might dull the seizure or keep it from happening altogether."

"Could it be that simple?"

He shook his head. "I doubt it, but it's worth looking into. I'm going to be with you on the full moon. I want to see how all this breaks down in the end."

Break down. That's exactly what it was like. I didn't say it aloud, but instead, moved on to study his home theater system, trying to put the lycanthropy problems out of my thoughts.

Like me, Gibson indulged himself in films, but I would have sold Baba to have a setup like his. He had an impressive rack of vids, and I was drawn to them, wondering if there was something I might borrow. There were a few movies, but mostly he seemed to collect medical documentaries. I picked one up and read: *Neurology and the Mind: Where the Metaphysical Meets the Physical.* Dr. Anthony Davis. Another read: *Neurophilosophy, the Misunderstood Science.* Dr. Shelia Morrison.

My brain must have had an explosion of glucose at that very moment, because it made a connection.

Toward Human Extinction. Dr. Philip Ligotti.

The Moral Question of Saving the World. Dr. Philip Ligotti.

32

As I SAID, my one indulgence is watching vids. I have an eclectic interest in life that leads me from documentaries to musicals to action adventure films. So, the next morning, I went to my favorite disk supplier, Blockbuster Bill.

Renting and buying vids is pure back door stuff, because the government feels that it needs to control the informational aspect of society. It wants people to die of boredom watching the approved shows and movies. The district also tries very hard to confiscate the inventory of hardworking dealers like Bill.

The Vid King, as he likes to think of himself, has an old house next to St. Ophelia's Memorial Park. At one time the structure was part of the graveyard and belonged to the groundskeeper. It has a damp basement that, while not climatically controlled for the illegal disks, makes a good storage area for the approved ones. The contraband is kept nice and dry in his family unit's private mausoleum. This is where I found Bill dusting off his stock in anticipation of a close-out sale to make room for new disks.

He greeted me with his usual stink of beer breath and dirty teeth and then pointed to the vid stack wedged between the coffins. "I'm glad you stopped by, Ty. I was saving a few films for my best customers. I'm selling cheap this time. I have a new load coming in from District Ten and I have to make room." He held one up. "This is that werewolf movie you liked so much. It's yours for five credits."

"Five credits? Why don't you throw in another one for that price? What about a copy of *The Sino Injunction*?"

"Ah, you like Presley Steele. All the women like him.

He's mostly naked throughout that whole film, right? Yes, I can see why he wows the femmes. OK, it's a deal." He searched through a blue plastic trash can looking for my request. That's when I hit him with another.

"Bill, do you have any taped lectures available?"

"You mean from the university? You know I have some of those. You've rented practically all of them."

"The ones I'm looking for probably aren't approved. If they exist, they'd probably be underground cuts."

He handed me the vids. "If they exist? Don't you know?"

"I'm playing a hunch here. It's part of a murder investigation I'm working on right now, and we're yanking at threads at the moment."

"Ah, murder." He winked. "I have six disks from *The Masterpiece of Suspense* series."

"But do you have the last episode; the one where our man in District Sixty-four finally catches the killer?"

He looked sheepish. "That's volume seven, and it's trashed. One of my customers had a bad machine and it scratched up the disk. Still, I'll sell the six to you for a good price."

"If you get the whole set, give me a call. Today, though, I'm interested in the lectures."

"All right. Give me names, and I'll see what I have."

I started with the hardest one first. "*Government Intervention and Reasons for Today's Trend Toward Selective Breeding*."

Bill stared at me with a surprised expression corrupting his flabby features. Then, "What other ones?"

"*The Moral Question of Saving the World* and *Toward Human Extinction*."

"They're not exactly taped lectures, Ty."

"Well, what are they?"

"Porn flicks."

"You're joking, right?"

"I wouldn't kid about illegal shit. That's what they are, and there are more than three in the series."

"Do you have them on hand?"

He nodded. "You want to take them home for a viewing?"

"Yes. All of them. Are they rented frequently?"

"Porn flicks are always rented frequently."

"Do you keep a list of renters?"

"That's classified information, Ty. Folks don't appreciate having their names spread around, especially when it comes to renting a sex movie."

"I'm not going to spread them around. I just need to know who's watched them."

He pursed his lips and then released them with a smack. "How does this help with a murder investigation?"

"The killer may have made references to these films. Knowing who's rented them might provide us with a clue to catch this bastard before he knocks out someone else."

"Ah, a serial killer. I have a few movies dealing with this subject. Interested?"

"Not really. What do you say about the list, my friend?"

He fumbled with his moral obligation before answering. "All right. You can see the names, but you have to buy something else."

I smiled. "Do you have *Duvalier's Whip*? I'd like that one for my library. It's one of Baba's favorites."

He returned the smile. "I have an unopened copy. It's yours for another five credits."

After Bill got done with me, I was going to have to borrow money from LaRue to see me through the rest of the week. "I'll buy. Now, where's that list?"

"In the house, of course." He led the way back to the rickety building and into what he called his office. It was a back bedroom containing a crooked metal filing cabinet.

Pulling out a heavy sheaf of papers, he offered them to me. "They're organized by movie title."

He left me to search the list. I made myself comfortable on the floor, listening to the creak of termite-nibbled hardwood as I sat down.

There were, indeed, several films in this porn series. The final three movies were called *The Genius of the People*; *Resistance, Reclamation and Survival*; and *Global Transformation*.

Scanning the pages of renters took over an hour. I didn't find the elusive Blackburn and I didn't find Jack's name. I did, however, find his brother, Max.

33

IT WAS A tough job, but someone had to do it: watching ten hours of porn flicks; eating a whole pan of Baba's homemade flat bread; trying to follow a very weird story line; and finally, living through another lycanthropic stretch.

Yes, another one. It hit me just as I was rewinding one of the disks. The heat exploded in my stomach like the blast from a flare gun. It practically clubbed me with pain, causing me to drop the remote control and fall right out of the chair. I lay on the floor for a good five minutes, unable to do more than whimper, moan, groan, and keep from crying out. After a bit, it subsided, and I'd entered a new phase in my lunar month.

It was a different kind of stretch as compared to the one that changes my dress size, but Gibson was sure to notice the differences. My hair, which normally goes every which way, thickens up and turns so unruly that Baba's best efforts with a curling iron can't even tame it. My nails grow, my eyes carry more flecks of gold than they usually do, and I get an irritating ringing in my ears, which signals a change in my hearing.

Aside from these physical changes, there are alterations in my energy. I find that sleep is hard to come by, but when I finally manage to exhaust myself, the light goes out for hours. I get the heebie-jeebies and, like a cocaine addict, I can't sit still. It was a good thing I managed to get through the movies before the stretch came on, because the edginess settled in immediately.

Baba was off sorting through trash somewhere, so I had the flat all to myself. I walked off the length of the room a couple of times before deciding on a cup of tea and a phone call to Gibson.

He was with a patient, so the clinic nurse took the message and told me he would call back after he was done in the examination room. I resigned myself to the wait by slugging my tea, walking the room again, and trying to figure out the porn films with which I had soaked my lycanthropic brain.

They had nothing to do with a government plot to wipe out selected groups of unproductive individuals. They had everything to do with sexual prowess and quantum smuggling. The lead actor for each play was a husky dark-haired fellow who escaped bumbling marshals, saved damsels in distress, screwed around, then moved on to another adventure while trying to shift his load of drugs from one district to another.

Stranger yet, the whole thing was filmed as a documentary series, given credible titles, and directed and produced by Dr. Philip Ligotti. I had my doubts that Dr. Ligotti was a real person.

A commotion on the street dragged me to the window. I pulled back the trash curtain on an overcast afternoon and a fistfight on the sidewalk below. Two men punched, lunged, and rolled around with each other. A crowd gathered, and though I couldn't see the exchange of money, I knew bets were being taken on the outcome. I watched the brawl for a couple of minutes before I grew bored and then I busied myself by studying the faces of the people who yelled for the conclusion of the boxing match.

According to books and vids, there are many different types of lycanthropes. They align themselves with various animals such as cats, horses, foxes, and bears. From what these so-called authorities report, it's clearly a delusional state and nothing more. If that's true, then, I'm one in a million in the way my affliction works. This fact was not only borne out by Gibson's conclusions, but by the simple reason that I'd never met another person who would admit to having the same condition.

I stared down at the group and imagined them to share my supernatural legacy. In my mind's eye, I saw swishing tails, cloven hooves, and smiles bracketed by long, eloquent, saber teeth. I colored the fantasy with leopard spots and black fur, graying muzzles and sepia manes, and just as I started to focus upon the noises these odd creatures might make, the phone rang. It was Gibson.

"Is something wrong, Merrick?" he asked.

I had my excuse all ready. "No. The murder investigation. I need to ask you a question."

He sighed. "All right. Fire away. How can I help?"

"Have you ever used quantum in your research?"

I could almost hear his surprise. "That's a controlled substance, Merrick."

"Of course. Have you?"

"Let's just say I know something about it and leave it at that."

"Then tell me how it works on the brain."

"Quantum stimulates the neural pathways. Remember the ten activation levels I told you about?"

"Yes."

"Quantum affects the firing sequence, as far as we can tell."

"It was a designer drug in the beginning," I said. "Scientists must have had some clue to what it did in the brain."

"We usually don't know. It was years before we figured out how certain antidepressant drugs interacted with the brain's chemicals. In the late twentieth century, we had people running around on substances I wouldn't give my dog. Quantum was the same kind of thing. It just got away and hit the streets. It's a cinch to synthesize and the ingredients are cheap."

"Do scientists know why it heightens the feeling of self-worth?" I asked.

"It probably stimulates some part of the temporal lobe by altering the chemical composition associated with emotions and changing the serotonin balance."

"What happens when the brain starts to break down from frequent use?"

"The physical problems associated with it are easily detectable. The drug kills off neurons, and the brain has to form new pathways and synaptic junctions. Use it enough and the gray matter turns to gray mush."

"Do these new neural pathways actually stimulate creativity? Or is that a bogus claim?"

"Not bogus. That part is real. Those initial changes in brain patterns allow the user to make leaps of imagination.

If scientists could figure out how to curb the destructive effects, the future of the world would be forever changed."

"What are some of the outward signs of a quantum user traveling toward dementia?"

"There are no detectable physical changes. They're all mental. Sleeplessness, fluctuating moods, forgetfulness, confusion. Actually, once you get to the confusion stage, it's just a hop, skip, and jump to lunacy."

"Lunacy? Could the person become crazy enough to find justification in killing?"

"Most definitely," he said. "Most definitely."

34

THE SERIES OF porn movies had made my own neurons feed down an unusual pathway. Each film was set in a different locale, in a different historical setting, and addressed a different ethnic culture: Chinese, Russian, Greek, Italian, Irish, and Portuguese. Since four of the six scrolls translated matched the films, it was my idea that the mystery languages would coincide with the last two movies. I took the chance and went to see Stonehenge Tilly.

On the back door, Stonehenge Tilly is considered a marketing genius. She dabbles in what she terms gray witchcraft, that invisible magic that leans a little more toward the black than the white. She's been known to lay on a few curses, love triangles, and demon hexes, but her best claim has nothing to do with the magic itself. She swears she's the sole heir to the lands that were once Salisbury, England, and the ancient structure known as Stonehenge.

According to Tilly, she has the deed and family unit rights to it all. When she showed proof of ownership to the government, they gladly crushed the sacred site for her and put up a fake one in its place just to appease the tourists. They then sent her all the broken rock. From that day forward, she has always had a ready supply of holy stone chips for sale.

Tilly is reed-thin and as you would expect, wears a long, black shift reminiscent of the clothes worn during the Salem witch trials. She talks in nasal drags and always wears her hair in pink sponge rollers. Of this last fashion statement, she will tell you that they are necessary to collect astral vibrations needed to enhance her magical powers.

"How's business, Tilly?" I asked, as she showed me into a small, neat parlor.

"Great news. Did you hear?"

"No. What's up?"

"I've had another ancestral claim verified. Mayan. I own one of the ancient temples in District One Hundred Nineteen. It's through my mother's side."

I smiled but didn't deter her delusion. "How much is the rock worth from this temple?"

"Plenty. It was once covered in gold leaf, you know. The government is dismantling it for me right now and the sacred stone should be ready for sale by the end of next month. Shall I put an order in for you? Only a credit and you can have Mayan magic."

"I already have Stonehenge magic. I think I'll stick to that, but if I hear of anyone looking for some different rock, I'll send them to you."

She grinned and poked at a curler. "Fair enough. Now,

what can I do for you? Do you have need for a curse or a spell? I'm running a special this week."

"I need a translation. We're working a murder investigation that involves some pretty cryptic clues. We have a document that I believe is written in Gaelic. I remember you said something once about having an Irish grandmother who taught you to read and write the language. Is that right?"

"That's right. For years, it was all we spoke at home. You have a good memory, Ty. Where is this document?"

I handed her the paper. She angled it to pick up the soft glow from a propane lantern sitting on a nearby table. As she read the scroll, her face grew into a heavy scowl.

"This is evil," she murmured. "I can feel the vibrations that linger on it."

"Can you tell me what it says?"

She nodded. "It says: 'The family units unaffected by the isotope have within them a survival gene that cannot be provoked. This genetic quality can be found in all races of the world, but I have discovered that it is especially common in obese, white females.

" 'I maintain to this day that the government enacted a secret program to study these individuals to see why no changes were encountered after the use of the hormone. Their findings have remained classified, and all requests for information have been denied me. I have taken it upon myself to open a new scientific examination using private funds and various volunteers. These subjects will supply the necessary genetic material necessary for this investigation. While I have a timetable for success, I will in no way compromise the results by rushing the study.' " Tilly squinted over the next line, momentarily fumbling for the words. " 'It is vitally important to destroy the isotope and expose a corrupt government before it's too late. *Resistance, Reclamation, and Survival.* Dr. Philip Ligotti.' "

35

WHEN I GOT home that night, Baba was in the bathroom cursing.

I glanced into the closet to see her leaning over the toilet, brandishing a bloody butcher knife. "What's going on?" I asked, and after doing so, I realized how stupid the question sounded.

"There's a goddamned snake in the commode!" she answered. "Now, you tell me how a creature like this could travel up five stories." A silence. Then she addressed the serpent. "Why don't you go back into the sewer where you belong?" Another pause. Then, "Ty, dear, I think it's a mutant. I just cut off its head and the bastard is still swimming around. Do you know where the plunger is? I'm going to send him back to Hades."

I took her knife to the sink and returned with the appropriate tool. She accepted it with a gentle smile and turned to viciously slam the plunger into the hole. As she worked, she began to hum her favorite hymn, "St. Ophelia's Madness."

I left her to her chore to change into a clean uniform. Each district marshal is required by contract to serve two nights a month patrolling a specified portion of the locality and I could no longer put off my extra duties.

I'm supposed to wear a kevlar vest when I do my patrols, but I never do. The thing makes me hot and restricts my movement. LaRue always yells about it to me, but I ignore him, and so the thing is sitting in my clothes closet, buried under a stack of trash blankets.

The standard issue running shoes always squish my toes

after I grow, so I had to invest in a pair a half size bigger to accommodate the splay in my feet. I buckled up the boots, pinned on my ID, and checked the charge on my flashlight and the bullets in my service revolver.

I finished stuffing my utility pouch and collected my gloves, leaving the apartment to the sound of Baba's muttering as she complained about having to clean up serpent blood.

Pausing on the building's stoop in a wind loaded with freezing rain, I glanced up to watch thick clouds mottling the sky. I didn't need to see the moon to know how close I was to the turn. I could tell just by the way my skin felt against my bones.

My patrol section is twenty blocks long and encompasses a litter-strewn public park, the coking plant, the supply docks, and the tent camp running a few muddy streets along the Black River. I stepped into the weather and headed for Marley Street, slowing my steps as I came upon the vagabond community.

Because of the freezing rain, people huddled inside their canvas houses. The feeble lights from propane lanterns backlit the residences, making the occupants appear as shadow puppets against the walls of their flimsy homes. I heard a child cry out and then a curse from an adult. A dog barked in the distance and a bus gunned its diesel engine as it rumbled up the street. After that, there was only the sound of the sleet, my footsteps, and a world that had turned into crisp shapes and delicate icicles.

Taking a turn down toward the East Avenue Jetty, I paused to check out a drunk sleeping in the gutter. He was alive, so I radioed the district hyperthermia unit to come for a pickup and moved off into the shadows among the cargo storage buildings lining the river's bank. Aluminum roofs formed corrugated porticos that kept the rain from pelting me. I flipped down my hood, paused to take a deep breath, and smelled the hard-edged odor of sewage. It was then that I realized that I'd picked up a tail. He slithered in behind me, using the angles of the building to try to obscure his presence.

As I said, my hearing changes as I settle into my lycanthropic disposition. It becomes pinpoint precise, and I can pick up the little noises filling the world. Doing my poetic self justice, I like to think of these sounds as arias on the wind, because it seems to me that there is an opera being sung just below the threshold of normal hearing.

In this case, my ears told me that the person following me wore rubber-soled shoes and they smacked slightly with each step he took. I halted, sliding into a shadow on the lee side of a recycling dumpster. The stalker copied me by finding his own dark space, but before he did, I saw a momentary glint as the barrel of his weapon reflected the light of a bare bulb hanging over a nearby bay door. He carried an auto bow. I suddenly wished I'd listened to LaRue and had worn the vest, for unlike the mythical werewolf, it doesn't take a silver bullet to kill me.

The ban on automatic weapons had been in effect for years. Anyone who was caught with such a gun in his possession was immediately arrested and executed, usually without a trial. So, to thwart this strict regulation, some enterprising inventor devised the auto bow. It was a variation of a single-shot crossbow, with a major difference: It could sling one hundred, tiny, deadly arrows in less than a minute. Some assassins dipped these darts in poison just to add to their killing power and, though the weapon was heavy and unwieldy, an experienced shooter could feed replacement clips at a furious rate. The government should have done something about these murdering machines, but despite the protests from the law enforcement community, their existence was still unofficially recognized.

The sleet slowed and the drumming force of the rain gentled. As we each took refuge, I clearly heard the bolt being drawn back on the auto bow.

There was a cat sitting in the darkness where I'd settled in. It stared at me and swished its tail, adding a menacing hiss and meow, clearly piqued about the fact that I had invaded its territory.

Now, you may have heard how lycanthropes can control other animals. All the vids and books on werewolves claim that this link with the lower species is a telepathic power of some kind. I'm sure if Gibson were to give a dissertation on it, he would undoubtedly say that I'm working from the influence of the reptilian portion of my brain. Whichever is right, science or myth, there's one fact that I can affirm: Animals don't talk back, so it's hard to know if your thought patterns are getting through.

Still, it was worth a try. Without some type of diversion, I was going to end up a pincushion.

Carefully, I drew my revolver, knowing what a waste it would be against the auto bow. I was bothered by questions of who he was and why he was following me and obviously intending violence. Because of that, it took me a few seconds to calm down my jumping concentration, before trying to get the cat's attention telepathically. The man moved into another dark patch several feet from my position.

The cat and I looked at each other and I did my best to press my thoughts into its head, but I have a feeling that he knew if he willingly walked out of the shadows as a decoy that he would be skewered like a barbecued chicken. So, when my mental coercion didn't work, I did the only thing left to me: I kicked him into the open.

He yowled when my foot contacted him and he flew through the air in an arc, twisting as he did, but landing on his feet. My assailant fired blindly, peppering the concrete, but oddly enough, missing the cat. Arrows bounced off the building behind me, coming in with such lethal force as to explode the bricks and send dust showering over me. I squeezed off a couple of shots, which sounded hollow and inconsequential against his response. He stopped just long enough to reload and adjust his position, confidently striding from the shadows as though he was unconcerned about my gun. I gave him pause, though, because when he moved into my range, I popped another shot off. He ducked and I heard him curse. Though my lycanthropy gives me many seemingly supernatural advantages, one of them is not echolocation. I had no idea where he had gone.

I remained statue-still for a minute or two until my ears separated the soft sound of the sleet from the rustle of his clothing. He grunted and I realized he had managed to come up on my unprotected right side.

Funny, how a person can long for the oblivion of death when day-to-day problems become overwhelming, but when actually faced with the possibility, the survival mechanism turns on and surrender becomes impossible.

I took a deep breath, recited some vague prayer about protection and, hugging the side of the building, dashed toward a concrete loading platform. A volley of darts followed me, falling short as I pushed my speed. The darkness was intense in this area, with no light to give me away. I listened for the stalker's approach, but the rain had resumed its beating cadence to shield the sound of his footsteps.

I took a chance and finished out my ammo clip, at the same time trying to hurl myself around the corner of this building. Just as I cleared the edge of the delivery dock, he sprayed the landscape again. One of the darts pierced my right shoulder. As small as the arrow was, it still contained enough force to knock me to my knees. There was that moment of complete silence that comes right after being shot, when time and space seem to be suspended as you try to figure out exactly what has happened. These are the vulnerable seconds that a true assassin would use to finish his job, but luck was with me and my assailant didn't continue. I did everything I could to climb to my feet and not scream out from pain.

Remember that extra lycanthropic strength I told you about? Blood streamed from my wound, but my vitality allowed me to escape this deadly stranger and make it to Gibson's flat.

He threw open the door in response to my pounding and stood there surprised and staring. I staggered into his arms. That was all she wrote for me.

36

I AWOKE WITH a start from a nightmare in which I was being crushed under an enormous woman who looked just like Maria Raynor. My eyes, though, opened to see the welcome face of Gibson. He studied me silently with that squinty look of his, and then he smiled.

"Your partner and Baba are in the other room, prepared to give you a scolding about not wearing your bulletproof jacket," he said. "I want you to know how lucky you are that I keep medical supplies amid all this junk, and that LaRue shares your blood type."

I tried to speak but was too weak to open my mouth. He understood and patted me tenderly on the hand. "You looked like you walked into a firefight when you got here last night—dust and pebbles in your hair, an auto bow wound that has matching stitches on both sides of your shoulder, and your uniform was shredded in one spot. You bled on my floor and colored up my robe. And how you managed not to go into shock before you got here messed with my mind greatly, until LaRue told me your lycanthropic seizures give you an added vitality and strength. Another thing you forgot to mention."

He stopped talking long enough to don a stethoscope. Gently, he pulled the blanket back to listen to my heart. That's when I realized I was completely naked. His fingertips brushed along my breasts as did his gaze, and as bad as I felt, there was something comforting in his touch. He continued in a low voice after removing one of the stems from his ears.

"Your lycanthropy saved your life. It's somehow altered your body's chemistry and made it possible for you to survive hits that would take out a normal person, but then, you've known this the whole while." He sat back to consider me before continuing. "From reading your files, I figured you would be like my other lycanthropic patient. He was a walking mental case, and he didn't change on the full moon, not even his dirty underwear. When I started this project with you, I was out to prove that a physical problem of the brain caused the onset of mental fragmentation, but that's not the way it is at all. You don't imagine you're a werewolf. You are one. Right down to your pretty, little knickers."

I closed my eyes and took a couple of deep breaths. His

words were the truth and the truth so spoken has a way of searing your insides. Lycanthropy did define me. I was as much the wolf as I was a human, and out of sheer mental and physical survival, I had learned how to integrate the two energies. My mind went to the picture Alex had given me. Thinking about how the artist had glued these strange elements together, I knew in my heart that I wasn't alone in this difficulty, and at that moment, I longed to touch another being who suffered the same as I did.

"Are you in pain?" Gibson asked.

I opened my eyes and managed a husky no.

"You ought to be."

"Tired," I said.

He nodded and wrapped a Velcro lead around my finger. I twisted a bit to see where it led and found that I was in his home lab, flanked by a stack of medical monitors. The one connected to me flashed slowly ascending numbers.

"The reason you're so tired is, one: you lost a couple of pints of blood, and two: your metabolic rate is charging like a stallion. That ring around your finger is attached to a machine that measures your caloric burn. You're down for the count and the monitor is telling me you're using the same energy as someone who is running. I've never seen anything like it in any other human." He shook his head and, picking up a pad of paper from a small table, he took a minute to scribble a note. "Get some sleep, Merrick. I think you need it."

I gratefully did as he ordered and returned to my nightmare, but this time, instead of sitting on me, Maria Raynor made a ghostly visit to talk. The dream was so vivid that I could even smell her musky perfume.

She explained in a pleading tone how all she had ever wanted was a normal life just like everybody else. Unfortunately, there were few people who understood this particular yearning and she felt that above all others, I would be able to sympathize. During the course of our encounter, she told me that she was a delightful, highly creative individual, but her weight added too much to her distinctiveness, and a jeering society had finally managed to destroy her zest for living. All she had in life was her imagination, and when that had started to disappear, the only way she could get it back was by using quantum.

37

I WOKE UP the next morning stiff, aching, and starving. Gibson told me I was hungry because of having expended so many calories during the healing process. He brought in a high-fat, breakfast: an egg omelette, perfectly seared pork chops, bread, and real butter. I ate like a famine victim, and while I did, I tried to put off LaRue's bitching about not wearing my bulletproof vest.

He sat at the foot of the bed, fierce and angry with me. His words seemed to stomp out of his mouth. "You deserve to be dead."

I picked up a chop and gnawed on the ring of fat enclosing the meat. Swallowing, I said, "I deserved to be dead when the furnace almost killed me, too. I've deserved to be dead lots of times." Another bite sent my teeth into the tender center of the pork. For just a second, I forgot he was there because it had been a long time since I'd had such a delicacy. After a few more mouthfuls, I added, "Thanks for the blood, partner."

"You would do the same for me," he said. "Just see that it doesn't happen again any time soon."

Gibson filled in an awkward silence that followed. "What's going on with this case that someone would try to kill you?"

"A cover-up," I answered. "We're just not sure that kind yet."

"And who's involved?" LaRue said. "Do you think it was Maria Raynor's killer who tried to bag you?"

I nodded. "It could be. Either that, or someone who's involved in this whole mess."

"A government representative?"

"That's what worries me about it. The fellow behind that auto bow knew what he was doing. I can't say he was a professional, but he didn't have any trouble using the damned thing. Maybe we really are getting close to something that the PHO doesn't want known."

"We've visited with a lot of people," LaRue answered. "Any one of them could have played ball. It's happened before, and frankly, a few of these turds we've been talking to make me wonder." He sighed. Then, "I'll tell you, Ty—this is one strange lot we're dealing with."

I didn't reply. Instead, I bit into a piece of bread and luxuriated in the feeling that the butter made on my tongue. Both men watched me but said nothing. I took another moment before speaking. "Tell me something, Gibson. Can quantum go undetected in the bloodstream?"

He thought a second. "It doesn't leave much of a pharmaceutical track because it breaks down into different chemicals." He paused to caress his chin, and the small movement drew my attention to his fingers. Continuing, he broke my momentary mesmerization. "When marijuana use was at its height, the governments tried to make people take blood tests to indicate drug use before they were given a job. Users would swallow massive amounts of goldenseal, an herbal stimulant that was supposed to cleanse the blood and mask the presence of pot. You could probably conceal a quantum trail the same way."

"Would chromium be a good choice?"

"I've heard of people trying all kinds of things so as not to be found out."

I broke off a piece of the omelette. "In your opinion, then?"

He shrugged. "I'd go so far as to say that if the mineral showed up in a high enough concentration in a person's system, I think it might attract more attention than the residual presence of quantum."

38

LARUE SAID THAT if I was getting shot at and finding answers in my dreams rather than when I was awake, then I had somehow stepped out of the bounds of perfect harmony. He thought that my chi energy needed to be pushed around by a Feng Shui priest and in this way I could safely recover my metaphysical balance.

Despite my protests, my partner dragged me off the next day to see his Uncle Carl. He said he planned this meeting to have a dual purpose: Carl could bring back my luck and translate the Portuguese scrolls.

The priest was working a community shift over at St. Ophelia's Soup Kitchen in Ward Nineteen. I was surprised to find that Carl was as big as Maria Raynor. He had the dark good looks of the LaRues, but they were strangely distorted by a pelt of fat. When he saw his nephew, he threw down his soup ladle and called out in a good-natured voice, "Andrew, my sister's invisible child. When was the last time you visited me?"

"Sorry it's been so long, Uncle. I haven't had a day off."

"That's not what your mother tells me. She says you have a new girlfriend to compete for your spare time." He glanced at me. "Is this her?"

LaRue smiled. "This is my partner, Marshal Ty Merrick."

Carl's features puffed even more as he grinned. "Now, you I've heard stories on." Then, back to LaRue. "What brings you down to the soup kitchen? A craving for my aviator stew?" With that he picked up the ladle and served up a bowl of chicken wings and broth, handing it off to the next customer in line.

"Not this time," LaRue said. "We need your help on two things. Ty, here, needs to get her chi in balance and we also need for you to read us something written in Portuguese."

"Portugal. Such a beautiful place. I spent my Feng Shui apprenticeship there, you know. What is it now? District Seventy-four? Yes, that's it. Not so romantic a name, though, is it?" Looking at me, he said, "I don't have to get near you to know that your energy is very fragile right now." Serving up another dish, he wiped his hands on his apron, called for a replacement behind the counter, and motioned us to follow him into the back.

He had a small office reached through a storage room that was lined with shelves packed tightly with institutional-size cans of green beans, corn, and applesauce. Outside the door to his retreat hung several strings of wind chimes. He noticed me studying them and explained as we entered.

"It is thought that the chimes direct the flow of chi, or energy, into a room each time the door is opened. But then, I have a feeling that you don't think there is anything to Feng Shui."

"I'm a skeptic, I'll admit it. I have to see it to believe it, and invisible magic is a little hard to get your hands around."

"Invisible magic? I've not heard it called that before." He left his comment at that and didn't try to convince me of the mystical powers LaRue claimed that he possessed.

The decor inside the office was functional but littered with more mirrors than I expected. Again, Carl explained. "It's believed that there are energy intersections where good and bad luck meet. To keep the flow of good luck, it needs to be reflected. A very simple premise."

"But is there anything to it?"

"The people hailing from the Sino districts have believed it for centuries. Nothing is done without consulting a Feng Shui master. He or she has the ability to find the places where there is the optimum flow of good luck. An adept can tell the best area to build a house or hold a wedding or even how deep to dig a hole for a burial. A person in touch with chi can even recommend what kind of transportation would best serve the individual."

I glanced at LaRue. "Did Carl have anything to do with you buying the Trabant?"

He shook his head.

"I thought it was a bad idea, but Andrew wouldn't listen. What is this fascination for old Communist relics, anyway? I just don't see the point."

"So the chi in the car is bad?" I asked.

"No, no. When I couldn't convince Andrew not to buy it,

I did the only thing I could. I had a Buddhist monk bless it."
He squinted at LaRue. "You haven't had any accidents, have
you, boy?"

"No, sir."

"Good. That means the luck is still holding."

He dropped the conversation while he changed from his
apron into a tent-size white linen robe. Stringing a sparkling
embroidered collar about his neck, he then turned to light
several incense burners sitting atop a teakwood cabinet. He
positioned me on a small circle of red carpet in the middle
of the room and told LaRue to point the shiny side of a hand
mirror toward me. He then began to chant.

I always find that I grow terribly uncomfortable when
made to perform such stupid rituals, but I wanted to get
LaRue off my back, so I stood there trying not to roll my
eyes and huff when Carl started splashing me with holy
water. After fifteen minutes, he was assured that my good
luck was back in place.

"Go home and drink a gallon of rainwater," he advised.
"That should cleanse you of any residual impurities."

I nodded and mentally patted myself on the shoulder for
not sneering at his prescription.

He removed his robe, hung it on a peg behind his desk,
and sat down heavily into the chair. It squeaked in what
sounded like an agonizing protest each time the huge man
moved. LaRue gave him the copy of the final scroll while I
sat on a leather couch positioned under a bank of mirrors.

"Please give it to us word by word," LaRue said.

Carl nodded, cleared his throat, and began. "'I am
convinced that the only way to solve the deadly riddle left
by the genetic isotope and, thereby, save the world, is
through a program of intense study. Yet, since the government has managed to keep its preliminary findings a
guarded secret, it's mandatory for me to start from the

beginning with my research. To do this, I must bring in many more subjects. This has a measure of difficulty to it because only the people who carry the survival gene may be used. They must first be prepared, not only mentally, but physically. In several cases, I have accomplished this through a rigorous program designed to cleanse them of residual negative energy. In this way, the results will be untainted by outside influences. *Global Transformation*. Dr. Philip Ligotti.' "

Upon hearing the words, our suspicions were confirmed. Our killer was going to take another victim.

39

As I SAID, I don't believe in invisible magic, and things like lucky charms are as worthless as the spit used to make them, but once in a while, things mysteriously drop into your lap. You see, Jack Raynor's brother, Max, was the youngest in the litter. He was, by his own admission, the designated black sheep of the family, and just before the end of our official watch, he was brought into the district lockup, charged with unlawful public assembly and illegal possession of quantum.

We sat in the interrogation room, listening to the man rant about his arrest. He couldn't see how three people sharing a street corner could be considered dangerous to civil order. It was my guess that he neglected to consider the verbal harassment thrown out at passersby and the drugs that floated openly between them.

A telltale sign of quantum use is that it makes your breath stink like garlic, and Max's exhales were overpowering. He also kept picking at a pimple on his cheek and smoothing down his greasy brown mane. Each time he lifted his arm, we were blasted with the sour milk smell of his body odor.

LaRue undertook the interview by flipping a chair around and sliding into the seat. He studied Max until the man wound down about his arrest. Then, in a voice carrying a full measure of menace, he said, "We want to know where Jack is."

Max snorted, blasting the small space with more stink. "I believe I have his itinerary right here in my pocket. Besides, what does that have to do with me?"

LaRue leaned in. "Someone murdered his wife. We want to talk to your whole family unit."

He stared at LaRue, and when he finally spoke, one word thudded into the next. "His wife is dead? Maria? Jack did it?"

"I didn't say that. We need to ask him some questions. And you." He placed both hands flat on the table before continuing. "Where have you been since you were released from drug rehabilitation?"

"Around. But that doesn't mean I know anything about Maria's murder. Shit. I can't believe it. She was a nice woman. Why would anyone want to kill her?"

"Maybe you can tell us. Again, where's Jack?"

He shook his head and muttered.

"You must have some idea."

"Did you try talking to his various female conquests?"

"We talked to Emily Church."

"Well, I can't help you. Before I went into the hospital, we had a fight. Not that we were ever on the best of terms, anyway. Jack isn't very impressed with my lifestyle. I'm a bum, you know. Never mind that I'm a brilliant bum, capable of such leaps of imagination that if properly funded, I could save the world." He chuckled darkly. "But that's Jack's domain. Saving the world, I mean."

"Explain that last statement to us, Max."

"It's just that. He wants to save the world."

"How?" I snapped.

He shrugged. This small action didn't do much for my patience. It made me reach across the table to grab him by the collar. I yanked only once, but I used my lycanthropic strength to make a point. "You better start spilling, you piece of shit, or I'll tie you to a tree by your tiny testicles. Got that?"

He managed a nod.

"Good." I released him, sat back in my chair, and donned some composure. "Now, Max, I've been shot at in the last couple of days and the shooter used an auto bow. Who, can you imagine, would want to kill me? Is it someone on the F-Project?"

He blinked, and his answer was slow to come. "I'm not sure what the F-Project is."

"But you've heard the term before? From Jack, maybe?"

"No. It was Maria. She mentioned it, but she didn't go into it. That's all I know."

"Jack told her he was involved in it?"

"Yeah, I guess. Jack couldn't get away from his early days, you know."

"What are you talking about, Max?" LaRue demanded.

"He missed going into the field and working right with the people. I lost count how many times he went into a sealed district when he first started working for Old Man Church. He loved it."

"Old Man Church? We're referring to Cecil Church?"

"Yeah. He's the one who got him the councilman position. Jack took it because the money was good, but every opportunity, he managed to weasel a gig outside of the office. I don't think the money mattered so much as the fact that he wasn't locked inside a cubicle pushing papers."

"What kinds of projects would he work on?"

Max considered the question by rubbing the stump of his arm over the table's surface. "I'm not sure. I wasn't exactly the person he'd talk to about his career."

"All right, Max," LaRue said. "You seemed to have been good friends with Maria. Can you tell us about her maid, a woman named Sun Ye Sung?"

He squeezed a look at him. "What about her?"

"Where did she come from?"

"One of the Sino districts."

"District Twenty-one, perhaps?"

"Could have been. I never asked. Jack was always importing folks for some reason or other. He had controlled visa authority because of his job."

"Controlled visa authority? Which governmental agency granted him that?"

"PHO, of course. He was in charge of health policy, after all."

"What happened to Sun Ye?"

"Jack got tired of her and was looking for an excuse to get rid of her. She was starting to act up, I guess. That and the fact that Maria truly liked her company. Anything that Maria liked, Jack managed to damage. He held up his stump for emphasis. "My brother has always had a vindictive streak."

"How long did Maria use quantum before she died?"

His face pinched up, and I thought for a moment he would deny it. "How do you know about that?"

"We're district marshals," I said. "We know a lot of things. How long?"

He shrugged. "A few months, I suppose."

"Did you turn her on?"

"No. You've got to believe me. It was their friend, Blackburn."

"What's Blackburn's full name?"

"I don't know."

"That's odd. You did associate with him."

"No, I didn't."

"You mean you didn't strike up a relationship?"

"No, never."

LaRue took over by getting up and slowly walking off the length of the room. He then turned like a panther and got into Max's face, despite the smell issuing from the man. "Axion Howard says you two scored quantum from him on a regular basis."

"Axion is the cheapest dealer around. We probably crossed paths."

"No. Blackburn told him he knew you really well. Make it easy on yourself, pal. Tell us about this man."

He sighed and rubbed his stump across his forehead. "Damn. All right. I know the guy. His name is Ronald Blackburn. I think his middle name is Orson. Whatever. That's what he likes to be called."

"How did this man meet the Raynors?"

"He met Jack during his humanitarian service. He was a blood tech or something. I think he did a few projects for him at the PHO."

"Could he have been involved in this F-Project?"

"Maybe. I don't know for sure."

"Where does Mr. Blackburn live?"

"I never asked. Contrary to what Axion Howard claims, we weren't that good of friends. In fact, he was closer to

Maria, especially after he and Jack had a fight. I think my brother stole his woman. That put the razor to the vein on that friendship. Jack just didn't know when to keep it in his pants."

"What was the name of this woman?"

"I've no idea. All I know for sure is that she worked for the company catering Maria's dinner parties."

"This would be The Macaroni Hut?"

He nodded. "I never talked to the woman, but she would be all over Blackburn during the parties."

I changed the line of questioning. "Did Jack ever hire you to do personal errands for him?"

"Once in a while. Especially when my paycheck wouldn't cover us."

"We understand that he sent you to a street scribe to have several documents copied for him. They would be Greek, Latin, Cryllic, Chinese, Portuguese, and Gaelic."

He nodded as I named them off. "Jack didn't send me. Maria did. It was part of a charm Blackburn was making for her." He rolled his eyes. "Can you believe that people actually believe in that stuff?"

I glanced at LaRue, knowing that he was wearing a freshly packed charm pouch given him by his mother. It was loaded with cinnamon, nutmeg, and clove, which meant it was only a short time until a full moon. After a few days of smelling like a pumpkin pie, he would give the bag back to her, and she would add some dried fennel and mustard seeds to increase the protective potency against werewolf bites.

Max continued spilling his guts. "It seems to me that these self-proclaimed sorcerers should at least use technology. How could it have hurt to type the pages on a laser printer? But no. Maria said that Blackburn had specifically said to take the pages to a female scribe who was between the ages of forty-five and seventy, who had access to naturally dyed, recycled paper and a narrow-gauge writing pen. She had to copy these pages between the hours of noon and three o'clock."

"What did you do?" LaRue asked.

"Hired the first street scribe I saw. Got her to do it for half price, too."

I dragged him back with my question. "Blackburn would make extra money selling charms?"

"Extra money? Try a lot of money. He charged hundreds of credits and Maria, for one, paid it. Jack was furious. He beat the shit out of her over it."

"When did that happen?"

"A few months back."

"What happened to Blackburn?"

"I don't know. Last time I saw him, he was on the street. He was pretty drugged out. He kept talking about what he called his new sideline."

"Which was?"

"Breaking and entering. It was all bullshit, of course."

I glanced at LaRue and could tell by his frown that he was thinking of Jolene Nebraska's ransacked apartment.

"Max," he said. "Do you know a gentleman by the name of Blockbuster Bill?"

He hesitated. "Yeah. He rents vids. So?"

"We have a list where your name appears several times. You rented some porn movies. You know the ones I mean, don't you?"

He scowled and his words husked out. "Yes."

"Did you share them with Blackburn?"

He shook his head. "No. I rented them for Maria."

40

BASED ON MAX'S confession, it was time to interview Edward
Polinato again. He came into the office immediately after
his summons, smelling of vodka and butter sauce, wearing
a bloodstained apron and a chagrined expression. As usual,
his hair was greased down, and each time he rubbed his
fingers through it, little oily beads flew into the air.

"Ed, you haven't been totally honest with us," I said.
"And we're not happy about that."

His words hooted like an owl. "Me? I've been honest.
What more can I tell you than I already have?"

"You can tell us about a gentleman who goes by the name
of Ronald Orson Blackburn. You do know him, correct?"

He hesitated, but finally found his voice. "Yeah, so what
if I do?"

"Who is he?"

"He used to date one of my employees; a girl by the name
of Christina Dunn."

"This is the same Christina Dunn who worked for your
catering business and who went unreported to the district?"

He glanced at the table. "OK, maybe I forgot to mention
her the first time we spoke."

"I'll say you did," LaRue answered. "Did she ever talk
about Blackburn to you?"

"Yeah, but I thought it was words from a kid's mouth. All
that lovey-duvey stuff."

"Well, what did she say?"

He sighed and slumped forward. "The usual things.
About how he was brilliant and working for the government. He was supposed to be rich, and they were going to

get married someday right after he figured out how to get rid of his wife."

"Did they get married?"

"It was all bullshit. He was into quantum and he didn't make a secret of it. That fellow was going down for the count, making up crap and talking crazy. I didn't pay any attention to him. Christina, though, thought he was the best thing to ever walk into The Macaroni Hut. I tried to tell her he was no good, but these teenagers don't listen."

"Did he come around a lot?"

"Practically every night."

"Stoned?"

"Yeah."

"Did he bother the customers?"

"Yes, that he did. Especially the women. I've lost some good customers because of him."

"Why did you put up with him?"

"Because for every one I lost, he brought two more in. I've never seen anything like it. The man must have known the whole district. It's how I got the catering jobs with Mrs. Raynor."

"Did he ever talk about committing burglary? Maybe he mentioned that he was fond of breaking and entering?"

He shook his head, releasing more oil into the air. "Not to me. No. Never."

"Did he ever mention his expertise with an auto bow?"

"An auto bow? He never said anything." His expression flatlined as he considered his next sentence. "It's strange you should ask about that, though."

"Why?"

"Because one of the parties that Mrs. Raynor gave was called Commando Nights. She called me one evening to finalize some of the plans and happened to say that she'd found an actual auto bow to use as part of the decorations."

41

RONALD ORSON BLACKBURN was officially dead. According to the district coroner's record, he had finally taken his last popper of quantum a year before.

He was born in District One and worked as a blood technician for the PHO. His wife, Nancy, divorced him after he lost his classification designation in a court-adjudicated dispute that asserted that he had endangered lives during a bloodmobile drive because he was high on dope. The information explained how he was placed in rehab and reentered into society at a lower job level, specifically as a clerical assistant, which if the guy had any ego at all, must have really galled him.

He had no relatives, and his school records were unavailable. His humanitarian service record had holes shot all through it, but it confirmed in bits and pieces what Max had told us. Jack had probably met him during his stint with the veterinary corps because they both moved on to the PHO's Department of Immunization. From there, he transferred to the Department of Mutagenic Studies, where he earned a demerit letter for insubordination. He then climbed aboard the district bloodmobile. After that, he was supposed to have died, but if that were true, then Maria Raynor had invited a zombie to her dinner parties.

LaRue came into our cubicle and slipped into his jacket. "We've got a visit scheduled with Nancy Blackburn," he said. "She seemed very anxious to talk to us."

I left the computer and followed him to the car, trying to gear up for the bumpy ride ahead. LaRue did his best to get my mind off the chuckholes by telling me how concerned

Gibson was when I showed up to bleed all over his apartment. He said that he kept talking to himself after he discovered my lycanthropic resiliency and extraordinary ability to heal. With the tearing of muscle tissue, I should have required several days to get back the use of my arm. As he told me that, I became aware of a thudding in my shoulder. Gibson was right about one thing: I was susceptible to suggestion.

LaRue kept going on about the doctor until we reached Ward Eighty-two, where he changed the conversation to give me his views on what he termed "a clusterfucking neighborhood."

To him, all the shacks and shanties in this region rambled over each other like a string of discordant lovers. In the pumpkin light of a setting sun, the hard angles softened into sepia shadows, relieved here and there by the twinkle of a propane lantern. It was ten blocks of poverty cast across a rumpled quilt of trash and cracked concrete.

We parked at the head of the block because the roadbed leading to Nancy Blackburn's residence was so chewed up that not even LaRue wanted to chance that many blacktop canyons.

Her home was a twenty-five-foot-long travel trailer that looked as though it had been rolled over at some point. It was shored up by the walls of two adjoining weathered clapboard houses, and it had a rotten wooden roof elevated above it. A tattered blue tarpaulin helped to keep the elements from intruding on this creaky-looking affair, and taking advantage of what must have been an open manhole in the sidewalk, an outhouse had been constructed of old paint cans and covered with a snag of corrugated aluminum.

LaRue knocked on the bright red front door, and while we waited the few moments for the answer, he pointed to the manufacturer's name painted in bright purple letters just below the cracked louver window: Donnybrook, Inc.

Nancy Blackburn responded, wearing a red checkered bandanna over her graying hair and a pair of dirty overalls without a shirt. Inside, the trailer was a tragedy.

The wooden cabinets and paneled walls were so rotten that they looked wet. A beat-up blue couch, a filthy mattress strewn with magazines, and a lumpy brown chair comprised this eclectic decor. Mold had crept into everything including the braided carpet and up the side of a small refrigerator. The electric was off, the cooler stood open, displaying not food but a rusty propane lantern and a greasy blanket.

"It ain't much, marshals, but you're welcome to have a seat," she said.

I sat down on the couch as gently as I could. LaRue joined me and when he did, the sofa groaned ominously under our combined weight. Thankfully, Nancy Blackburn made herself comfortable on the chair.

"Is something wrong?" she asked. "Has one of my kids started some trouble?"

"No, ma'am," I said. "We're here about your ex-husband."

"Orson? He's dead."

"We have reason to believe that he's not."

Her brown eyes widened. I thought she was going to start crying, because her voice came out cracked with emotion. "You must be mistaken. When he died, the government stopped sending me support payments."

"Is that why you're living here?"

She nodded. "I had to give up our house and move into this rat's nest. I only have a Class D designation, and you can't afford much on what I earn."

"What happened to your children, Mrs. Blackburn?"

"Workhouses. They're old enough to start fending for themselves. I certainly can't feed them. We had six, you know." She paused. "So you think he's alive, do you? That means the bastard found a way to stiff me out of my alimony and the government went along with it."

"Will you tell us a few things about your husband?"

"Of course. Anything I can."

"To your knowledge, before your husband died, was he working on any government projects involving genetic research?"

She snorted. "That's funny. He talked about being a scientist, but of course, it weren't nothing but the drugs talking. I knew it, and still I went along with it, 'cause I loved him. Love don't do people much good, though. I found that out."

"What do you mean?"

"He was cheating on me. And why? Sex. It was always available to him, too. I would have done anything to make him happy. Had all his brat kids 'cause he was against birth control. What did I get for it? Him with his nose in books all the time, and the goddamned clap from his womanizing."

"He liked to read?" I asked.

"Yeah. He liked to watch vids, too. Never did pay any attention to me. Always told me to shut up when his documentaries were on."

"What kind of documentaries did he watch?"

She shrugged. "I don't know. I never paid them no mind. I was usually screaming at one of the kids."

"Could your husband speak any other languages besides Barrier?"

She nodded. "He was real good at that. Had a talent for it. He taught himself a bunch of different ones, but don't ask me what they were, 'cause I just don't know. It's too bad he got so messed up on the quantum."

"What began to happen?" LaRue asked.

"It got so he couldn't tell what was real and what was

something that he'd seen in a movie or read in a book. He called himself brilliant, he did, just like Leonardo da Vinci. Said he had the answers to the save the world, but he was up against government bureaucracy, and no one would listen. He often said that he would make them listen. It was the drug talking. That's all."

"What made you finally decide to challenge the marriage vow?"

"His cheating, like I said. That's enough to get you out of any marriage."

"You're referring to an affair he had with a woman named Christina Dunn?"

She nodded and the bandanna fluttered with the movement. "She was one of them. He didn't even bother to try to hide the fact."

"How would you describe your husband's relationship with Jack Raynor?" I asked.

"That bastard? He's another one who can't think of nothing but sex. I heard they had a falling-out over that whore. Jack stole her away."

"Did Orson know Mrs. Raynor very well?" I asked.

"Sure. They were all his friends. He never invited me with him, understand. He didn't think I was high-society enough to fit in."

"Did you ever meet Mrs. Raynor?"

"I met her once or twice. Why do you ask?"

"Mrs. Raynor was murdered."

She blinked. "Oh, sweet St. Ophelia. And you think my no-good, nondead husband had something to do with it?"

"We're not sure, but there is a possibility," I answered. "Tell me, Mrs. Blackburn, did your husband have a side business where he made charms for people?"

Her surprised expression degenerated into a hooded look.

"That's illegal unless you got a government certificate or something."

"We don't care if you did or you didn't," I said. "We're not tax investigators and what you tell us won't go any farther. We promise you."

She hesitated. "Well, I don't know."

"Mrs. Blackburn, you won't get in any trouble if you tell us, but if you don't and we find out later, you could be cited as impeding an investigation. You could be brought into court and assigned to a labor camp."

Her mouth dropped open, but she made her decision quickly. "Yes. We had a business. I made the charms and Orson sold them. I know it weren't right doing the government out of their taxes, but we had so many mouths to feed."

"Did your husband ever make a charm bag for Mrs. Raynor?"

She frowned and glanced at the floor. "I can't tell you for sure," she answered, in a low voice.

I put on my most reassuring face. "What can you tell us?"

She squeezed her hands into little dirty balls and then looked up. "I just made regular charms, you know, protectors and love attractors; little stuff. Orson would get ahold of them and then start to add to them."

"How? Would he put more magical objects in them?"

"No. He would tell the folks that they had to do other things for the magic to work."

"Such as?"

"Such as telling them they needed to take special herbs and stuff."

"He would supply them with these ingredients?"

"Yes. He made us more money."

"What else would he do?"

"Well, he would score more credits by scheduling them up with appointments where he would pretend to boost the power of the charm. He didn't really do nothing, of course, but they believed him. He was a natural talker. I think he missed his calling. He should have been a salesman." She paused to insert a sigh. "We did real good for a long time. There was even enough money for us to afford an electric washing machine. Yes, indeed. That washer was the hardest thing for me to leave when I got kicked out of the house."

42

NOT LONG AFTER Max Raynor was released on a citizen's bond, he turned up dead, shot through the eye with an arrow from an auto bow. We got the word over the array, just as we were leaving Nancy Blackburn's house. Suddenly, LaRue and I became a bit more concerned over finding Maria's killer, so immediately upon locating Christina Dunn's address, we went to visit her.

She shared a house with her parents and a cousin. It was a small, worn, concrete structure sitting in the middle of a patch of bare vines and thorny creepers. LaRue decided that the owner had tried for an ivy-covered cottage but instead had made the place look like a piece of Styrofoam trash stuck in overgrown weeds.

Christina answered our knock. When we identified ourselves, she started to sweat, mumbling an apology about how warm the house was. She sat on a salmon-colored, leatherette divan, and pushed demurely at her calico-print dress and at a curl that had stuck to her forehead. LaRue joined her while I took a seat on a cloth-covered lawn chair. The seat was brittle with dry rot and there was a moment there when I was convinced my butt would go through it.

"Does this have to do with my job down at The Macaroni Hut?" she asked.

"In a way," I said. "We understand that you know both Ronald Orson Blackburn and Jack Raynor."

"Yes," she said, quietly. "But I haven't spoken to either of them for a long time."

"Did you know that Blackburn had invented his own death?"

She dropped her gaze to her lap and nodded.

"But you didn't report him to the authorities. Why?"

"I couldn't. I loved him. I still do."

"What you've done is against the law," I said. My sentence brought her head up abruptly and I continued in a serious tone. "It's called enabling tax fraud, and if you're found guilty, you go to a labor camp from ten to twenty-five years." I waited a moment for her to start to shake before I claimed her cooperation. "Ms. Dunn, you're young, and I would hate to see such a thing happen to you. If you talk to us, we'll see that you're left out of this whole ugly affair. What do you say to that?"

Her answer stammered out. "Yes, I'll do anything."

Satisfied that I'd laid the fear on her, I let LaRue take over the interview.

"Do you know who helped him invent his death?"

"No, I don't. You have to believe me. Orson was a brilliant man. He said he arranged everything himself. I didn't ask too many questions about it."

He tried a new tack. "Orson was using quantum. Is that correct?"

"Yes, but he only did it once in a while when he needed to feel better about himself."

"We understand you stepped out on Orson and dated Jack. Tell us about that, won't you?"

"I did do that," she whispered. Then, suddenly buckling, she crashed headlong into an explanation. "I'm not a whore, if that's what you think. I went to bed with Jack because Orson was having sex with Sun Ye, the Raynor's maid. I'm glad she got fired."

"You two had an argument?"

"She tried to tell me how to do my job because she didn't like the way the food was arranged on the plates. I told her to mind her own business, and something snapped inside of her. She shoved me. I had a tray of chicken in my hands and the whole thing spilled onto the kitchen floor."

LaRue and I both leaned close. "Then what?" I prodded.

"Well, I hit her back. She stepped away from me and started screaming something about how I'd better mind my manners, because Jack was a powerful man who had selected her to work on a special project. Like that was supposed to mean something to me."

"Is that when Sun Ye was fired?"

Her hand came up to scrape at her lips and then to rest upon her cheek. "What a scene. Jack came in just as she started screeching. He grabbed her by the throat and shoved her against the refrigerator. He told her to shut up and get out."

"Were you curious enough to ask Jack what his special project was about?"

"No. I didn't have to. He told me." She dropped her hand. "He said the quantum problem is worse than ever and once hooked, you're a lifer. I think he said that because he knew how I felt about Orson. He thought I was throwing my life away following him around. I didn't think so, and that's why I slept with Jack. I just wanted to get his attention, but it backfired. They had a huge argument and that was the last time Orson talked to me. I've dealt with it, though, because now I see that there was no relationship between us to begin with. When we weren't in bed, he was absorbed in his books or vegged-out on his vids. He didn't want to have anything to do with me during those times."

Well, at least the cad was consistent in the way he treated women. "Tell us about the project Sun Ye mentioned."

She thought a moment. "The PHO has a program where they try to help quantum addicts to adjust to the lifestyle he or she has fallen into. Jack's brother, Max, was such a person. So, apparently, was Orson."

"Did you ask how they helped him?" LaRue asked.

"Something about getting them to realize their full potential. That's all he ever said and I didn't take it any farther."

"Do you have any idea who else was working with Jack on this project?" I asked.

"No. He did mention that Emily Church's father had started the program years ago, though."

LaRue grunted and shifted the questioning. "Was Orson making a charm for Mrs. Raynor? Perhaps a protection bag like the one I'm wearing?" He flapped his mom's home-made werewolf neutralizer at her.

"Scamming? Boy, you know it. He talked Maria into all kinds of stuff, and she bought every time. The more she bought, the more expensive he made the next thing. He was smart about it, I have to hand it to him. He made even more money by convincing people that once they had one of his amulets or voodoo bottles, they needed other materials and luck spells to make the magic more effective. The customers usually did what he asked, paying through the nose for all the extras. I guess since they'd already spent so much for the initial charm, they didn't bother to balk at the increased prices he charged to fix them up further.

"I remember he bragged about how he'd convinced Mrs. Raynor that she needed to have a very expensive charm sack made for her by this special artist. She managed to get Jack to order it for her birthday. Well, Jack wanted her off his back, so he did what she asked, but when he found out how much it cost, he nearly lost his mind. It didn't matter, though, because she came up with it a couple of days later, anyway. She even told me how much it cost."

"And how much was that?"

"One thousand credits."

"Did she buy it directly from the artist?"

"No. I think she gave the money to Orson and he bought it for her."

"Did Blackburn ever talk to you about his interest in burglary?"

She frowned. "Orson was a lot of things, but he wasn't a thief."

"All right," I said. "Did he ever mention an interest in weaponry, specifically auto bows?"

"No. Never. He was a peaceful man."

"Even though he was bilking people."

She sighed. "Despite that."

"Let's go back to Jack," LaRue said. "He was very concerned with money, wasn't he?"

"Yes. Even though his wife was always running on about her trust fund. He was frugal, that's all."

"He had a lot of environmental waste meters in the house.

It looked to us as though he was also concerned about paying his taxes. Was he?"

She almost giggled, but composed herself before she erupted. "It was all a joke," she answered. "He had gauge after gauge, but not one of them was hooked into his house's computer system. They didn't measure anything, but Maria thought they did. Jack just loved getting one over on her like that."

43

I SAW A documentary once on Vincent van Gogh. It described how the artist's madness influenced his paintings. I watched that film several times and finally came to the conclusion that van Gogh had some form of lycanthropy. His painting, *Starry Night*, shows the same hard lines that I see after I stretch.

Shadows leap back and hold no secrets, and colors that normally have a muddy hue sparkle under the most mundane light. Misty rain turns into silver motes around me, and the reflections of the sun crackle intensely. Van Gogh caught this way of seeing with his brush and palette.

I was reminded of the painter as I stared at the 3-D effect of the patterns created by the crystal chandelier in the foyer of Cecil Church's mansion. It was late the next evening when we finally scheduled an appointment with the man. We also managed to step into the middle of his potlatch supper.

Potlatching became popular after Duvalier took over. Two family units would meet once a year to serve copious amounts of food and to exchange lavish gifts. The family that outdid the other with the magnitude of presents hosted the party the next year. All items would then be donated to a community service organization and could be claimed as a tax write-off. From the looks of things, Mr. Church would get a huge savings deduction from this party.

The butler led us to what he called the drawing room where cocktails were being served. He left us on the fringe of this event to fetch the master of the house. LaRue immediately got into a conversation about the benefits of distilling one's own alcohol rather than paying the exorbitant fees charged in the district's beverage stores. The man he'd cornered agreed and edged away, finally freed by the servant from having to listen to a discourse on Russian ingenuity and vodka making.

Mr. Church met us in the study. He was confined to an electric wheelchair and tethered to an oxygen pack attached to the motor. His long white hair was neatly pressed into a ponytail and there was some slobber on his Santa Claus beard.

An attendant, dressed in a crisp white uniform, started off with an apology. "Mr. Church suffers from Alzheimer's disease, Marshals. He may not be able to give you credible information."

"Oh, shut up, Dorthea!" he yelled. "It's all a lie concocted by that hateful daughter of mine."

"That would be Emily?" I asked quietly.

"No, that would be Jessica. I've disowned the both of them, you know."

Dorthea shrugged at us and went to sit on a mahogany love seat. She picked up a magazine and casually thumbed through it while the old man ranted for a few moments. Then he demanded to know why he had come.

Before answering, LaRue took a slow walk down a wall lined with bookshelves. He stopped to run a finger over the spine of one volume. Cecil Church turned his watery blue eyes on him like some ancient eagle who was enraged but helpless to prevent his territory from being invaded. "We're sorry to disturb you, sir," he said, finally. "It's a murder investigation, you see."

"I know which one," the old man hooted. "Maria Raynor. I read about it in the newspaper." He glanced over to his assistant who looked up from her reading. "Yes, Dorthea, I read the newspaper." Then, back to us, "They try to keep me in the dark, you know. Think I'm too far gone to figure out what's going on anymore. As you can see, I'm not."

"We need your help with a few things."

"Certainly. Anything I can do. I've always been a law-abiding citizen."

"Can you tell us about the F-Project?" he asked.

"What about it?"

"Well, for starters, what is it?"

"Good question." He frowned. "Can't quite recall the particulars."

"We think it has something to do with District Twenty-one."

"Oh, yes, that's right."

"What about District Twenty-one, then?"

"What about it?"

The attendant sighed loudly, but then settled into her magazine again.

"How did District Twenty-one fit in with the F-Project?" I asked.

"The plague, of course."

I looked at LaRue. "What plague?"

Obviously, some of his memory returned, because he plunged into an explanation. "It was years ago. There was an outbreak of Type-10 lupus. Wicked disease. Spread through the air. That's the worst kind, you know. It's damned hard to protect people."

"Did the F-Project address the problem?"

He stared at me for several seconds without answering, so I repeated the question. His answer popped out immediately after hearing it again.

"The F-Project was supposed to address the problem. We had scientists working on an immunization package." He frowned. "Yes, that's it. An immunization package. It didn't work. People were dying by the thousands. Nothing worked."

"What happened?"

"The PHO withdrew when it became evident that it wasn't going to solve the problem. They closed the borders and claimed it was a famine situation. They didn't want the word to get out because it would cause panic." He paused, and a startled look came over his face. "Oh, my, I wasn't supposed to talk about it. Ever. Forget you heard me say it."

"Yes, sir," LaRue said. He continued, taking advantage of Church's lapse. "Jack Raynor worked on the project, didn't he?"

"As I recall, he did."

"Does your daughter, Emily, know anything about this program?"

"Emily? She doesn't know anything but how to spend my money."

"We have a witness who said she was talking to Jack regarding the program."

"Isn't he a councilman, now? Public health policy or something like that?"

"Yes, sir."

"You were the one responsible for starting the F-Project several years ago," I said. "Is that right?"

"Looked into it then, yes. I left it up to my successor to handle." He shifted in his chair. "If you're really interested, I think the PHO included it in some documentary vid or something. Can't remember the name of the movie. Of course, if it exists, it would only be available through the university library, and to check it out you would have to be a medical doctor with a triple-A research rating." He grinned. "That leaves you two out of it, doesn't it?"

44

LaRue AND I stopped by the clinic on our way from Cecil Church's residence. There we found Gibson up to his elbows in kids who had the chicken pox. Depending on their infection level, they either screamed, cried, whimpered, or spit their germs around. The nurse pointed to his office and said she would tell him we were there as soon as she calmed a frantic mother. We walked down the hallway, hearing the commotion coming from behind the examining room door-ways. Someone had just gotten a shot; I could tell by the shriek.

We pushed into the doctor's office, and LaRue went immediately to study the titles of the medical journals crowded into a metal bookcase. He picked up a dense volume and flipped through the pages, and with that, he sat down in the sinking leather chair to glean more irrelevant information for his cornucopia of useless facts.

I occupied myself by staring at the photo display hanging on the wall behind Gibson's desk. The pictures weren't of his family unit, as you would expect. Instead, they were of his patients. A few showed smiling faces and blue hospital gowns; one showed him proudly holding a newborn with the parents looking on; and three showed him accepting some sort of award. I scanned the crowded collage for the one I knew would be there. It took me a moment, but I locked onto a photo with the man who claimed to be a lycanthrope.

I was drawn to it instantly, because there was something in his face that I recognized but couldn't verbalize. It was like the painting Alex had given me: a blending of wolf and human. Yet, if I was challenged to explain what I saw, I couldn't.

I had my nose an inch from the picture when Gibson entered. Silently, he walked directly to me, turned me around to face him, unzipped my cammies to my waist, pulled my sleeve down, and folded back the dressing on my arm. I stood there like an idiot without a protest. LaRue chuckled, drawing a lethal scowl from me.

When he pulled the gauze away and saw the neatly healed wound, he murmured something about me being a medical marvel and thinking he was in love. He leaned his butt on the edge of his desk while I fumbled with the zipper.

"I see you have an epidemic," LaRue said, glancing up from the book.

"The ward's public school had an outbreak. One kid gets it and then that's it. The whole place is under siege."

"I thought they immunized for chicken pox," I said.

"They do, but like everything else, you can't keep a good disease down. This is a different strain, just recently discovered. It's more virulent. And since you stepped into the chicken's den, you'd better let Nurse Exel pop the both of you."

LaRue groaned. "I hate shots. I'm worse than those screaming kids."

"We'll give you a lollipop." Then, Gibson said seriously, "It doesn't sound like it could be life-threatening, does it? If you're an adult, it can make you impotent, blind, and deaf. If you have other problems, it can make you dead."

"You're kidding?" he said.

"No. And the worse part? It's just the beginning. One school gets it and then another and then adults and seniors are up for the option."

"Why doesn't the PHO just do a mass immunization program like they do for the flu?" I asked.

"Because, Merrick, there's not enough of the vaccine. A whole lot of people are going to get left out on this one. Now, aren't you lucky you have a doctor who's crazy about the both of you?"

LaRue stood up, replaced the book, and grunted. "I'm first," he said. "Where do I go to get plugged?"

Gibson motioned with a nod. "Nurse's station."

After he left, the doctor turned back to me. "What can I do for you?"

"A couple of things, actually."

"Oh, here it comes. What do you need?"

I couldn't contain a grin. "We've tracked our killer to the university library. He may have been renting documentary vids and I need a card-carrying medic to get inside."

"Are you telling me the university won't cooperate with the District Marshals Office by supplying information?"

"Exempt status. They won't even talk to us, and anyone who can't verify a triple-A certification can't check out the information that we need."

"What about your forensic people? You've got a couple of doctors over there, don't you?"

"Not a triple-A among them. We just checked. You're a physician officially attached to PHO, and I'm sure you keep up with your university alumni dues. You can get us in." I paused. "If you don't mind."

He considered me before nodding. "Do you return vids that you rent?"

"Of course."

"And exactly what will you do in return for me?"

I'd considered this question before we came to him but still I hesitated, not sure I wanted to know the results of what I would offer. I hid my indecision by staring at the picture of the lycanthrope. Finally, I jumped in reluctantly. "What part of the brain controls the sight?"

I could tell he frowned without looking at him. "The occipital lobe," he answered.

Studying the picture, I said, "I really should get an eye exam one of these days."

45

AFTER I MENTIONED the eye exam, it took Gibson about three minutes to make a late-night appointment for me. He then told LaRue to take a hike and meet us in the morning at the university. I received my chicken pox vaccine, and an hour later, I was sitting in Dr. Jeffery Winegarden's ophthalmology unit at the local PHO medical service center.

Winegarden was a pleasant enough fellow who wore a thick pair of spectacles and too much cologne. When Gibson explained the reason for our abrupt appearance, the ophthalmologist grew an interested look on an otherwise bland face. He led us into an examining room and directed me to sit down before a large computer. He joined me and since there were only two chairs in the place, Gibson was forced to stand up.

"What are the numbers on your regular sight?" Winegarden asked.

"Twenty-twenty," I answered. "I just had a yearly exam for work."

"Have you ever had an eye disease such as conjunctivitis?"

"Pinkeye? As an adult? No. I can't tell you about my early childhood. I grew up in an orphanage, so it's possible. In that situation, kids tend to share everything."

"From your perspective," Gibson asked, "what happens to your sight?"

I thought about telling him of van Gogh's painting, but decided against it, fearing that I would look loonier than I already did. I shrugged. "It's just different. That's all I can say."

He nodded, but sighed.

"What do you know about the human eye, Marshal Merrick?" Winegarden asked.

"That we have two of them unless one falls out."

"It's safe to say there's a little more to it than that." He touched the rectangular examining bracket. "This machine is called an ophthalmoscope. It's used to check for abrasions and ulcers, among other things. Please place your chin into the restraining cup."

As I settled into it, he told me to focus upon the big E on the chart on the far wall. I did as he asked, and he ran the light around the inside of my eye. I saw the dark reflections of veins, specks, and stars. Gibson moved behind me and placed his hands gently on my upper arms.

"Just relax, Merrick. This exam doesn't hurt."

I realized then that I was so taut that my body was like a whipcord. I tried to calm my stiff muscles, but it did no good. Just as Winegarden asked me to blink, I had an explosion of irritability. I yanked away and twisted to stare at Gibson.

"Ophelia's mother! Why did you have to mention it?"

He laughed and his hands squeezed harder. "I swear, you need to be tranquilized. He let his touch slide down my arms before he released me. "I'm sorry."

I gave him a curt nod and went back to the chin cuff.

"Do you see better in the darkness or in the light when you realize the change has occurred?" Winegarden asked me.

"Everything is just sharper somehow."

He finished looked through the scope and turned then to the computer, punched some buttons, and returned to me. He pointed to a hood hinged to the top of the chin brace. It was shaped like a small welder's mask, so he hurriedly attempted to stall the frown that I knew came to my face. "I won't hurt at all. That's an ocular sensing device. It's hooked onto the computer and gives me vital statistics on your eye." He pushed the lid down over my face. "You'll see a dull red glow when the hood is activated. Can you sit still for a couple of minutes while it does the diagnostic?"

"Yes," I said, feeling the fidget growing in my knees.

The machine hummed and clicked. I sensed that Gibson had retreated to lean against the counter that ran the length of the room. The other man moved slightly as he studied the computer's analysis. Neither doctor spoke.

When it was over, Winegarden read the file through, crossed his arms, and swiveled his chair to study me with a quizzical expression.

Gibson leaned in. There was that annoying intensity to his voice. "What did you find, Jeff?"

"Something extraordinary." He, in turn, leaned toward me. "Marshal Merrick, humans normally have eyes that are considered diurnal. They have many more cones than they do rods. This machine can give me a fair estimate about how many of each are housed in the eyes of a particular individual."

"What are rods and cones?" I asked.

"They're photoreceptors. They channel visual information to the brain by a series of electrical impulses. The eyes of humans and higher primates have mostly cones, which allow us to see sharply primarily in the daylight. Rods allow for the processing of dim or dark surrounds. Your eyes have evidence of housing duplex retinas, and a significantly higher rate of rods than should be normally found. The shape of your eye has changed as well. It is now what we call arrhythmic."

"My God," Gibson murmured. "How can this be possible?"

"What?" I asked, feeling a touch of panic coming on. "What?"

Winegarden finished up. "The arrhythmic eye, Marshal Merrick, is found in large land mammals such as lions, bears, and wolves."

46

I just wasn't prepared for Dr. Winegarden's strange analysis. My wall of resistance, the thing in me that is marked with my personal graffiti of assurances, was suddenly chipped up by his words. I could feel it crumbling and I must have moaned when I heard his analysis. Gibson physically buoyed me as he led me from the ophthalmology center by placing his arm around my waist to guide me in a straight path down the street toward my flat. He said nothing, obviously giving me time to assimilate this latest information. I followed along like a robot, trying desperately to find my engage button, unsure of why I was so stunned.

He was the first to speak when we entered my apartment. "It's warmer in the hallway."

There was a scrawly note on the kitchen table left by Baba. She was spending the evening with Craia and I was invited down if I couldn't get the heat working.

Hard reality snapped me back. I wasn't anything romantic like a werewolf living in London; I was a werewolf living in poverty. Trying to light the stove for some heat, I found that the propane canister was dead. I growled and manhandled the counter drawer and then spent a minute irritably searching for a crescent wrench to see if I could fix the portable furnace. Gibson watched without a word. His expression, though, was one that made me think he was counting the number of calories I consumed while I dismissed my anger. He sat down beside me as I flopped onto the floor to wrestle with the orifice from the heater's gas line.

It took a few minutes before I could yank off a sentence. "Did you know that Duvalier was a lycanthrope?"

Gibson humored me. "I hadn't heard that."

"Haven't you read his poetry?"

"Of course. It was required reading in my third year at the university. As I remember, it was frightfully bad."

"I don't think it was."

I fumbled as I unscrewed the valve. He gently interceded, taking the wrench from me and working it with fluid movements that spoke of a person familiar with torque and pressure, scalpels and stitches.

"The clues were all there of a man consumed by moon madness," I said. "Maybe you should read his works again with a new appreciation."

"I'll do that." He held the orifice to his eye, and then, seeing the problem, gently blew into the opening. A chunk of rust flew from the chamber. Then, "Tell me, who else do you suspect of being a lycanthrope?"

I pulled my knees up to my chin and hugged them. "They can be found all through history: Jack the Ripper, Gacy, Manson, Dahlmer, Vertal, Beazley."

He stopped wrenching down the orifice to stare at me. "They were all killers and all insane. You're not."

I didn't reply, lost in my own thoughts while he finished installing the valve. The more I learned about the actual biological changes in me, the more loathsome the upcoming full moon stretch seemed. It made me wonder just what evolutionary track I'd gotten off on and if, indeed, during that final lunar seizure, my brain didn't break down all the way.

Gibson signaled my attention by knocking a knuckle against the propane bottle before lighting off the burner with an engraved silver lighter. He then sat forward to consider me, asking in a quiet voice, "You are going on with this exploration of your lycanthropy, aren't you?"

I hadn't really thought of stopping. I wanted to know what had hold of me, though the obvious disintegration into another species suddenly scared the hell out of me. In a world where superstition is the food of the day, it was easier to see myself as something supernaturally special, not biologically corrupt.

"Will you?" he asked again.

My throat was tight, so I answered with a nod.

He stared at me, placed his fingers tenderly on my cheek, and then he kissed me full on the lips.

I'll have to admit I could have swooned into it. He was a great kisser, but I recovered and pulled away. "Is this sexual interest or professional interest?"

"Both." He didn't wait for me to reply. Instead, he kissed me again with the intensity that so characterized him. Releasing me, he murmured, "We have to get your hearing checked."

I almost smacked him, but abruptly decided that I'd been batted around enough in the last couple of weeks. I did like the body before me. It was available, no matter the strings attached, so I took it.

And the whole while we made love, Gibson whispered about lairs, lycanthropy, and full moon stretches amid hard breaths, grunts, and sighs.

47

———————— ■ ————————

THE NEXT MORNING, we met LaRue outside the university library. My partner gave me a questioning look by wigging his eyebrows, but beyond that, he didn't ask me why I hadn't responded to his call over my com node the evening before.

Gibson acted like he owned the place. He took the granite steps leading to the Parthenon-like structure two at a time, and stretched or not, I had to race to keep up with him. He yanked at one of the huge bronze doors, holding it open for us to enter an immense marble atrium. Both LaRue and I stopped dead to stare.

I had never suspected the inside of the library to look like the Cathedral of St. Ophelia, but it did. The far end of the building was a stained glass masterpiece that showed a scene from the Battle of Duvalier, when the dictator finally vanquished the UN resistance and formed the new world order. Sunlight glimmered through it to form colored patches on the pearly stone floor. Mahogany, polished to a liquid beauty, rose up everywhere: the tables, the chairs, the cabinets, the walls, the molding, and the bookshelves. Amid this refined beauty, I saw several scholars working quietly at their trade.

I felt a nit of jealousy that this was denied to the common man, but before I could express it, Gibson went into action. He walked purposefully to the librarian's massive desk and then leaned casually upon it. The woman sitting behind it was a pretty little thing with light brown hair and a thick-lipped smile.

"Ah, Amy," he said. "I haven't seen you in a while. But I must admit, you're a fetching beauty, still."

She giggled and then covered her mouth. "Oh, Lane, you've been keeping yourself scarce. I thought I was invited over for a free exam any time, but you never called like you said you would."

He tossed her a wild-eyed look. "You know where the clinic is, babe. Come by."

She grinned and then gave me a caustic review. Gibson explained. "These two friends of mine are district marshals, and they're trying to solve the murder of Maria Raynor before another person dies. Did you read about that?"

Her searing gaze gentled when he said that. "I did." Then, in a conspiratorial tone, "Is it a serial killer?"

LaRue stepped forward. "Yes, ma'am, it does appear to be so. We're working against time."

She glanced at Gibson. "So, what can I do to help?"

"Well, we understand that the killer may have a library card. He seems particularly interested in documentary vids and we were wondering if you could look over the borrowers catalog for us. The marshals would like a printout of the films he may have checked out over the last few months.

She squeezed her expression. "I'm not supposed to, Lane. I could get into a lot of trouble. You know the rules. Only academics can use the facilities and equipment."

He nodded and laid on a silver-tongued innocence. "We wouldn't ask if it wasn't vitally important. I understand that these officers don't have university credentials, but I do. Can I get copies of the vids?"

"Up to ten. Any more than that and the chief librarian will notice. A flag comes up to signal overages."

Gibson turned to me. "Will ten vids do?"

I nodded. "It will get us started."

He swiveled back to the beauty behind the desk. "Amy,

we appreciate it. You should receive a citizen's medal for humanitarian deeds."

She blushed and touched the region of her cleavage. "Lane, you make my day when you stop by. Tell me, what are you looking for?"

"Whatever has been checked out recently under the name of Ronald Orson Blackburn. He may have also used the name Orson Blackburn."

She moved to her computer console and, humming quietly, she called up the checkout lists. Several minutes went by as she flipped through the screens. Shaking her head, she turned back to us. "There's no triple-A designation listed for either Ronald Blackburn or Orson Blackburn, and the name doesn't appear under any other authorized governmental designations, either. If he checked something out, he didn't use his own library card to do it."

I stepped forward and leaned on the desk. "Would you please look under the name of Jack Raynor?"

She nodded and went back to work. It was only a short time before she was signaling a hit. "Mr. Raynor's name appears often under his PHO designation. He's borrowed several historical documentaries and a few medical vids, as well."

LaRue jumped in. "Is there anything regarding something called, the F-Project?"

She scanned the list, shook her head, and went to a summary page. "I don't have anything under that title, but I do have a reference to it in a vid called *Formosa Under Siege*."

My partner grew a smile. "Can we get that one?"

"It's available, according to the database. I will have to check in the stacks to make sure it did come back in. Sometimes we lose track of those things." She frowned slightly as she scrolled through the screens. "He's been renting a lot of vids in the last few months. And he still has one that's several weeks overdue. He shouldn't have been allowed to check out anything else until that one was returned."

"Which one is it?" I asked.

She placed her finger on the monitor's glass and said: "*Great Scientists of Our Time.*"

48

AFTER OUR VISIT to the university library, Gibson returned to his chicken pox problem, telling me he would call me once he set up a hearing test for me. I reluctantly agreed, figuring I had gone this far already. The good doctor had used his card to check out ten vids formerly rented by Jack Raynor and so LaRue and I returned to my flat loaded with movies to find Baba back in residence and working at her loom.

Sometimes I think she's a psychic. She knew exactly what had gone on between Gibson and me the night before, and of course, she wouldn't let go until I admitted it.

"What's he like in bed?" she said loudly.

LaRue laughed, but didn't enter the conversation. Instead, he busied himself loading one of the vids into my player.

"Baba, that's none of your business," I said.

"Will he bring more food?"

"I don't know."

She scowled. "You had him in bed and you didn't talk him into provisions? Pardon me for asking, my dear, but where was your mind?"

"It wasn't on food," I answered more sharply than I intended.

LaRue snorted this time and I glared at him.

"What is it with you two? Can't a person have a little privacy?"

"I still think you should have cornered him into giving up some more food," Baba said.

"That's something a whore would do," I said.

"No. Whores want money, my dear. Food is different."

I couldn't fathom her logic, so I let it drop by changing the subject. "Andy, is that thing ready?"

He nodded. "I suppose we should have popcorn or something."

I joined him on the couch and said in a low voice, "Don't get her started."

He grinned and settled in around the poking springs. After a moment, Baba joined us, thinking she was going to view a Presley Steele movie and when she found out they were mostly documentaries, she huffed, but wiggled in between us, anyway.

Jack Raynor had an eclectic taste in films. He had rented such titles as *Confucius and I Ching*, *The Holy Roman Empire*, and *College-Level Calculus*. There was an old *National Geographic* documentary on how Duvalier saved the whales and one on the active volcanoes along the Sino Belt. His taste ran to the exploration of angels, ghosts, and the energy of crystals, as well as Halloween. He rounded out his viewing pleasure with poetry readings, a biography of Einstein, and a dramatization of a Sherlock Holmes mystery.

As far as we could tell, the vid on the F-Project was the only medically related disk he'd rented in the last few months and it was a dry one. In fact, the narrator had such a droning voice that I almost lost interest. LaRue started yawning about ten minutes into the documentary and at about eleven minutes, he was asleep, leaving me to work through the monotony alone.

At one time, District Twenty-One had been called Taiwan, but when Duvalier took over, he used the former name of Formosa. The figures on population and indigenous species were unremarkable as was the short geophysical lecture about this island locality.

It wasn't until halfway through that there was a mention of the F-Project. My partner came instantly awake.

The scene cut from one of idyllic beauty to one inside an infirmary, where every available space was taken up by an obvious famine victim. There were whimpering children whose heads were too big for their shrunken bodies, bamboo-thin old women, and men who were walking sacks of bones. The narrator expressed this horror in the same monotone voice he'd used to express the lush countryside.

"The F-Project was formed to halt the infectious spread of Type-10 lupus, a deadly disease thought to come from the tuberculosis germ that was so prevalent in the mid–twentieth century. Type-10 lupus was first discovered during a famine situation in District Twenty-One, but has never appeared in any other locality because of swift government intervention to contain this microbal murderer.

"PHO developed an immunization program in response to this killer and organized the district into a test center, sealing the borders of this remote island to avoid worldwide contamination. Scientists discovered that once this airborne virus lodges in the lungs that death occurs as quickly as three months later.

"Though an effective vaccine was never developed, the researchers found that some people had a natural immunity to this virus. Further studies suggested that these individuals were born with a specific survival gene and it was thought that if this genetic quality could be amplified, then future generations would be free from the attack of Type-10 lupus.

"District Twenty-One has been maintained as a closed locality to this day, with visa issuances officially terminated."

LaRue thumbed the pause button on the remote and turned to stare at me. "My head is starting to hurt from all this. Do you think the Sung family is one of the healthy family units somehow allowed to leave?"

"Why would the government let them go? Wouldn't it be easier and cheaper to lock them up with the lepers?"

"Maybe the experiments have dumped over into new localities."

"And maybe it's all bullshit and the scrolls have it right."

"Either scenario scares me senseless."

The phone rang, interrupting the images our brains were cooking up. I answered it to hear Gibson giving an order to someone standing in the room with him. "Merrick?" he said after a moment.

"Yes. What's up?"

"Are you free tomorrow afternoon? I'd like to meet you for a late lunch at the district's automat on twenty-ninth and Sydney. I'm buying."

"And then?"

"To the Hearing Research Center for a quick scan."

I didn't answer right away, so he hurried on. "Are you still having a hard time accepting these new findings?"

I nodded, even though I knew he couldn't see me do it. Knowing now how my lycanthropy worked, it seemed that to separate the wolf from the human would come down to splitting atoms, and I wondered what that might do to me. As startling as the truth was, I had years enough to get used to this fusion. I had alternately denied the disease and accepted it, but with the revelations Gibson had made, I was now strung up somewhere between these opposites. On the one hand, it gave me a trifling power, but on the other, it didn't help me pay my bills. If I could just ease the agony of the seizures and still have the benefits of the rising wolf, life might be all right.

I must not have said anything, because he called gently to me. "Merrick? Do you want me to come over? Do you need to talk?"

"No, I'm fine. I guess it's better to know exactly what happens during the changes." I let a little despondency creep into my voice just so I could get some sympathy.

He heard it. "We need to know what happens to you so we can begin to formulate a treatment. You know that."

He wasn't very good at the poor baby routine. "Can you seriously believe that there is an effective treatment?"

"I'm sure of it. We just need to find the key that controls the change."

I thought he was going to add something corny like "Take heart, all is well," but he didn't. "Tell me something, Gibson. How long do you have to devote to this project?"

"Before the money runs out or before the PHO yanks me off it?"

"Both."

He refused to be specific. "We have time on each account. Don't worry. My personal interest won't let me leave you hanging without some kind of help. I honestly find you too fascinating to walk away from this relationship."

Fascinating? I was glad he'd chosen that particular word to describe me. In my own thoughts, the word *oddity* surfaced as being more appropriate. I sighed, "All right, Gibson, you win. I'll meet you in the lobby of the automat." I hung up to the stares of my roommate and my partner.

LaRue spoke first. "What's wrong?"

I looked down at my feet. "Nothing's wrong."

"You're lying, my dear," Baba said. "And doing it very badly, I might add."

I shook my head and pumped the button on the remote. It was damned hard to be a freak. I didn't need to try to explain it.

LaRue stared at me for another minute before dropping his probing look back to the vid screen.

Fifteen more minutes of worthless, boring data almost drove my partner to sleep again, but when the narrator came down to the last part, his attention snapped back. It was an overview of the economy, short and to the point, and I almost missed it because it was so fast and the facts were so dry.

Apparently, District Twenty-one had a limited agricultural base, so Formosa supported itself by processing electronic parts, pharmaceuticals, and designer drugs. At one time, this included the manufacturing of quantum.

49

THE WATER RESTRICTION instituted by the government was lifted for each ward on a rotating basis and the next morning I could actually take a bath. The water was only lukewarm, but it was a luxury, anyway, and I scrubbed like a demon, hoping the clean would hold until the next cycle came around. When I was done taking off the dirt, I spent more money I didn't have by emptying the tub and refilling it. I then took my time to look over the case notes while I sipped at a cup of tea that had gone cold while I bathed.

After finishing up with the vid on Formosa, LaRue and Baba had fled, leaving me to spend the entire afternoon watching each documentary. I found them all interesting, especially the film on angels. Although I wouldn't admit it to anyone, I watched it again, because it talked about spirit animals. They were otherworldly guardians tasked with protecting humans. The animal that the individual chose represented the power and strength he wished to manifest in his life. Those who sought communion with a lion identified with the animal's ferocity and yes, those who identified with the wolf longed to match its lethal prowess.

My spirit animal obviously didn't know he was supposed to be living in another dimension and not inside of me. Its presence showed up in little insidious ways that I had never mentioned to any doctor, and I never will—not even to Gibson.

Take my feet, for instance. After one of my stretches, my toes kink as though something is yanking on the muscles and preventing them from straightening completely out. The ball of my foot puffs into three segments. Look at it and you see the deep grooves formed between the little balloons of flesh. My arches flare at a higher angle and sometimes my heel will ache from imprecisely touching the floor. A podiatrist would have a field day with my feet, but the most unusual thing can't be seen by looking at my peds at all; it's when you look at the print and then you can see the paw.

I finished off my drink, felt my empty stomach protest, and poured a little more water into the bath. Ignoring the growls from my midsection, I let go of my thoughts on lycanthropy to study the information given to us by Wainwright.

Maria Raynor chose the most unusual themes for dinner parties that I'd ever heard of. One gathering, in particular, caught my fancy. It was called *Ramses' Ninety Brides*. According to the documents, the party was supposed to remind the guests of being trapped inside an ancient Egyptian harem. The foods included stuffed grape leaves, grilled free-range chickens soaked overnight in fresh lemon and spices, date and nut pudding, and flat bread baked with camel's milk cheese and coriander.

An expense sheet was attached. The camel's milk cheese cost five hundred credits alone.

Ronald Orson Blackburn's name showed up on many of the guest lists, especially for the more interesting parties. He was there for the Greco-Roman tribute, *Cleopatra and Mark Antony*; around for *The Last British King is Dead*; and found eating at *Duvalier's Last Supper*. He came unattended as far as I could tell, and never failed to appear.

I heard the phone ring and Baba answer it, knowing right away without being told that it was LaRue. I climbed from the tub just as she came into the bathroom.

"Andrew is holding for you, my dear. He says it's important."

I nodded and started to dry when I noticed her look to the

tub. "The water is still warm, Baba. Why don't you jump in?
I'm done for the night."

"I think I will." And with that she stripped off her shirt
and dove for the bucket even before I collected my glass and
papers to leave the room.

LaRue was still waiting for me. "What's up, Andy?" I
asked.

"I heard from Axion Howard," he answered. "He says
he's just seen one of Jack Raynor's friends."

50

AXION HOWARD SAT in the homicide unit interrogation room,
sweating, coughing, and generally looking nervous. He
smelled like a garbage dump, especially since my own stink
was lessened. LaRue smiled at my entrance and kicked a
chair out from under the table. I slid into the seat and tried
not to take a deep breath.

"And the purpose of this visit?" I asked.

"We were just getting started," LaRue answered. Then,
cutting Howard a frown, he said, "Take it from the top,
please, and don't leave anything out."

The man jerked his neck which, I assumed, sufficed as a
nod. "I ain't never snitched on no one before, but I figured
that youse and me could come to an agreement."

"What kind?" I asked, wearily.

"The kind that says youse will stay off my back. Look the

other way, so I can run my business without youse hassling me."

I scratched my ear and put on one of those pained, skeptical looks. He charged into the interim.

"I got good info. Do youse think I would willingly come marching in here if I didn't? Do me a favor and I'll make it worth your while."

"All right," I said. "We won't bother you if you don't commit a murder."

"That's not what I mean. Tell the blues to ignore me. Them damned ward cops are making things difficult, and I know I can help youse once in a while. Come on, what do youse say?"

I wanted to say that I didn't dictate to the ward cops and wasn't about to start. I lied instead. "OK, the fix is in. You're good to go, provided the information is something we can use. Now, will you please explain?"

Satisfied, he grinned, and I noticed he was missing two front bottom teeth. "Jack Raynor's floozy came in to see me."

"Which floozy?" LaRue demanded.

"The rich one."

"Emily Church?" he asked.

"Yeah, that's her."

"How do you know it was her?" I said.

He punched me with a scowl. "I ain't so stupid as youse might think. I take myself down to Washing Machine Park once a day to read the public bulletin board. That's where I saw her picture. It was right there in the newspaper, just yesterday, and I ain't wrong about that. I scanned the whole article, I did. It was about how her family has reported her to be a missing person. Gone. Poof." He shook his head. "Bullshit."

"Did she want to buy quantum from you?"

"No. She wanted to sell it."

LaRue grunted and turned to stare at me. Then, leveling his Rasputin-like gaze upon Howard, he demanded, "How much did she want to sell?"

"Over four kilos."

"St. Ophelia," he murmured. "Think of the street value."

"Did she say where she got it from in the first place?" I asked.

"She mentioned something about it having come out of another district. It was being used in a medical study, but now the project was at an end and she wanted to unload it."

"Didn't it seem funny that if the quantum was from a medical project, that she didn't turn the stuff back in to the proper authorities?"

"Yeah, and that's why I'm here. I don't like to hear words like medical project when I'm buying supply. You never know if what you're getting is quantum. The goddamned PHO diddles with that shit, and I got a rep to uphold with my customers." He paused to suck in a breath. "She was looking to make some heavy pocket change."

"Did you buy it?" I asked.

"No. Where would I get that kind of credit?"

"What did you do?"

"I told her that I needed to get front money from my customers, and if I could do it, then I would get in touch with her."

I leaned over the table and grabbed him with one of my steely stares. "How would you get in touch with her?" I growled.

"I'm supposed to leave a message." He rifled through his pocket, pulled out a puff of black lint, a rusty knife, and finally a piece of wadded paper. Unfolding it, he angled it toward the bare lightbulb hanging precariously over the table. "I'm supposed to leave a message at The Macaroni Hut."

I never let up on my intense scrutiny, hoping that my expression would convince him to help us. "Mr. Howard, we'd like you to leave that message. Today."

51

—■—

WE NEEDED TO gain Emily Church's cooperation, even if it meant getting the boys from vice to help us set up an arrest. Axion Howard was suddenly even more affable when the drug boys offered to drop a pending court hearing if he helped to corner the woman. It took us an hour to get him straight on what he was to do, and then, fired up from all the planning, LaRue and I immediately went to take out some of the energy on Edward Polinato.

We found him in the back room with an Instamatic camera pointed at a customer perched atop the DaVinci Chair. Just to scare him into answering some questions, I came through the swinging doors with my weapon drawn, my stance wide, and a belligerent look on my face. Polinato had only a moment to lower the camera and stare at the gun before LaRue grabbed him by the apron straps and slammed him against the wall. The Sheetrock cracked from the force and the camera clattered to the floor.

There was a woman sitting on the potty who froze in fear when she saw me brandishing the firearm. I released my attitude and went to her, wearing a reassuring smile.

"I'll bet your wish doesn't include us, does it?" I said, in low voice.

She shook her head and swallowed hard.

"Has Mr. Polinato taken your money yet?"

Again, she shook her head.

"Have you made your wish?"

She nodded.

"Good. Then you got a freebie. Go home and don't ever mention that you saw us here. Understand?"

She nodded furiously, leapt from the throne, and flew through the doors, dragging her red knitted scarf behind her.

I turned back to see what my partner was doing.

I love to see LaRue squeeze someone. He's not a big man, but his hands are so fast that they remind me of the charging pistons on a car. He literally hammers the suspect with his fingers, and I've seen evidence of where he has bruised a person so badly that his chest looked like it better belonged on a leopard.

So when the DaVinci Chair was vacated, LaRue used his balance to swing the man around and dump him into it. Our friend whimpered and tears melded with sweat and grease. "I don't know anything," he whined. "Nothing. You've got to believe me."

I joined LaRue to caress the barrel of my gun along the man's jaw. He held his breath, but his puckered lips worked just like a pump. I backed off a step and LaRue started punching him with those fingers of his. Polinato winced at each contact. I finally started the interview.

"You're going to jail," I said in my most threatening voice.

"I haven't done anything."

"Oh? Well, then, why would Emily Church tell a known quantum pusher to give her a call here?"

"It's a lie. I don't know her."

"You do, and I think you know even more about the F-Project."

LaRue beat a rhythm on him, never saying a word.

"The F-Project, Polinato, what about it?"

He shook his head. "I don't know. I never heard it called that." LaRue tapped him some more and finally, his confession started to leak out amid a whimper. "I can't say. They'll kill me. They have automatic weapons." LaRue stopped pounding him so he could talk.

"Who has automatic weapons?" he demanded.

"The government. They told me if I squealed, they'd finish me off."

I leaned in again with my gun. "Ed, you have choice. I could kill you with a single bullet through the head right now, and being officers of the law, we won't have a hard time suggesting that you resisted arrest. Or you could take your chances and tell us the complete truth."

Sweat trickled into his eyes and he blinked against it, slinging a little salty water as he did. It didn't take him long to decide to answer after I placed the revolver's nose against his temple. "All right, all right! You win. I'll tell you what I know. Just please, don't shoot."

Snot seeped from his right nostril and that was enough to make me step away. "Explain everything and don't shade one fact or your choices disappear."

He nodded furiously. "They came to me earlier this year."

"Who, the government? People from the PHO?"

"No, well, yes. They said they were working for the government. Jack Raynor and Emily Church."

"Why?"

"They wanted to use my basement for a project they were working on. Orson told them about it. I didn't ask questions because they gave me money up front."

"How much?"

"Twenty thousand credits."

LaRue whistled. "That's a lot for rent. They must have wanted you to keep it very hush-hush. Why? What were they doing?"

"I don't know. Honest. People would come over and stay downstairs for a couple of days in a row."

"Who would come?" LaRue pressed.

"Emily, Raynor, Orson. They'd usually have a couple of Chinese with them. Different ones. They would come a few times and then new Sinos would show up."

"Is there anyone in your basement right now?" I asked.

"No. Since this thing with Maria Raynor, they've been careful. No one's been here in a week."

"Not even Emily?"

"Yeah, yeah, besides her. She said some guy was going to call with information she needed. Why she had him call here and not at her place is beyond me, but it's the first thing they've ever asked me to do aside from keeping their presence in the basement a secret. Mostly, they wanted to be ignored."

"No one else has showed up? Not Jack, not Orson?"

His expression widened when he realized he'd been caught in a lie. "Orson, yeah. He did come a couple of times, now that you mention it."

"Did he go downstairs?"

"Yeah."

"Why?"

"I'm not sure. He was mumbling something about experiments. He's crazy, like I said. The quantum has turned his brain to pudding. I don't pay any attention."

"You got your money, huh?" LaRue said.

"That's right, and I did what I was told. It isn't every day the government pays you when they take over your property."

"When was the last time he was here?"

"About five days ago. I swear; that's the last time I saw him."

"We're interested in seeing this basement, Ed," I said.

He shook off a nod. "All right. Let me up and I'll show you."

We gave him room and he came to a jerky stand. I thought he would go through the kitchen to some back stairs, but instead, he pulled the DaVinci Chair from its place of honor and touched a rusty spot on the far wall, revealing a swinging door hidden in the Sheetrock.

"Well, I'll be," LaRue murmured.

Polinato flipped on a light and we followed him down a rickety wooden staircase. He talked as we went. "I haven't been down here, honest. I don't know what we'll find."

What we found was a makeshift lab that would have impressed Gibson. The space was large and filled to capacity with five metal folding tables, three canvas cots, six computer stations, a wall unit stuffed with various pieces of medical equipment, a thirty-five-inch vid, a refrigerator/freezer combo, a tall shelf lined with books, and right beside that, an empty pharmaceutical safe. At the far end of the vault, a gray cabinet drew my attention. I went to it as LaRue commanded Polinato to have a seat in one of the hard-backed chairs available.

He did as he was told like a scared, greasy jack rabbit trying to hide from a hungry wolf. "I didn't know all this was down here," he repeated. "My God, I didn't."

There was a flimsy padlock on the chest and with a good hard yank using my lycanthropic muscle, I broke it. Inside, I found medical instruments, including a portable laser. I pulled it out to show LaRue. Upon seeing it, he immediately resumed the interview.

"When was the last time Jack Raynor showed up?" he asked.

Polinato thought a moment as he wiped at the mucus edging his nose. "The day his wife died."

"He was supposed to be out of town."

"Well, he was here. Around the clock. I never saw him leave. That is, until Orson came in."

"Orson came in? On the day Mrs. Raynor's death was announced?"

"Yeah, I'm pretty sure. I think he told him, because Jack came upstairs looking pale. He might have been crying, too. I had customers out the ying and didn't have a chance to notice much more."

"Did Orson come out with him?"

"No. He was in the basement for the rest of the day and into the evening."

"Was he whacked out on quantum?"

"Always. I've never seen him when he wasn't."

"What do you think he was doing down here all that time?"

"I don't know. He was quiet. That's about everything I can say."

"Were there occasions when the group got rowdy?"

He nodded and swallowed hard. "Sometimes they had arguments. The last one was a couple of days before Mrs. Raynor was murdered. I was upstairs with a customer on the DaVinci Chair and I could hear them pretty clearly. I had to ask them to hold it down one time."

"What were they arguing about?"

"I don't know."

"Well, you heard them."

He buried his head in his hands, got grease all over his fingers, and finally looked up. "They were talking about

District Twenty-one. Something about solving the plague there."

"Is that everything you remember?" I asked.

"Orson was screaming something about having the answer to the problem. He said he couldn't prove it, though, until he had the right material."

"Anything after that?"

He blew a heavy sigh. "Raynor said he would see what he could do."

52

WE LEFT ED Polinato at The Macaroni Hut under the supervision of a plainclothes marshal until we could get something set up to draw Emily Church out into the open. She had, indeed, been reported as a missing person, and though we figured she made the call herself, the person filing was recorded as being Jessica, Emily's sister.

Jessica lived in the mansion with Cecil and just happened to be home waiting for word on her sibling. She was nothing like her beautiful sister. In fact, she was dowdy and colorless and weighed almost as much as Maria Raynor had. She wore a beige A-line dress, sensible shoes, and her graying hair in a starched-looking bun atop her head. The only expression of her obvious wealth was a pearl choker, but the ring of fat around her neck partially hid it.

She greeted us in the foyer with a breathless question. "Have you found her?"

"No, ma'am," I answered. "We're here to get some more information."

Her face grew hard. "I told the Marshals Office everything I know."

"Yes, ma'am." Then casting my gaze around the room, I said, "Is there some place we can talk?"

"Of course." She stomped by us and that's when I noticed she wore thick support hose over varicose veined legs.

We followed her into a small parlor where a cozy blaze burned in the fireplace. The room, done in Victorian prints and pale green colors, opened out onto a glassed-in conservatory. The porch was filled with blooming flowers and the scent was heady. I moved directly toward it while LaRue labored with the interview.

"When did you first realize that Emily may have been missing?" he asked.

"When she didn't come home after three days."

"She's a grown woman. Perhaps she went away and neglected to tell you."

"It's not like her. She travels, yes. She has interdistrict visas to the ends of the earth, but she would always let me know when she would be on a trip, so I wouldn't worry. No, she wouldn't do that."

"You and your sister were close?"

"Very. After Mother died, I raised her. She was a midlife baby, you understand. I couldn't bear having her subjected to a series of nannies like I had been. You see, my mother was a concert pianist for the District Symphony and my father was always working to save the world."

I snorted to myself, even as I poked my nose into a ruby red rose. Rough life.

"I remember her," LaRue said.

His statement was enough to make me look at him. "You do?" I said.

"Sure. Hester Peterson Church. She was one of the greatest musicians the district ever had. She was so good that she made several recordings. My grandmother was a great fan of hers. She did *Dark Allegro*, didn't she?"

I knew right then that he'd gotten the information from the district database, but it was enough to get the woman started.

"Yes, yes, she did. That was my father's favorite piece until . . ."

"Until he came down with Alzheimer's disease?"

"Yes."

"When did that happen?"

"He was diagnosed just a year ago, but apparently he'd had it for a while—you know, the forgetfulness, the confusion—by the time anyone noticed he was starting to have some bad days. When I realized something was wrong, I couldn't even bring myself to take him to the doctor. I didn't want to hear the verdict firsthand." She sighed, threatened to break a tear, and then sat down heavily onto a cushy chintz sofa. "Bless my dear Emily. She took him for me. Father kept screaming that they hadn't gone to the doctor at all. He said my sister took him to a park and they fed pigeons all afternoon. That hurt her, even though she knew he wasn't himself. She's always taken him for his checkups after that."

LaRue let a lull seep into the conversation. The short silence was all that was needed to get Jessica to talk some more.

"Do you like flowers, Marshal?" she asked me.

"I love them. These are beautiful."

"Emily created this room. It's her special hideaway. I think she has an artistic flair for decorating. Don't you?"

"Yes. It's very tasteful."

She nodded and breathed another sigh. Then, "She's

always been creative, my little sister." More sternly, she added, "I instilled this importance in her, mind you. She comes from a gifted family unit of thinkers, artists, and musicians. Because my parents trusted the stability of the government, they invested in short-term treasury bonds, the payoff of which enabled her to have the wealth to pursue her talents. I'm proud to say, using her imagination became a driving force in her life. Since I have no special abilities, it's done my heart good to see her excel."

"We don't have her listed in any labor designation," LaRue said. "What does she do?"

"She doesn't need to work the nine-to-five shift, Marshal. She takes artistic commissions when she feels like it. She decorates people's homes for them."

That got me thinking, and I pulled out of the conservatory to ask, "Did she decorate Jack Raynor's house?"

"Oh, that man." She gave a mock shiver. "He's loath-some. I never have liked him, even when he was a young pup out of the university."

"So, did she decorate his house?"

"No. She decorated for Mrs. Raynor's theme parties until Jack coaxed my sister into bed and the situation changed drastically. She couldn't get near the house after his wife found out what was between them. I can't blame her. And Emily wouldn't listen to common sense. She kept dating him. Then he did what I knew he would do; he found another woman."

"That would be Christina Dunn?" LaRue asked.

"Christina was her first name. I never heard Emily refer to her by her last."

"I'll bet Emily was furious," I said, joining her on the sofa.

"She hated her and did everything to break them up. Why she wasted her time, I can't understand. Mrs. Raynor was not going to give her husband a divorce. Emily mentioned it over and over to me." She glanced at her sensible shoes and wrung her knotty hands. "I suppose she'll marry him now."

"We were under the impression that they weren't seeing each other anymore."

"Jack broke up with Christina. He called Emily again." She looked up from her feet. "Do you think Jack Raynor had something to do with Emily's disappearance?"

"It's likely. We don't know where Jack is, either. He's not at his home."

"Have you tried his condominium?"

"What condominium?" I asked.

She frowned slightly. "Well, let me see. Emily talked about it several times, too, but I only half listened." She closed her eyes momentarily, as if this would help call up the information. "I'm sorry, I really can't recall where it is. I do know that he would go there to get away from his wife and meet with my sister. She said he shared it off and on with a man he knew from his humanitarian service days, but she didn't elaborate."

"Did she ever mention a Ronald Orson Blackburn?"

Upon hearing the name, I could have sworn she recognized it, but her answer strangled my hope. "No," she said. "Never."

53

WE'D JUST LEFT Jessica Church when dispatch directed us to see a lady in an alley just off Riley Avenue. When we found the right alley, we also found Brown Hilda. It took over a half an hour to get the old woman to come to the point of why she had called us, because the wind was whipping trash from a nearby recycling bin and her attention kept being drawn away by Styrofoam treasures and half-used napkins.

"I've got an appointment in a few minutes," I said finally. "Can we get on with this?"

She glanced up from a project under her magnifying glass to follow the track of a tumbling wad of aluminum foil. She looked at me, pointed to the prize, and like a trained retriever, I fetched the ball for her, tossing it into the cart. I had just done that when she noticed a fairly clean paper plate trying to launch itself from the runway of the alley's dirt floor and sent LaRue to abort the takeoff. She hunched back over her work after he dropped it on her makeshift desk.

"The Gettysburg Address," she muttered.

"I beg your pardon?" I said.

"The Gettysburg Address. I wrote that once on the back of a stamp just to see if I could do it. I was young then, and could see better than I do now."

"What did you do with it?"

She looked up and grinned. "What did I do with it? Why, I put it on an envelope and mailed it, of course." She cut loose a cackle and it was then that I noticed how rosy the wind had made her cheeks. Sobering, she said, "He was here just last night."

"Who?" I asked, leaning toward her.

"The man with the red three-ring binder. Well, it wasn't the same person who came last time. This person had both hands, but it was the same notebook. I'm sure of that."

LaRue fished out the photo of Jack Raynor. "Was this the guy?"

She studied it until drawn off by another piece of flying trash.

"Brown Hilda," he snapped. "We're running out of time here."

She pursed her lips and nodded after a few seconds. "That's not the man who came with the notebook." Diving back toward the magnifying glass, she added, "When he wasn't looking, I tore a page out of it."

I tried to keep the interest from showing in my face. "Do you still have it?"

She glanced at me. "I can't give it up for nothing."

"This man could possibly be a murderer, Brown Hilda."

"So?"

"That's withholding evidence."

"So?"

"It's against the law."

"So?"

I could see I wasn't going to budge her without laying out an offer. Patting down my cammie pockets, I looked for a trade item. I came up with a comb and the moon madness tobacco ball that I'd gotten from Madame Janetta. She nodded toward her cart and then stared down LaRue. He threw in a coupon for a free pair of socks at the district-run dry goods center and a broken wristwatch. Satisfied, she reached inside her coat to pull out the paper.

The page was written in the Barrier language and included a diagram. It also explained in intimate detail how the killer gathered his genetic material.

54

LaRue dropped me off in front of the automat and went on to do some legwork concerning Jack Raynor's mystery condo. Gibson was waiting for me at a cracked Formica booth. As I entered the cafeteria, I caught him drawing pictures with his fingers on the steamy window. He grinned, waved me over, and when I got there, he made a show to wipe crumbs from the orange vinyl seat. There was already an array of plastic-wrapped food on the table.

"I took the liberty of choosing dinner," he said.

"Looks so inviting," I answered. "So much . . . bread."

He laughed. "The sandwiches are the only things worth eating here. That and the microwaveable french fries. Do you like onion rings?"

"Only if they're greasy," I answered, having already zeroed in on a roast beef and rye.

"They're swimming in it." He pushed a cardboard container toward me. "Try some."

I did while he talked.

"I hope you're feeling better about the information we got the other day. This thing that happens to you is extraordinary, and I'm going to go so far as to say that it's not a disease."

I stopped pushing a potato in my mouth long enough to stare at him. He continued, and I noticed he hadn't touched a bit of his dinner.

"Clinically, your metabolic and physical changes meet no real criteria to be classified as the symptoms of a disease from what I can tell. Nothing actually goes wrong with you. On the contrary, you grow stronger and more sensitive, and if you gauge the transformation by your outward appearance, the changes are so subtle as not to be readily noticeable. You have to be looking for the differences to really see them." He sat back, took a swig of coffee from a dented Styrofoam cup, and studied me over the rim. "Do you know that I asked LaRue what changes you went through after each seizure, and he couldn't tell me? I'll bet you Baba can't, either. They're around you so much that you look normal to them no matter what lycanthropic stage your in."

"What about the stretches themselves?" I asked. "Isn't pain an indicator of disease?"

"Most certainly, but unless it's associated with an identifiable abnormality, then how do you look at it?" He took another sip before continuing. "It's considered painful for a baby to be cutting teeth, but it's a normal physiological occurrence that signifies natural change in the body. As agonizing as the seizures are, I think they're nothing more than growing pains."

I almost choked on my sandwich. Not because it was so profound, but because I'd come to this same conclusion years ago. He didn't give me a chance to clear my throat so I could say something.

"Merrick, I'm going through all this because I don't want you to be afraid to find out everything about your lycanthropy. You may, indeed, have a neurological illness. I'm not ruling it out, but I can't track it if I don't know the extent of the changes you go through."

I finally swallowed my food and pointed a slippery french fry at him. "Is this supposed to make me feel better about the upcoming appointment?"

He smiled sheepishly and nodded.

"Well, I appreciate the concern, but I'll be all right. The thing with the eye doctor was just unexpected."

His gaze grew intent once more. "I need to know everything about your condition, Merrick. What are you keeping a secret?"

There were so many things I could tell him about my lycanthropic experience—from the enticing lure of shiny objects to the sensitivity of my gums and teeth—but I had a feeling that these symptoms would do nothing more than support the unexplainable.

"I've told you the big stuff," I said.

"Are you sure?"

"I don't think I've left anything out."

"What about the full moon seizure itself? You've been quiet about it. I'm going to need to know what happens to you so I can be prepared."

"I thought you talked to LaRue."

"I did, but I think there's a conspiracy going on here. He started giving me all this metaphysical bullshit, and he refused to speak of it in any other terms."

I chuckled but didn't reply.

"What exactly is this stuff he refers to as past life fragments and demonic debilitation?"

"You've come to know LaRue. He's into charms and spells and magical incantations. It's a nice, harmless way to see the world."

"I'm looking for the truth, Merrick. What happens from your point of view?"

I shrugged and pointed to his dessert. "Are you going to eat that piece of apple pie?"

55

GIBSON TOOK ME to my latest appointment. The ear, nose, and throat exam was painless, although the doctor had a case of bad breath that would have knocked over a sasquatch. I came out with my eyes burning from it, but at least I came out as ignorant as I went in. His tests weren't as immediate as Winegarden's had been. I had a little time to mentally prepare for the answers.

I had no sooner reinstalled my com node when I heard dispatch hailing me. I stood there in the middle of a busy waiting room trying to talk past the array's usual static while Gibson conferred with his colleague.

"Merrick responding. Go ahead, dispatch."

Instead of the professional response I was hoping for, I got: "Ty, Andy has been trying to reach you for an hour. Are you all right?"

"What is it, Sylvia?" I asked, sharply.

Her reply blasted through, and surely must have damaged my eardrum. "He said to tell you that Axion heard from Emily and the meet's a go-ahead. Got those names? Axion and Emily."

I checked my watch. Damn! I had about twenty minutes to reach the drop point. "I got them. I'm on my way, and do me a favor and relate that to LaRue. The static on the array is sending shock waves through my body. I'm turning off."

"Ten-four, Merrick. Watch your posterior."

Definitely not a professional police dispatch. I left before Gibson appeared from his consultation with the doctor, chugging up the street in an all-out sprint. People stared at me, but seeing my black uniform, they swerved to veer out

of my path, while I kept checking for ruts and chuckholes in
the shattered sidewalk.

Running is the one thing that the werewolf myths have
gotten right. It feels good to break into a sprint. The nervous
energy is finally released, and it pushes through me in what
feels like arcing electrical bolts.

The district marshals who work substance abuse maintain
several places around the locality where they set up their
sting operations. They're easily defendable areas that allow
for cover and surveillance when a drug exchange goes
down, so for our game, they assigned us Duvalier's Monument.

It wasn't really a monument. It was a district project that
hadn't really gone anywhere because the funds were di-
verted after only a third of the building had been erected.
The structure sits at the apex of Battery Hill, the highest
point in the region. It was supposed to resemble a Greek
temple when completed, and so tons of marble were shipped
in from distant quarries, but the money dried up before most
of it could be cut. What was left litters the area: half-carved
columns, busts, and statues, all of which make the place
look like Medusa's playground.

The district councilman in charge of restoration projects
decided to get some of the money back by turning the
monument into a tourist trap. He managed to divert enough
funds to install ornate, cast-iron streetlamps throughout the
shattered grounds. He also ordered a contractor to pour a
curling sidewalk between the mountains of stone, and added
picnic tables, benches, and a public rest room. Then he
invited interested people to plop down five credits apiece to
take in the view.

I pushed up the hill and through the front gate of the park.
Flipping on my com node, I found out LaRue's location. It
took me five minutes of weaving through a stand of

immense Ionic columns before finding him at the far end of
the building, hiding behind the enormous statue of our
beloved dictator posing as the Greek god, Zeus. He had six
ward cops fanned out along the perimeter, two acoustical
technicians monitoring the situation from the cover of a
marble outcropping, and Axion Howard wired for sound.

"I was worried you weren't going to make it," he
murmured.

"Sorry. I got here as soon as I could. Is Howard doing his
level best to cooperate?"

"He's sweating, but he'll be all right. I just wish we didn't
have to go through all this shit."

LaRue said the same thing on every sting we ever set up,
but the point of law is clear: A person cannot be arrested for
a crime unless he's caught in the act of committing it.
Period. It made our jobs all the harder to do, and there were
a lot of thieves and sex maniacs loose on the streets because
of it, but it was in the original covenants written by Duvalier
and, therefore, nonnegotiable. As stupid as it was, it was the
basis for our limited civil rights and the people wouldn't let
it get away from them. Riots had broken out in the past
when rising young political stars had tried to strip away this
humanitarian right.

We wanted to hold Emily Church in custody, and there
was no other way to do it except to boondoggle her. LaRue
and I held our position behind the statue's huge, sandaled
foot and after twenty minutes of nail biting, our mark
stepped into the dim glow of the lamps wearing a black
cocktail dress and stiletto heels. She didn't come alone,
either. She brought Jack Raynor with her.

LaRue hissed when he saw the man walk by, but when I
glanced at him, I found that he was grinning. The clouds
made the sky as black as printer's ink and so the trio was
forced to meet for the exchange under one of the fancy

streetlights near our surveillance spot. My partner adjusted his com node to listen to the conversation. I just used my ears.

"Youse were supposed to come alone," Howard said.

"I brought a friend, who has a gun," she said. "He'll make sure nothing goes wrong."

Raynor remained silent, but opened his jacket to show that he did, indeed, have a weapon stuffed under the waistband of his pants.

Seeing it, Howard suddenly acquired a shake to his voice. "I don't want no trouble, and I ain't never cheated no one. Do youse want to sell or not?"

"You found customers quickly," she said.

"Popular stuff. One call is all it took. Now, are youse going to show it to me, or not?"

She stared at him before opening a large black bag she carried, but thinking better of it, she stopped. "Show me the money first."

We had provided Howard with a hefty wad of bills, which he pulled from a purse he wore clipped to his belt. As quickly as he flashed the money, he replaced it. Emily showed him the goods, and with a short nod from the buyer, they traded bags. That's when LaRue called for the cops to go in.

They jumped from their concealed positions, screamed their usual, "Don't move, district marshals," and aimed their rifles. Howard slipped back and did a momentary tussle with Emily as she tried to reclaim her sack of quantum. He pushed her to the ground, and she yelped when she hit. Jack, obviously the courageous one, took off running. He avoided the ward cops to leap into the forest of stone surrounding the place. LaRue and the unit officers lost him in the dull light, but I had a good lead on him and tracked his trajectory in my mind as I spun off in pursuit.

He jumped from boulder to capsized statue, using the shadows as well as the man who had tried to kill me on the dock. I followed him with that in mind, determined that I wouldn't get in the way of his gun. He rounded a corner and ducked behind a boxwood hedge. That's when I realized he was heading straight for the bathroom.

Why he didn't keep running is still a mystery to me. I suppose he thought the light was dim enough to hide his escape, and normally it might be, but he hadn't expected a wolf-eyed, lycanthrope to mark his trail. I dashed after him and stopped a few feet from the men's room to contact LaRue on the com node. In a moment, we had the small building surrounded. My partner and I went in the front, hugging the curving tile wall. At one point, it made a sharp turn, and we halted.

Now, if someone could be so stupid as to run into a john with no back door, he deserves to suffer. At least, that's what I decided in Jack's case.

It's rare that I have the opportunity to use various weapons in my personal arsenal, but this situation gave me the perfect excuse. I steadied myself on the slimy linoleum floor and, unzipping my sleeve pocket, I slid out one of my homemade cherry bombs. It takes a while to collect the supplies to put together these little explosive packs, so I use them sparingly.

LaRue handed me his butane lighter when he saw what I had in mind. I knocked the end of the flame against the M-80 and as I tossed the bomb into the urinal, we jumped the corner. It exploded with a tremendous noise. Jack screamed, flying like a projectile from the toilet stall, intent not on shooting me but bowling me over in his getaway. He didn't reckon on my strength, though, and ran into my fist.

56

JACK AND EMILY were clearly terrified, and it picked up my mood right away. They were cuffed and booked and thrown into solitary confinement. LaRue chose Room E, which was in the basement of the Marshals Office and which looked like a small dungeon, because the cell was constructed with one side open to bare bedrock. The ceiling was claustrophobically low, and LaRue had to stoop to stand up inside. There was a rusty bucket serving as a chamber pot and a rotten mattress on the filthy floor. Our detainees sat upon this cushion, trembling.

I took a flashlight to the meeting as there was no electricity. Emily kept staring at it.

"You can't leave us here," she whimpered.

"Oh, shut up, Emily," Jack growled. "They can do anything they want."

"That's right," I said. "We can, and we will. You're both missing persons as far as we're concerned. You can stay missing a long time."

"No," she whispered. "Please."

I studied her and then moved my consideration to Jack. He was a handsome devil, all right, with neatly cropped dark hair and light blue eyes that must have felled many a femme. I caught his gaze with the light beam. He blinked against it, so I held it in his line of sight.

"Jack," I said, drawing out his name until it sounded like gravel hitting the floor. "We've been looking for you."

"I didn't kill Maria," he said.

"We think you did," I answered brightly.

"I wasn't home."

"Where were you?"

"With Emily."

"Oh, good alibi, Jack."

"It's the truth. I didn't love Maria, but I didn't kill her. I couldn't."

"She had all the money, didn't she? Knock her off and if you watch your pennies, you're pretty much loaded for life. You could retire."

He shook his head but said nothing as he tried to dodge the light.

"You liked to beat her, didn't you, Jack?"

"I only did it when it was necessary."

"Necessary?" LaRue said. "When could it have been necessary?"

"You didn't know her. She was belligerent, arrogant. She spent too much money on foolish things."

"Like buying very expensive charms from a man named Ronald Orson Blackburn?" I asked.

They both glanced at each other despite the light. "Orson saw an easy mark. He was trying to rip her off. And me."

"Why didn't you stop it? What did you do to Orson?"

He shook his head and tried to avoid the light by glancing at the floor. "Nothing."

"Why not?"

When he didn't answer, I practically shoved the flashlight up his nose I got so close with it. "Is that because he knew too much about the real F-Project?"

He frowned. "What does that have to do with anything?"

"Councilman Raynor, if you talk to us, I'll take the light out of your eyes and maybe we'll let you go back upstairs after we're finished."

Emily moaned softly and yanked at her dress, which had crawled up her legs. "Please, Jack, it's over now. Tell them. My father has powerful friends. They'll help us."

He cranked his neck to stare at her. "I thought there was more to you than the conceited, spoiled bitch everyone warned me about. You're not only that, you're a coward, too."

"Please, Jack," she whined, ignoring his slanderous remark. "Please."

"Yes, Jack," LaRue said, "tell us about the F-Project."

He blew a heavy sigh and slumped forward a bit. His words slid out dryly. "The F-Project was an immunization program I worked on years ago."

"We're concerned," LaRue said. "We understand that something called a genetic isotope was invented that was introduced into the population."

Jack looked confused. "I don't know what you're talking about. I've never heard of a genetic isotope before. The F-Project was started in an attempt to thwart a plague."

"Well, the experiment we know about involved a hormone that was injected into test subjects. It was deadly. Once under it influence, the person literally starved to death while filling up on food, because his body could no longer use the resources afforded him. We understand the government has been enacting a genocide program against certain elements of the population, starting with District Twenty-one. This makes us very nervous, as it should. What do you know about it?"

He set his nice, square jaw before answering. "It's the most foolish thing I've ever heard. The government wouldn't do that. This is a humanitarian society, in case you haven't noticed."

Some people will believe anything. "Do you know a man named Dr. Philip Ligotti?" I asked.

He thought a moment. "Why does that name sound familiar?"

"Well, it was written all over a bunch of dirty movies that Max rented for Maria. Did you watch them with her?"

He shook his head. "No. I certainly would have remembered that."

"Did Orson watch them with her?"

"I don't know. I'm not home that much. Maybe. I wouldn't put it past Maria. She was always trying to get back at me for my indiscretions."

"Can't say as I blame her," LaRue said.

"You rented a lot of vids from the university library," I told him. "Why?"

"Is that against the law now?"

"Don't play with me, Councilman."

"All right. Yes. I rented them for Maria to help her come up with ideas for her dinner parties. That's it. Harmless."

I gave him a momentary break from the light by shining the beam into the corners of the small room. A rat ran for cover. Emily saw it and barely turned a scream into a gasp. It was then back to pester Jack.

"Please," he muttered.

"The sooner you start talking, the sooner the beam goes out."

"I'm answering your questions."

"You're buying time. You haven't answered anything yet. No one knows you're here, Jack. And no one will, if we chose to bury you. Don't try us."

Emily buckled all the way. "Tell them everything, you sonofabitch, or I will."

I crowded Jack again by hunkering down before him. "Your wife was a quantum user. Did she get the shit from you?"

He brought his hands up to rub at his mouth before answering. "No. I swear. I'm not a pusher. I'm running a serious research project here." With a defeated sigh, he finally started the story. "You're right about a plague, but it wasn't caused by this isotope you referred to. It just happened, like plagues do. The PHO went in to handle it and discovered that it couldn't be controlled. We tried everything, but nothing worked, so we closed the district's borders and let everyone die who would die."

"You were there, according to reports, why didn't you get it?"

He would have spread his hands if he could have. "That part is genetic. We discovered that certain people have a survival gene that wards off the disease. I was just damned lucky. A lot of the scientists and researchers weren't."

"Then there were some family units who survived?" I asked.

"Yes."

"And it's possible that these people could be carriers of this plague?"

It took him a moment to answer and when he did, it came out in a whisper. "Yes."

I glanced at LaRue and knew he had the same tight feeling in the pit of his stomach as I did. Turning back to Jack, I said, "You risked bringing some of these people out of the district. We know of the Sung family unit in particular. Why?"

"It was my idea," Emily answered.

"Yours? Now, isn't that interesting. Please explain."

"We considered it a minimal risk. As Jack said, everyone who would die, did. Years ago."

"So, why did you bring the Sungs out?"

"Quantum." She paused, glanced at Jack, and continued. "I watched my father's frustration to get adequate funding to produce a vaccine that would work. The government doesn't practice genocide as you're thinking, but they might as well call it that. He fought the bureaucracy until there was no fight left in him. They yanked the plug on the project and doomed thousands of people to death."

"Did the plague ever run its course?"

"Sure. They almost always do, and then when you least expect it, they pop up again in a newer, more virulent form. There have been reports of new outbreaks in he last few years, but the PHO is remarkably resilient when it comes to ignoring these situations." She inserted her own defeated sigh. "I've always been a pampered child. You must know this by now. But I'm not as shallow as some would suspect. I wanted to leave my mark on the world, too; and yes, I had a crazy idea that just might work. I needed help, though, and that's when I went to Jack."

"Exactly what was your idea?" LaRue murmured.

"There was a study done some years back concerning the use of quantum. It was thought that if users could be placed in a controlled environment, then the creativity that's the hallmark of the drug could be funneled and directed for the betterment of society. Unfortunately, the program was never approved because the government decided that quantum was just too unpredictable and that it should be contained immediately."

"So you thought you could control such an experiment?" I asked, with a little more surprise to my voice than I intended.

"Yes. I was specifically interested in applying quantum-inspired creativity to the problems caused by this newer form of the plague. There were no answers coming from the mainstream scientific community, so why not?"

"What did you do to set up the program?"

Jack picked up the discourse then. "Emily came to me. I have connections, it's true, and when she told me her plan, it made sense." He looked at her. "I don't know what I was thinking.

"My marriage was hell, and my job was boring me to tears, so I followed her in and once in, found we'd created something we couldn't keep under wraps.

"When I first went to District Twenty-one, I met the Sungs. They were immune to the effects of the disease. Not one person in their entire family unit ever died from the plague.

"You probably know by now that this locality had in the past produced quantum. When it was outlawed, the little cottage industries sprang up. People had labs in their bedrooms and their basements. It doesn't take much to produce the drug and being cut off from the world and with government aid sparse and unreliable, the citizens did what they could to survive by exporting the drug through whatever channels were available to them. I'm sure your drug enforcement section can give you the particulars on various smuggling operations."

"We want to hear about yours," LaRue said.

He nodded. "The Sungs maintained a large lab. They weren't wealthy from it, but they could enjoy a higher standard of living than the normal citizen of District Twenty-one. It didn't do much good to have a little money, though. There are very few imports on food and luxury items. We needed their product to start the program, so I contacted Mrs. Sung and offered her a deal. I have the power to grant interdistrict visas. It's a limited capacity, and I don't even know why I have it, but it came with the job. I used the authority and I promised her that I could manage a transfer from District Twenty-one to District One for several of her family members. We needed money as well as quantum to get the project off the ground. I told her that the cost of the visas was ten thousand credits a piece, but I would cut that figure in half if she could supply us on a regular basis with quantum. She could and she did for about three years."

"Three years?" I said. "This has been going on that long?"

"Yes," he answered.

"How did you get the drug into the district?" LaRue asked.

"It came over with different members of the Sung family. Brothers, sisters, daughters, aunts, uncles, whoever we managed to get out."

"I take it Qi Pak is the latest arrival?" I said.

"Yes. A year and a half ago, the government cracked down on illicit production and our supply was cut off. They burned the Sungs out and destroyed everything. They also levied a back-taxes penalty on them and took all their money.

"The government didn't really stop the quantum production on the island. Mrs. Sung had contacts and she told us that if we were willing to supply visas to get more of her family out of the district, then she would see to it that they brought the drug in with them."

"It sounds like you were bringing it in by the donkey load," I said. "Why did you need more?"

"Our project grew, and we still didn't have the answers we needed."

"How many people are involved in this project?"

"Over the course of the program? About one thousand."

"One thousand? You've turned one thousand people into quantum addicts and managed to keep it a secret?"

"About half of the subjects were already users when they came to us. And as we said, this is a research project. Everything is done in a controlled environment. It's not like we were pushing the drug the same as Axion Howard. We're not in it for the money."

"No, you're in it for the glory," I said. "How could you be sure that the government officials wouldn't have a problem with your experiment when you presented them with the results?"

"Emily's father has contacts. We were sure we would have gotten through it with approval."

"And it never crossed your minds that one of these drug users could flip out and do the project irreversible damage?"

He glanced at the floor. "It was a chance we took. We made sure we selected our subjects carefully. They were screened for mental instability before they entered the programs. Many were poor and we paid good money for volunteers, and over the course of the project, no one talked. Besides, those from District Twenty-one wouldn't squeal. They would have risked having their visas revoked."

"How many of your subjects are from this district?" LaRue asked.

"About seven hundred."

"Each with the capability to carry the plague?"

He nodded. "Another chance we took."

His admission made me shiver. Here I was so concerned about finding answers to my lycanthropy when, at any time, this plague could resurface to kill the world. "Where does Blackburn fit in with all this?"

He chuckled darkly. "Orson. The one who caused the fall."

"You knew him from your mandatory humanitarian service days, didn't you?" LaRue said.

He nodded. "Orson was brilliant. He really was. He longed to be a scientist, but unfortunately, his family unit didn't have the money to send him to the university to attend an entire program. He managed to secure a secondary degree as a blood technician before the funds ran out and he had to leave. I liked him from the start, and when I received my first assignment under Mr. Church, I offered him a position to help confront the plague. He traveled to District Twenty-one and spent several months there. When it became apparent that nothing could really be done, the PHO assigned him to another operation. We did keep in touch, though, and he was the first person I thought of when Emily and I organized our project."

"Was he a quantum user then?" I asked.

"Yes. I never found out when he started taking it, but I thought he was stable enough to join us. I was wrong."

"You should have subjected him to the same screening procedures as the others," Emily snapped. "You should have listened to me."

When Jack didn't defend himself, we took the interview down a new street.

"He and his wife had a little charm-making business on the back door market," I said. "Is that correct?"

"Yes. Orson could talk anybody into buying his products. He was doing all right, not great, but he could pay his taxes. Then, the stupid bastard screws up his job on the bloodmobile and loses his classification designation, his house, his wife, and his kids. The government put him in rehab for a couple of months and there wasn't anything I could do to prevent it. When he got out, I felt sorry for him and let him stay at a condo that Maria's parents gave her when we were married. I even went so far as making it possible for him to fake his death, but I wouldn't relent and let him back on our project. I was too afraid he'd start abusing the drug again. He came to me a hundred times begging for a place on the team."

"We understand he came to the lab you set up in Ed Polinato's basement."

"Yes, he came there a lot, but it didn't change my mind about anything."

"How did he get hung up with your brother, Max?" I asked.

"Max wanted to borrow money from me, and Orson happened to be visiting when he came begging. He knew a little about what we were doing because my wife had a big mouth.

"Well, you know how quantum addicts are: They stick together, and they thought of an ingenious way to get the drug. Orson talked Maria into trying some of it. When they got her hooked, they told her that they would save her the trouble of having to deal directly with the pusher. She paid them to buy it and they skimmed the quantum before bringing it to her."

"How did she get started taking the chelated chromium?" LaRue asked.

"Orson told her that it would help her lose weight and she believed him."

"Was he selling her the chromium?"

"Yes. He was getting it wholesale through a friend and making a bundle on her. Everything he could think of to soak her on, he did. When I found out, I was furious. I'll admit, I beat the shit out of her. After that, I tried to tell her that chromium wouldn't help her lose weight, but it led to another argument, and so I dropped it. At that point, I didn't care whether she lived or died, but I didn't kill her, as much as I wanted to."

"What happened then?" LaRue demanded.

Emily answered. "Orson became belligerent after he found out that Jack was having an affair with Christina Dunn. He threatened to blow our operation if we didn't let him back in. I refused."

"And?"

"He went off the deep end. He started screaming about knowing how to solve the more virulent version of the plague, but he wanted regular access to the laboratory we'd set up in the basement of The Macaroni Hut. He ranted, mentioning something about needing special genetic material for his experiment. He's crazy. Jack tried to calm him down by telling him he would see what he could do. And then Maria came up dead and mutilated. Orson did it. He killed her."

57

JACK GAVE US the address of the condo he had offered to Blackburn so we could check it out. We then decided to leave the pair in Room E for a few hours so that they would be nice and supple, should we require anything more. Emily started screaming right away and Jack kept barking for her to shut up. It was carnival time in the old lockup.

Ronald Orson Blackburn fit the scenario as described by our councilman, and now, knowing how fragmented and confused he was from his abuse of quantum, we also knew how capable he was of acting on his drug-induced ideas. It wouldn't be long before the predator hit the street to slay another victim—if he hadn't already.

After hearing Jack's and Emily's confessions, I was certain that the weapon-wielding assassin who tried to bag me was also Blackburn. While LaRue sent two undercover ward cops over to the apartment, I went back to my desk to make some calls, but I was still staring at the phone when my partner walked into our cubicle.

"What's wrong, Ty?"

"Do you think a plague can kill a werewolf?" I asked.

He frowned and sat down, studying me with one of those looks that said he was going to break out into a metaphysical discourse at any moment. "That would suggest that a werewolf isn't a supernatural being."

"What defines supernatural?"

"Everything that we don't understand."

I saw this strange scenario in my mind's eye: a decimated world where only lycanthropes, vampires, and zombies roamed, all living in a paranormal state of grace. That was worse than the thought that I just might be one of those who would contract the plague.

LaRue went on to give me his opinions concerning the great thinkers of our time and their take on mutating viruses, chicken pox, and what constituted paranormal powers. I listened until he wore down. I have to admit, I was glad when he decided to check the database to see if there was an outside chance that Blackburn's district photo ID hadn't been deleted following his phony death.

I forced off thoughts of an apocalypse and a coming supernatural world order by dialing up Jacob Tompkins at the bar and grill where he worked as a janitor. Jacob was a tumper, which meant that he could tump up practically any weapon you might want to buy. I could hear the live band in the background when he answered the phone.

"Hey, Jake, it's Ty Merrick."

I could almost hear this big black man smile. "You don't call me like you used to, Ty. What? Is no one killing each other with guns anymore? Or maybe you finally decided to buy that .350 Black Colt you like so much."

"There are still plenty of murders with bullets, and as much as I'd like to buy that revolver, I don't have a single credit I can put down on such a deal."

"I'll throw in a free silencer kit and give you a discount on a box of concussion grenades."

I didn't have time to dicker with him. "I don't have any money. I called because I need information."

"Well, information pays well, too. What kind of guns are we talking about?"

"Not a gun. An auto bow."

"Do you have a name for me?"

"Yes. Ronald Orson Blackburn. He may refer to himself simply as Orson. This guy has used about one popper of quantum too many. Can you get some skinny for us? It's important. The guy is on the rampage."

"Who isn't, anymore; at least, in our fantasies?"

"Can you help?"

"Give me a couple hours, Little Girl."

He hung up before I could yell at him about the nickname. As I did, I heard LaRue curse softly. He shook his head and knuckled his eyes and ended his act with a sigh. "I'm going to have to get a composite from those two geeks downstairs."

I could see he was hedging the job, so I patted his arm and pushed back my chair. "I'll do it. I like scaring the hell out of Emily. It's fun."

58

I MANAGED TO intimidate the woman for over three hours while she and Jack tried to describe Blackburn to the office's criminal artist. When we were all done, I threw them back into the hole, issued an APB, and told LaRue I was going home for the night. I arrived at my flat about dawn to find Baba clacking away on her loom. I went to the sink to draw some water to wash my face and hands.

"Don't bother," she said. "They must have rotated the rations this morning. We're dry as a bone."

"Dammit," I muttered. Walking straight to my lumpy couch, I crashed right there, not even bothering to change from my cammies. I must have been tired, because I didn't wake up until Gibson's voice intruded on a dream I was having about a future where only lycanthropes remained. The doctor sat at the table with Baba, helping her eat a large plate of beef ribs.

"Good afternoon, Merrick," he said with a smile. "Come join us."

I sat up and stretched. He watched me with his usual wild-eyed squint, and I knew he was imagining the ripple and pop of muscle and tendon beneath my uniform. Plopping down in a creaky chair, I reached for some food.

"How's the case coming?" he asked.

"We seem to have a definite ID on our killer now."

"Is that why you ran out of the specialist's office before I had chance to finish talking to him? Or didn't you want to hear the preliminary observations?"

"Both." I didn't ask him for the results. I just sat there tearing at the meat and getting grease on my chin.

He waited until I'd downed two of the bones before speaking. "The word came in this morning."

A dollop of uncertainty mixed with my gastric juices to churn up the meal. I selected another rib as though that action would stall his report, but it didn't. He wiped his hands on a battered napkin and began. "Your sense of smell remains undetermined, but you may spontaneously grow more olfactory nerve twigs after your seizures."

When I shot him a confused look, he explained. "You have two little organs in your head called olfactory bulbs. They're connected to the olfactory nerve, which transmits the electromagnetic equivalent of odors to the brain. The bulbs, in turn, have something called nerve twigs. These are found in the nasal lining and they're the fibers that actually start the process of smelling. We didn't detect any changes in the bulbs themselves or in the signals to the brain, but the number of twigs could have increased with your seizures. So tell me, is your sense of smell any different after a stretch?"

"I suppose so, but it's hard to tell most of the time, because my sinuses are usually clogged from the damp weather."

He nodded and continued with his report. "We did discover that your vocal chords show signs of scaling, though. Does your voice get lower when you have the full moon seizure?"

"LaRue has commented on it before. What about my hearing?"

He frowned a little. "When I went into this, I thought there would be some significant alterations to your inner ear, perhaps equivalent to the changes in your eyes. I figured you would be able to hear at a higher frequency, but no, according to the tests, your range remained consistent for humans."

"That's nice to know." As I said it, his expression flattened. "What?"

"Have you ever heard of phenomenon called the Taos Hum?" Gibson asked.

"No. What is it?"

"In the late twentieth century, in what was then New Mexico, certain people in the town of Taos complained that there was an eerie hum that backdropped everything. Some thought it was a mechanical noise, others thought it was the sound created by an energy vortex, and some even thought the government was conducting mind-control experiments. The bottom line was that the noise was driving people to their wits end."

"Did they ever find out what it was?"

"Scientists measured it, but couldn't say for certain. So they then closed in on the people who could hear it and started studying them."

"I'm afraid to ask what they discovered."

He tossed me a gentler look. "What they found was that people affected displayed symptoms that indicated various degrees of temporal lobe dysfunction. You will recall the changes that occurred in your brain mass were significant in this region."

"What does all this have to do with my hearing?"

"The Taos Hum turned out to be the by-product of the normal electrostatic current of the planet. The people who were affected were capable of hearing on a one-second delay at certain frequencies. The brain processed the sound differently and this, in turn, opened up their awareness to underlying noise. I think something similar happens to you."

59

THE PHONE RANG before we got in another word about my hearing. I mechanically rose to answer it. The caller was Jacob Tompkins.

"I've got a line on your man," he reported. "See a greaseball by the name of Hi-Test Doherty. He pumps gas in the district's heavy fuel distribution point."

"Does this fellow subcontract from you?"

"You mean weapons? I don't hire anyone. I'm strictly solo and it stays that way."

"How does he know our suspect?"

"He bought an auto bow from me about a year ago on the time payment plan. Well, his credit sucks. When he couldn't pay me, he had to sell it before I broke his legs. I called him up and asked him who he sold it to, and what do you know? The guy appears to match your description. Hi-Test knows for sure that he was a quantum user, so it might be him or it might not."

"Thanks for the info, Big Guy," I said. "The payment is in the mail."

"It better be." With that, he severed the connection.

I immediately contacted LaRue via my com node, asking him to meet me at the fuel depot. I signed off quickly because I was suddenly and painfully aware of the static interspersing the district's array. Gibson never said a word to stop me as I ran out of the flat.

As I rushed to meet my partner, I tried to put this latest finding into perspective. It wasn't that I felt bad about it; it was that I suddenly felt like I had a fat head. The change in my eyes had been startling, I'll admit, but like the alteration of my skeletal structure, I would get used to the idea. I would eventually catalogue this aberration as I had my lycanthoropic vigor and supernaturally unruly hair. Still, as I walked down the street to the subway, I couldn't help rubbing at the bones over my ears and wondering why I had never noticed the tenderness there before.

LaRue was already at the fuel depot when I arrived, busy casting a stern eye over the man pumping the petroleum into the Trabi. His greeting was a nod as he refused to take his gaze off the attendant. He whispered as I came up beside him. "You have to watch them, Ty. They see a classic car like that and they steal the windshield wipers. I know, it's happened to me before." Then, louder. "Do you know how hard it is to find those things, anymore?"

I humored him. "How hard, Andy?"

"Tough. When did they close the auto factory here?"

I shrugged. "It's been years. Before we were born, anyway."

"It won't be long until you can't get parts for these antiques." He sighed and lovingly stared at his beat-up piece of junk. "I suppose when she goes, it's back to feet. I sure won't ever be able to afford another car."

I changed the subject, because I could see he was getting maudlin over it all. "Have you talked to Hi-Test, yet?"

"No. That's him, the guy getting too close to my windshield wipers."

Hi-Test was a jaunty young man with dirty brown hair. As he came up to us wiping his hands on a dirty rag, I noticed the letters of his nickname tattooed down each middle finger.

"Mr. Doherty," LaRue said, flashing his ID, "we're district marshals and we'd like to speak to you."

For a moment, he looked like he might bolt, but he visibly

calmed himself before doing something stupid. "Yeah? So, what do you want?"

"We want to know if you've ever seen this man." LaRue pulled out a copy of the composite, flapping it in front of Doherty's face.

"I might of. We get a lot customers in here."

"Oh? What might he have been driving?"

He stared at the picture. "An old Vespa scooter. Why do you want to know about him?"

"Because he tried to kill me," I said. "In fact, he used an auto bow that you sold him."

"Did not."

"Did too. Jacob Tompkins told me." We began to guide his steps backward, wedging him between us and the car. "Relax," I said. "We don't care about you or your little schemes. We want the man you sold the weapon to."

Doherty blinked at us for a minute but finally answered. "He called himself Orson. No last name. He used to come in here for a fill-up for his scooter. He stood out because he was a big guy, and he was riding this little motor bike."

"When did you sell him the auto bow?" LaRue demanded.

"A few months back. I haven't seen him since."

"Where did you exchange the goods?"

"A dark alley over on Prescott."

"Did he do any talking?"

He thought a second. "He mentioned he was scamming charms and that's how he managed to get enough credits to buy the auto bow. I didn't care how he did it, so long as he had the right amount."

"Did he say anything else?"

"I don't know. He kept the conversation going. I was busy counting my money. I didn't pay much attention."

LaRue pinned his neck under one of his battering ram hands. "Think," he ordered, and then let loose.

Doherty's reply came immediately. "He said he was hitting up rich old broads, making charms and spell sacks for them. He called himself a shaman and he wanted to know if I could turn him on to anyone who might be interested. Who the hell believes in that garbage anymore?" Then he noticed LaRue's werewolf bag dangling free from his jacket. "Oh," he said. "Sorry. Didn't mean to offend."

My partner ignored his apology. "Did he mention any names?"

"Yeah, he did. It stuck in my mind because my old lady has been pestering me about going to the cathedral on a more regular basis."

"The name," LaRue growled.

Doherty looked at him like he was stupid. "Don't you get it? Cathedral . . . church? The name was Church. Jessica Church."

60

AFTER TALKING TO Hi-Test Doherty, we were certain that Jessica Church was Blackburn's next intended victim, so we contacted her immediately and told her we were on our way to talk to her.

LaRue was running on about Trabants and the fall of the Soviet Union while we drove. He kept talking about how plague and pestilence were signals of a society heading for collapse. He proved his hypothesis, at least to his satisfaction, by saying that the universal life force dictated these reorganizations.

By the time we reached the Church residence, he'd started a one-sided dialogue regarding the perils of a centralized world government and when he did, I was damned happy to get to the house.

Jessica Church rolled into the parlor where the butler had parked us. She looked tear-stained and frumpy and I suddenly felt sorry for her. She had wealth and status, but not much more.

She settled carefully on a heavy settee and then blew her nose into a pink silk hankie. "Is there news?" she asked. "Have you found my Emily?"

LaRue fielded the question. "Ms. Church, your sister is fine. We've heard from her. She's concerned about you."

"Me?"

He kept his expression bland as he worked into the lie. "Yes, ma'am. She tells us that you know Ronald Orson Blackburn. Why didn't you tell us this when we were here the last time?"

She snorted, but then I realized it was a sob. Several moments passed where she was attended to by the servant, who brought her what look like a glass of dry sherry. She knocked it off in one gulp and sputtered as the liquor stung her throat. "I don't know. I didn't think there was any connection. What can I say? Is he the one who kidnapped Emily?"

"Ms. Church, Emily wasn't kidnapped," I answered. "She left this house of her own free will."

"But why?" she wailed. "Why did she worry me so?"

LaRue steered the subject away. "How did you first meet Mr. Blackburn?"

"He's a friend of Emily's. A nice fellow. Jack Raynor had a dinner party and I was invited. I went and that's where I met him."

"How long ago was that?"

"About a year, I think."

"Has he been keeping in touch with you?"

"Off and on. Emily doesn't speak of him anymore. They had some sort of disagreement."

"Does he come here to visit you?"

She pursed her lips as she chewed on the question. Then, "That wouldn't be proper."

LaRue ground the question in. "But does he come?"

She blew her nose before surrendering. "Yes, he sees me about once a week when Emily isn't home. There isn't anything going on between us.".

"What do you do when he comes?"

"Have tea and talk."

"About?"

"Everything. Orson is a refreshing individual. He has a great mind and speaks several languages. We listen to Italian opera and have long talks about the music. Ever since Mother died, I haven't had a friend who can discuss the great composers. You see, I don't get out very much and it's nice to have the company."

"Did he ever tell you about a project he was working on with your sister and Jack?"

"He told me he was working with Jack. How could he be working with Emily? She does artistic commissions, as I said. Orson is a scientist."

"What kind of a scientist?"

"A biogenetisist."

I glanced at LaRue before asking, "Did he ever tell you what he does as a biogenetisist?"

"He looks for cures for virulent diseases. Orson says that

such things are spawned because of genetic mutations and he's determined to make a name for himself by solving some of our more difficult problems."

"Did he ever mention a disease known as Type-10 lupus?"

She puckered her lips again before speaking. "I don't recall that one."

"What did he mention?"

She thought a moment. "Well, the one he spoke of most was Ligotti's disease."

LaRue grunted.

"Did he ever explain the symptoms of this disease?"

"Oh, yes. A person literally starves to death because he can't absorb nutrients from the food. It's a problem at the subatomic level, whatever that means. He did mention that he was sure women," she cleared her throat, "large women, that is, carry a survival gene that can somehow be manipulated and used to combat the disease. He also said a Chinese scientist during the late twentieth century had been interested in finding bioapplications for population management and invented the hormone that caused all the problems. You'll have to forgive me but I've forgotten her name."

LaRue grunted again and made eye contact with me. I read certainty in his expression.

I turned back to Jessica Church and asked the kicker question. "Have you paid Mr. Blackburn to make any magical charms for you?"

They say that lycanthorpes have the ability to tell when a person is lying, but from her strained expression, I didn't need any supernatural skills to tell she was considering a fib. Something must have made her give up the truth, because she said, "Yes. He swears it will help me to find emotional balance in my life, which will then allow me to lose weight. In fact, he made one for Maria Raynor. I called her to ask if it was working and she said she had dropped twenty pounds, so I thought I'd try it. I've never held much store in those things, but I have a bad heart and high blood pressure and can't seem to get to a normal weight. If I don't, I'll die."

"How much did you pay him?"

"Fifteen thousand credits."

Hearing that figure made my eyes water and I had to take a breath before speaking. "Did he deliver it to you?"

"Yes." She pulled forth a pouch that was hidden in the dark pit between her breasts.

"Can you tell us what it has in it?"

She carefully opened the bag and pulled out tiny, pastel-hued scrolls wrapped with silver threads. "These," she said, holding them in the palms of her hands. "They've all been properly blessed. That's why this charm is so expensive."

"Would you mind if we examine one of them?" LaRue said.

She hesitated. "Orson said that I shouldn't disturb them."

"Ms. Church, this man can be considered extremely dangerous."

After a moment, she nodded.

We both watched as he carefully slipped the sparkling bands from one of them. He needed only to unwrap the first paper and we knew Blackburn was playing the same game as he had with Maria Raynor. Our expression betrayed us.

"What's wrong?" Jessica asked.

LaRue says that my tact was destroyed when I became a lycanthrope. I'm not sure if that's the complete truth. As far as I'm concerned, I just get impatient with people. "Ronald Orson Blackburn murdered Maria Raynor," I blurted, "and we believe he intends for you to be his next victim."

After I said it, I knew I shouldn't have. Her face turned red, and she became hysterical. There was nothing we could do until the butler managed to calm her down and by this time, she was perspiring at a furious rate. The sweat smeared out over her dress and an incredible montage of perfume and body odor made me realize that Gibson was right: My olfactory twigs were extremely sensitive.

LaRue took command of the situation after she finally settled down. "Ms. Church, we need your help."

"I can't help. It's impossible."

"But you can. In the end, it may be the very thing that keeps you out of harm's way."

She stared at him with bloodshot eyes and then had the butler pour her another drink. After downing it, she said, "All right, I'll try. At least now I know Emily is fine. What do you want me to do?" The BO pumped off her with each word she spoke.

"First, do you know of anyone else who has received such a bag from him?"

"No. He's never said."

"When are you to meet with him again?"

"On the night of the full moon."

"Why?"

"He told me that he had another object to add to the bag, but it had to be done at a specific time. Apparently, the full moon changes a person's gravitational response and alters the aura."

I could see LaRue mentally filing this last bit of metaphysical fluff and I was sure that he was going to later apply the concept to my lycanthropy.

He rose, dragging me to a stand. "We're going to assign a ward cop to serve as a bodyguard until we contact you with the details of an operation that will allow us to legally arrest the man."

"Will the policeman come tonight?"

"Yes ma'am. He'll be right over. If you like, we'll have one assigned to your father, as well."

"Oh, yes, that would be fine. I'll even donate to the District Marshals Fraternal Fund, if you send over a third."

"We'll see what we can do. Are you supposed to be alone when Blackburn comes?"

"Well, yes. Others can be in the house, but we must have complete privacy." Her eyes grew round. "Do you think he really intends to kill me?"

LaRue shrugged. "It's a good possibility, Ms. Church."

We left after that, when a sob started to bubble up in her. Standing outside on the flower-covered veranda, I looked at LaRue and jabbed a finger toward his head. "So, do we have a plan?"

He smiled, darkly. "Ty, my partner, we have a full moon and plenty of inspiration."

61

As I MENTIONED, LaRue has been with me on many full moons. He knows what happens and tends to explain it by using his usual irritating metaphysical associations.

The final stretch for me is the most painful of the lunar month. Following the agony of the immediate seizure, I'm up for twelve hours of paranoia and schizophrenic episodes. I'm coherent in a lethal sort of way, but when the night is done, I forget much of what happened. According to my partner, I become a fragmentation of past lives, because he says extraordinary things seep through that he can't explain any other way. I suppose Gibson's theory on it will be to say that I'm accessing some sort of primal memory contained within each human brain. To be honest, as much as I think it's all bullshit, I like LaRue's idea better. It, at least, lends some romance to the misery.

We climbed into the Trabi and he looked at me before jiggling the key in the ignition. "Do you think my Uncle Carl weighs more than Jessica Church?"

"By about a hundred pounds would be my guess."

"Mine, too. I think he'll help us catch this killer."

"Decoy?"

"He'd have to be. That woman will break down. We can't let her in on the heart of the sting. She'll blow it before it starts with her histrionics."

"I think that was an excuse so she could drink."

"She must have put away an entire bottle of sherry while we were there."

He turned quiet after we decided to visit his uncle and I have to admit I was glad for the silence. I had a feeling I knew what idea LaRue was turning over in his head: a simple scam, one that would veer Blackburn from his prime killing objective.

We found Carl at home, firmly ensconced in a huge, blue checkered cloth chair that seemed to conform perfectly to his bulk. He was reading the Epistle of St. Ophelia and drinking a glass of white wine when his daughter showed us into the modest room he called a study. His smile was engaging, and he pointed to a couch scrunched into the space beside his throne, but he didn't bother trying to rise to greet us.

"What brings you two here this evening?" he asked, pouring out two more glasses from a wine carafe decorating a small side table and handing them off to us.

"Do you remember the church play you directed me in when I was a kid?" LaRue asked.

"Well, let's see. You did one on angels, one on St. Ophelia's rapture, and one on the covenant and statutes."

"What about the one where I played the wise man from Ithaca?"

"Oh, Andrew, that wasn't religious. That was celebrating our humanitarian way of life. It was during the Energy Resources Festival. I thought I taught you better than that."

"Uncle Carl, we would like you to help us catch a murderer."

He was about to take a sip of wine, but LaRue's words stopped him. He pondered the question, staring at us over the rim of his glass. Then he took a slug, set the goblet on the table, folded his hands over his stomach and said, "How?"

LaRue cleared his throat before speaking. "I'm not sure I can put this delicately."

"State it as it is, Andrew. I've told you that before."

"Yes, sir."

He hesitated again and so I jumped in. "Carl, we need your fat."

He looked at me for a moment. A smile slowly crossed his jowly face and that was followed by a couple minutes of a loud belly laughing. He stopped when the tears started to soak his cheeks. "Forgive me," he said, in between chuckles. "I would love to give you my fat. Any ideas on how we'll get it off me?"

Our plan, as wet as it was at the moment, was to take advantage of Blackburn's quantum addiction. The effects of the drug had made his thinking confused. His actions suggested that he had intertwined reality with imagination to the point where he was lost. We intended to play on this fact in an effort to coax his interest away from Jessica's corpulence and toward Carl's. LaRue's uncle considered the danger for only a moment before agreeing to help us. We would use one of the office's safe houses, throw a SWAT team around it, and set up Blackburn in the act of trying to separate Carl from his natural insulation. It was easy in concept, but for all its simplicity, I was worried about the haste with which we concocted the sting.

We had to convince the killer to attempt it on the upcoming full moon. If we didn't, he would go after Jessica to check the energy of the charm and make mincemeat of her thighs. I knew there was no other choice with the time left us, but it angered me that I couldn't be in on the collar. It was just too dangerous. In my madness, I could spoil the whole thing.

It was after midnight when LaRue and I pulled up in front of my apartment building. He placed a hand on my shoulder just as I was opening the car door.

"Don't be too upset, Ty," he said. "You'll still get credit for the bust."

"I know, Andy. It's just that it feels like I've read through a book only to find that the last chapter's been torn out."

He nodded, but didn't say anything; not even good night.

62

WE LAID OUT our plan for Jessica Church and Uncle Carl, strung a surveillance camera to record the meeting with Blackburn, and then all met at the mansion at three thirty the next afternoon.

Carl, who proudly emphasized his experience in directing the passion plays over at St. Ophelia's, admitted to me he'd always wanted to be the lead in a play, and though the danger to his personal safety was enormous, he was excited to see how convincing he could be. He came wearing a black silk shirt, black slacks, and a charm bag crocheted with gold thread.

Jessica was fussing with the surveillance techs who were trying to check a hidden vid camera in the room Emily had decorated. She winced when they were forced to drill a hole above the door lintel and started turning scarlet when one of the boys accidentally bumped an expensive-looking vase sitting on a small, round table. LaRue mananged to calm her down and get the two in their places while we watched on a monitor in the next room.

At five minutes until four, Ronald Orson Blackburn showed up.

Clyde Smith had been right about him. He was a big man, tall and heavily muscled. His ice blue eyes had a lurking way about them, and I was reminded of a predator seeking his next meal. He had shaggy dark brown hair that scraped the collar of his stained linen shirt. The stubble of a goatee gentled at the flat line of his thin lips, but despite his effort at keeping a blank expression, I noticed a snarl threatening to roll off his gum line. He didn't seem doped up, and sitting lightly in the available chair, he paused to cast a stern expression over Jessica and Carl as they weighed down the opposite ends of the same settee.

Jessica kept fiddling with the charm bag Blackburn had given her, but when she spoke, she managed to hide the nervousness in her voice. In fact, she managed a society drawl. "Welcome, Orson. So glad you could come."

"My pleasure, Jessica."

"Let me introduce my friend, Dr. Philip Ligotti."

His expression turned to surprise and the impact of his sentences was dulled by the long pause between them. "Philip Ligotti? It's not possible."

Carl didn't answer right away. Instead, he took his time to fish into his shirt pocket to remove the box of nippers we had traded for Madame Janetta. He popped one in his mouth and waited patiently for the attentive butler to stoke it with a jade lighter. He took a puff and then studied the cigarette before answering. His voice was smooth and syrupy as he looked at Jessica. "Please, my dear, would you be so kind as to leave us alone? I wish to speak to this gentleman concerning a delicate matter."

"Yes, of course." She rose with a grunt and added, "I'm so glad I could bring you two together. I know how much Orson appreciates your work." With that, she stomped out of the parlor and came to join us in the surveillance room.

Carl really went into his act, then. "To answer your question, Mr. Blackburn, it is possible for me to be here. Have I changed so much since we served together during the outbreak of the plague in District Twenty-one?"

Blackburn's mouth hung open, and this time the pause remained complete.

Carl continued, pasting on a smile that was more akin to a sneer. "I see that you don't. I remember you, though. A brash young man so full of himself, even though he was nothing more than a blood technician serving on the project. I was in charge. I wonder if you remember that?"

Blackburn frowned. From his expression, it looked like the confusion between reality and imagination had started to grind together. "Yes," he said, tentatively. "I remember that."

"Good. Then you'll also remember that I'm the one who invented the genetic isotope."

"No. It was Sun Ye Sung." He squinted. "What game are you playing with me?"

Carl chuckled. "Not a game, Mr. Blackburn. Serious business. Sun Ye Sung was my wife. Surely, you recall how you stole her from me."

"Stole her? You're mad."

"Unfortunately, I'm not. She did have your child, after all."

"I have no children."

"That you know of. Why do you think I sent her away? The affair was bad enough, but then to find out she was pregnant by you. That was too much." Carl adjusted his weight, took a puff, and added, "By the way, she died giving birth to your bastard."

Blackburn rose mechanically. I thought he was going to leave, but instead, he stalked around the room, stopping to stare at objects, pick at the plants, and clear his throat several times.

Carl kept it coming. "And as to these preposterous scrolls you're putting inside of charm bags—"

Blackburn spun on him.

"That's right. Jessica showed me hers. You claim that my work was used by the government in their program of genocide, when in truth the genetic isotope was invented to thwart the effects of the plague and nothing more."

"My research shows otherwise."

"Your research. What credentials do you have? None. You don't even have a job and your so-called work is ridiculous."

Blackburn muttered and static in the pickup prevented us from hearing it. He took another walk around the room, his neck twisting with each step so he could stare at his sudden opponent.

Carl dragged on the nipper, blew a smoke ring in Blackburn's direction, and then pulled out the folded paper that Brown Hilda had given us. He unwrapped it carefully. "This page, I believe, is from one of your so-called research notebooks."

"Where did you get that?"

"From Jack Raynor, of course."

"Jack?"

"That's right. He called me when he realized that you intended to slander my research with this tripe. I felt that it was my right to confront you. When Jessica mentioned her association with you, I found it a fortuitous opportunity."

"This is madness. This isn't how it is. I don't know who you are, but you're not Philip Ligotti."

"In the same way that you're not a scientist?"

Blackburn's face seemed to swell. "How dare you!" he spat.

"I do dare. You've had the audacity to attach my name to this pitiful, mad excuse for medical research. This particular sheet of paper mentions your project; a project that, I remind you, has a focus that doesn't exist. Further down the page, you remark on your efforts at collecting genetic material, supplying the gruesome details of this despicable process. Mr. Raynor tells me that you regularly use quantum and have for a number of years. Obviously, you can't tell what is real and what is not, anymore."

Blackburn worked on getting the words to come out, but

they didn't. By this time, he had a lovely red sheen on his face. Carl went for the hoop.

"Regarding this notebook from which this excerpt was taken: I'm reasonable in assuming that you intend to self-publish your so-called findings. That will not happen. I let you get away with something precious of mine once before, but this time, Mr. Blackburn, you will not succeed in stealing my research and making me the laughingstock of the professional community.

"I'm at a point of breakthrough, and I'll be announcing these facts at midnight tonight before the Medical Congress of the PHO. You see, you won't have a chance to discredit my work with your absurd claims." Carl smiled. "I'm going to beat you at this game you're trying to play and see, at the very least, if I can't have you committed to a high-security mental facility. I shouldn't think that it will be too hard, either, because once the ETA finds out you faked your death, they're going to want their back taxes, and then they'll come after you."

Blackburn blinked at him and then abruptly stormed from the house. When he was gone, we went in to see Carl.

"You were beautiful," LaRue said, shaking his hand.

"I rather enjoyed it. Did you see how his blood pressure mounted the stairs? I was worried he was going to burst a blood vessel as we talked." He rubbed his hands together. "So tell me. What are the odds he's going to take the hook?"

"I'd say he's already in the pickle barrel," LaRue answered. "We've made you a mandatory target, and he'll come after you."

"Well, I'll say a Feng Shui mass when I go home. The luck will be complete. Don't worry, nothing will go wrong."

63

THAT EVENING, A pounding rain came in. LaRue's sacred windshield wipers refused to work, so we were both forced to stick our heads out the side windows to see where we were going. By the time he dropped me off at Gibson's apartment, my hair took on the classic wet poodle look and my cammies were soaked straight through.

The onset of my full moon stretch is preceded by what I can only term as a series of squeezes. These strange contractions start at my feet and chug steadily up my body until they reach my torso, where it feels as though someone is applying a vise to my lungs. No matter what I do, I can't gather a deep breath. I'm sure that my poor brain is starved for oxygen, because it's at this point that I get night terrors, tiny hallucinations that confuse and befuddle me. The muscles in my ankles were starting to cramp by the time I reached the lobby of Gibson's building, only to find that the elevator was out of order.

I hobbled to the stairwell and began to slowly climb the eight flights leading up to his flat. I had just cleared the third floor when I pitched forward onto the landing, half paralyzed by a tremor that constricted my abdomen. This dry labor sent steam through my arteries and there was nothing I could do but whine. Finally, the cramp released me, moving as it did, into my solar plexus. I struggled to stand and slowly mounted the steps again.

When I reached Gibson's floor, I found him nervously pacing the hallway. His hair was loose, and he was wearing blue denims, a university-emblazoned sweatshirt, running shoes, and a District One baseball team cap. He came to me immediately as I sagged against the stairwell door. Without a word, he guided me gently into his flat and onto his couch. He studied me for a moment before speaking. "I didn't think you were going to make it."

"Business," I huffed. "Sorry."

"Can you get out of your wet clothes, or do you need my help?"

"No, I can do it. Just give me a minute." He did, filling the seconds by going to his knees and removing my shoes and socks. After he was done, I used his shoulders to boost myself to a stand. I turned a bit to fumble for my rucksack sitting on the sofa, but the strap suddenly transformed into a greasy, red worm, its body ringed with hundreds of tiny, sharp teeth. It took a moment before I realized it was a fake, but that came after I gasped, pulled my hand back, and yes, cried out. Gibson embraced me with a choking strength and whispered something that didn't make sense. I yanked from his grip, wobbled to the bathroom and, slamming the door behind me, I dropped the lid on the toilet and sat down.

Following the tremors, there is what I call a warm-up period. My body temperature rises dramatically. Gibson would undoubtedly say it's the effect of a fever, but during this surge, I begin to experience a sense that I've grown lighter in my entire form, as though a layer of bone has been blasted off by the heat convecting through me. Sitting there on the potty, I could feel the first flushes come over me and I could hear my wrists pop as I unzipped my uniform. I had just stripped off the jumpsuit when the seizure ambushed me.

There I was, lying in someone else's bathroom, shivering, coughing, and slobbering, wearing nothing more than a pair of pink panties and the notion that I was now linking with the wolf. In my tortured mind, I knew Gibson had been wrong about the effectiveness of the light therapy. The last full moon stretch had been easier. I was sure of it.

He abruptly appeared, pushing the door back and squeezing into the space with me. He held me down, sitting on my legs, catching up both of my flailing hands into one of his. With the other, he pushed on my solar plexus, even as I squirmed, howled, and tried to shove him away.

Pain shot down my spine and back up again until the cruel ache stabbed me in the center of the forehead. I couldn't close my eyes or my mouth; the lycanthropic grimace had taken hold, making me imagine that my nose was sprouting into a muzzle and my teeth into fangs. Worse yet, I was coherent through it all, knowing that when it was over and I looked into the bathroom mirror, not one goddamned change would be readily evident.

I twitched for another ten minutes before the physical pain of the stretch finally let go. It was another five before Gibson climbed off me.

"Can you stand?" he asked.

"Yes," I rasped, and did just that, avoiding the mirror as I clung to the sink.

"Let me help you with your cammies," he said, and remained undeterred as I balked.

He didn't bother to zip up the jumpsuit; instead, he led me again to the couch before going to a nearby box and digging out a stethoscope.

The full moon makes my skin sensitive to touch and the chill of the instrument almost blasted me off the sofa. He apologized, but forged on with his examination, the now all-too-familiar intensity predominating his expression. When that check was complete, he grunted and replaced the stethoscope in favor of an electronic thermometer. He pushed it into my ear and hissed at the reading.

"One hundred two point six."

"I'm all right," I whispered.

He nodded and disappeared into his lab, returning with a large hypodermic needle.

"What are you going to do with that?" I asked.

He smiled. "I want to get a blood sample, Merrick. Don't worry. I'm great at this."

For some reason, my mind went to Ronald Orson Blackburn and his own talents regarding the tools of the medical field.

I stared at the procedure, watching as Gibson pinched up a vein in the back of my hand and inserted the needle. A moment later I was transfixed by the red fluid flowing into the plastic chamber.

Some books and vids assert that lycanthropy is a vestige of the Stone Age, when bands of semicivilized people started avoiding those individuals still concerned with cannibalism. At that very moment, as I watched the extraction of my life force, I knew that claim was true. Never before had a blood lust come on so completely as it did then. It was all I could do to fight down the urge to attack Gibson and sink my teeth into the fleshy part of his neck.

He didn't seem to notice anything amiss as he slipped the needle from me. "I'm going to put this in the analyzer. I'll only be a couple of minutes."

I nodded, because there were no words in my throat; only a growl.

As he retreated into the other room, I rose to stalk the perimeter of the living area in an effort to dissolve the violent desire that had so suddenly come upon me. I stopped before the glass door leading to the balcony and for a moment studied the pens of chickens and rabbits. It was good Gibson returned before I had a chance to walk outside

He was silent, clutching a computer printout, and he

watched me as I paced the room. It was then that I realized his gaze had gone to my feet and he had noticed that I was walking on tiptoes. I immediately worried that he might notice the appearance of paw pads, so I came back to the couch and slipped on my shoes. When I couldn't remember how to tie them up, he placed his printout on the sofa and knelt before me again, a concerned look replacing the intense one.

"What does it say?" I croaked, pointing to the paper.

He sat down beside me before answering, and ran a fingertip along the page. "Not much. I was hoping for some definite changes, but you're pretty normal as far as the red stuff goes. Your cholesterol is all right and the fat content in your blood is nothing to jump about. Everything else looks good, though you're low on folic acid." He glanced at me. "Folic acid is iron, Merrick."

I just stared at him. He continued with a frown so slight that it merely peppered his brow.

"The low folic acid content could be a result of the lycanthropy, but I think you're just short on it anyway. It's something that women usually lack in their bodies."

When he said it, my thought patterns turned from circles to squares, because my brain immediately formed an image of Blackburn standing over a naked fat woman with his laser scalpel ignited and a pleased smile on his face. In one hand, he studied the missing page from his notebook. So surreal was the cast to it all, I had to drag my words beyond it. "What did you say?"

"I said your iron deficiency may be a result of your lycanthropy, but I don't think so." A pause, then, "Is your hearing all right?"

My ears were perfect, but my neurons fired me deeper into the fantasy and I didn't answer.

"Merrick?"

It took me a few moments before I could realign my thought patterns. "Yes?"

"Where were you just then?"

"I'm not sure. I didn't recognize the surroundings."

"What does that mean?"

I shrugged. "I saw our perp. He was ready to make another killing. And it seemed that I was there in the room with him. The colors were so bright they hurt my eyes. It was like a dream, but it wasn't."

"So, since you don't recognize the surroundings of this particular illusion, do I understand that you do experience feelings of déjà vu?"

"Yes. Sometimes."

"That might be a form of temporal lobe epilepsy." Gently tapping my head just above my ear, he said, "This part of the brain is responsible for those feelings of having been there before, and dramatic, colorful scenes are common when there's a seizure."

His statement brought up an irritability that I wasn't prepared for. "I'm one big medical chart to you, aren't I?"

He leaned back, looking as though he had just dodged a silver bullet. "I'm sorry. I only want you to realize that what happens to you isn't some supernatural transmission of energy."

"But all in all, you're not sure what it is. This is probably as fruitless as Jack Raynor's so-called research."

"Oh? And what was he doing?"

"Farming the heightened creativity of quantum addicts and then making them regurgitate their ideas for fun and profit." Having said it, I must have gotten another jolt through my temporal lobe, because I was off with a new image, one where Jack tossed Blackburn a popper and then sat back with a pen and notepad to write down the gleanings of a tortured psyche.

I winced, and Gibson whispered my name. I forced my way out. "Sorry, but I've put in so many hours on this last case that I can't stop thinking about it."

"Obsessive thoughts? Is that something that plagues you during a full moon?"

Plagues. I zeroed in on the word and was gone from him again. This time I saw Blackburn cutting the dermis from a woman ravaged by his genetic isotope. "Yes," I muttered, still transfixed by this internal image. "Obsessive thoughts."

"Are they usually violent?"

"Yes."

"Do they excite you?"

That did it. I came out of it enough to snap, "That would make me an animal. I'm not."

"I didn't say you were. I'm just trying to get a feel for what's going on inside of you right now."

Inside of you right now.

"The study of the brain is a complex procedure, Merrick. We're still exploring how combinations of chemicals work to form the personality."

"I'll admit, I don't know what you just said."

He smiled. "Think about a quantum addict—you've gotten a good taste of one during this investigation. The compounds in the drug affect the brain and the personality. It inflates the ego to the detriment of the superego."

He went on with the explanation, but it didn't make sense because of my lycanthropic state. One thing did happen, though: I suddenly knew for a fact that as enticing as it was, Ronald Orson Blackburn hadn't taken our bait.

I rocketed to a stand, and Gibson followed my rise. There was a moment of confusion as I stared at him while trying to pull myself back into reality. He placed his hands on my upper arms, but I backed out of his grasp and staggered for the apartment door.

"Call the office and get LaRue on the horn," I ordered. "Tell him that Blackburn isn't going after the mark. He's going to kill Jessica. Tell him to hurry. There's a couple of ward cops on duty who might go down, too."

He headed me off and blocked the door. "Where do you think you're going?"

"Stand aside, Gibson. The house is in the next ward. I might be able to beat the bastard there."

"Merrick. You can't go anywhere. You don't even know what you're doing. This madman could kill you before you get a chance to catch him."

I snarled and grabbed him at the waist, and with my lycanthropic strength, shoved him to the floor. "Call LaRue!" With that, I left him staring at me and ran for the stairs.

The rain came down so hard that with my lycanthropic sight, I could actually see the arcs made by the drops as they bounced off the sidewalk under one of the streetlamps. For a moment, my steps slowed as I became enthralled, but I managed to recover and picked up speed again until I was in a full-out gallop. Halfway there, I realized that I didn't have a gun.

64

RONALD ORSON BLACKBURN had an enormous ego, if what we had discovered about him was true. His own research was paramount; his ideas were the only ones to consider, and in his mind, he'd published his views through his scrolls.

He claimed that obese women carried the specific gene necessary to combat the isotope, and whether he believed our fake Ligotti or not, it didn't make any difference. He was caught in his particular madness, the same way I was caught in mine. We had missed the biggest clue of all.

I tore up the next two blocks and made a slapping turn at the corner of Edgerton and Birelli, but then I stopped short when I realized my cammies were unzipped down to my navel. Of course, the zipper was hung up on the fabric. My patience, being what it is at this time of month, didn't last long. I managed to get the pull up part of the way before my frustration got the better of me and I ripped it off. I growled and let it be, starting back into a trot.

Concerning my temporal lobe déjà vu problem, I had one of those irritating situations surface as I dashed along.

If there's a time when I coalesce with the wolf, it's during these intermittent, full moon, brain explosions. I lose a sense of self and degenerate into a primal focus. I suppose Gibson would matter-of-factly say that my thought patterns are momentarily confused by altered synaptic cues. To me, it feels as though I'm wearing fur on the inside of my skin and my muscles and tendons are stretched and quivering. When one of these past life fragments eclipses reality, I have no choice but to work through it, and on this night, I was also battered by paranoia.

The street fizzled on me, the scene changing to a remote wilderness of hard shapes and steep canyon walls. In my mind, I wasn't running to stop a murder, I was trying to escape one—mine. There were people chasing me. I could hear the clutter of a hundred voices behind me. I pushed harder, my lungs starting to burn under the rush of caustic air that not even the storm could gentle. A cargo tram rumbled by, splashing me with water that stung my hide and made me yelp. My pursuers were getting closer. I could hear the rattle of Iron Age weapons and was certain in the knowledge that a shaman traveled with them, liberally sprinkling spells along the path I'd taken, hoping one would be strong enough to ignite my trail like gunpowder to the keg.

I passed an alley and glanced down it, seeking some protection from the ghosts in my mind. In the shadows, I saw an old woman sitting in a side doorway, trying to huddle against the weather. I heard a consumptive cough erupt from her, and the sound was enough to snap me back into total coherence, but it was also enough to make me stop again, because in my frenzy, I'd overshot the street leading to the Church residence.

By the time I realized it, I also realized that the rain had stopped and the full moon was dodging the shifting clouds, appearing, then disappearing. I paused to stare at it. Despite the mounting medical evidence suggesting that I was an assortment of biological aberrations, I still wondered how all that was connected to another world.

I forced the thoughts off and doubled back, taking the appropriate turn, and finally finding myself on the quiet, manicured avenue I needed. Checking my watch, I saw that it was almost 10 P.M. If Gibson had done what I'd told him, LaRue would already have the killer apprehended, but as I came up to the wrought iron gates protecting the entrance of this mini plantation, I saw no signs of his arrival. I also saw no lights anywhere.

I buzzed the main house at the box. There was no answer. After jiggling the gate, I cursed myself for not thinking about bringing my rucksack. I carried a portable electronic lock pick, which would have saved me from having to scale the stone wall surrounding the mansion, but since I was alone with nothing more than my strangled wits, I settled for scraped hands and bruised knees.

The rain had made the attempt slippery and compromising. It was a few minutes before I found a place where I could wedge my fingers and toes to pull myself up. Once I reached the crest of the wall, I had to gingerly avoid the broken glass bottles cemented along it. I did use the vantage point to squint into the darkness, trying to see beyond the thick, overgrown garden that obscured the back of the house. There was no movement and no odd sounds, so with a heave, I threw myself over the side, landing not as a sure-footed animal would, but as a clumsy human might—on my rump.

I groaned, stood, wiped at the seat of my pants like it would make some difference to my comfort. Looking around, I saw no signs of life.

We'd assigned those three ward cops that Jessica had asked for and one of them should have been patrolling the perimeter. In my haste to stop a murder, I had also neglected to bring my com node, so there was no chance to contact the sentry and ask for a location. About this time, the wind kicked up and I realized that I'd forgotten my jacket, too. Imaginary fur on the inside of the skin does nothing to keep a person warm.

I didn't move from my spot for about a minute, sniffing the air for signs of life, but all I smelled was smoke belching from the stack of a nearby plant. To my left, there was a long, high, boxwood hedge cut to match the serpentine crawl of a brick walk. I started out, wishing that if magic were real, that I could materialize a gun.

Fifteen steps later, I found the body of the ward cop. She lay in a knot near the bushes, several tiny arrows from an auto bow pricking her torso and arms. One had pinned her in the heart. I stopped to rifle the body for a weapon. Her side arm was gone.

A sound came to me just then; the breeze was slapping at something. In my state of mental flux, I lost my concentration as I tried to figure out where it came from and what it was. Images consumed my mind's eye with threads of thoughts that had no true place within me but nonetheless instilled me with a momentary fear. I saw a hangman's gallows from the barred window of a street-level cell, heard the whine of taunting voices, felt the pelt of stones as they were slung into my prison. Instinctively, I knew I was being executed, because I was a werewolf in a time when no one could conceive of this madness beyond the myths handed down by Lucius Apuleius Plato, Olaus Magnus, and St. Augustine. The feeling of déjà vu came up again, and if LaRue was right about his blasted past life fragments, then I had, indeed, died some wrongful deaths.

The noise battered me out of the delusion, and I took a step back into the present. While suffering my hallucination, I had walked without knowing it and had almost reached the house where I found the source of the sound. The French doors opening onto the second story balcony were ajar and flapping.

I climbed the circular concrete stairs, hanging in the shadows of the patio for a few heartbeats before scraping along the house's exterior wall. I came to the door, and peering into the darkness, I sensed nothing threatening, so I slid inside. That's when I found the hunched, lifeless form of Old Man Church sitting in his wheelchair. His throat had been cut. Lying on the floor beside him was his nurse, Dorthea, who had suffered the same fate. The blood covered her crisp white uniform and the freshness of the bouquet made me wince. I moved on, coming out into the dimly lit upstairs hallway.

The mansion appeared to house hundreds of art objects. In this one passage alone, I padded by antique tables graced with expensive knickknacks made of crystal, ivory, and gold. Large oil paintings framed in precious woods lined the walls, showing what could only have been generations of Church ancestors staring down sternly upon those who traversed this corridor. The carpet looked expensive, too, and I felt a tinge of guilt as I dripped water and mud all over it. When I reached the second floor landing, I found another ward cop who had been killed like his comrade. His weapon was missing as well.

I descended the huge, curving stairs leading to the now-familiar foyer. At the halfway point, I heard voices again. It took me another few seconds to realize that they weren't produced by my brain, but instead were coming from one of the rooms below me.

I silently followed the noises and found myself hiding in the shadows just inside the kitchen door.

The room was immense and in near darkness, the only light coming from a kerosene storm lamp attached to the far wall. My flat, Gibson's, and possibly LaRue's would have fit into this space. Pots and pans hung like giant wind chimes from ceiling racks and stainless steel preparation tables filled the expanse. A restaurant-size stove was wedged between a huge freezer and refrigerator. Beyond that, there was a bank of sinks with several spigots, a dishwasher, micro-wave, and not one environmental usage meter.

The voices came from a walk-in pantry. Heading toward

it, I tripped over the third ward cop and skidded on the pool of blood in which he lay. The sounds from the other room stopped, and I dove for cover behind a large bread rack that was heavily laden with several fragrant loaves.

From my vantage point, I saw Ronald Orson Blackburn step from the pantry. He held his auto bow in one hand and a stolen service revolver in the other. I froze as he stalked right by without seeing me. Glancing at the floor, I noticed that I'd left bloody tracks to my hiding place. Thankfully, he didn't see the marks and returned to the pantry. After a minute, I followed.

The illumination was brighter in this space and I was forced to pause as I looked in to give my eyes a chance to adjust. When they did, I saw that Blackburn had his back to the door. He hovered over Jessica Church, who was bound at her feet and hands and lying facedown on the floor. Her blue dress was hiked up around her thighs. I could see her quivering.

Blackburn set his weapons on a nearby ledge next to a box of instant rice. Jessica begged for her life, but he ignored her as he unwrapped his laser kit, intent, I'm sure, on sadistically flaying the flesh from her while she was still alive. Glancing around for some useful weapon, I noticed the block of butcher knives sitting on the sparkling counter. As quietly as I could, I crept toward it and selected a nicely weighted boning knife. Returning to my place just outside the door, I took the instrument by the blade and waited for the killer to hunker down over his quarry. That's when I slung the knife at him. The projectile landed true, zipping into his right shoulder.

He screamed, more in anger than in pain. He scrabbled to rip the blade out and tossed it toward the door. I heard him go for his weapons once more and then cock the bolt on the auto bow. I lunged for the shadows behind the bread rack, slipping another knife from the block as I did. Of course, the wolf chose that moment to eclipse my concentration and throw me into another delusion.

I found myself lurking in a deep forest, concealed from the hunter by thick, chunky overgrowth and shadows formed by surrounding boulders. In my thoughts, this man with the bow had killed those closest to me and now sought to end my life. The reasons weren't clear, though my fear and rage was. He had to die; that was all there was to it.

I watched him walk to the sink and turn on the tap, knowing in the back of my mind that it was a sink and a tap, but in the front of my mind, thinking that it was a cleft in the rock from which a waterfall sprang. He opened his shirt and flushed the wound and in his exaggerated effort, he flung handfuls of water along the floor. Turning from his chore, he to stalked the kitchen as if he knew he was in perfect control of the situation.

All this time, my imagined rage escalated. It almost felt good to let go, but I knew if I did, I would lose hold on reality. I had to maintain a sense of place. I had to know I was in a house and not some hard-surfaced, geometrically shaped woodland. I tried to contain my composure by taking long pulls of air, but unfortunately it did little to keep my logic from clicking on and off. Like a battered neon sign, I was now open for business every ten seconds.

I smelled the fresh blood draining from the killer's shoulder, and then I heard myself growl. He turned in my direction, but for some reason became sidetracked. Instead of coming straight for me, he marched down the center of the room, stopping to check behind a table and inside of a large cabinet. I crouched, using the shadows behind the bread rack like they were a part of me. Placing the knife in the deep calf pocket of my cammies, I inched forward along a narrow aisle separating two large work counters.

The man took a step closer.

I held back a shiver as I pushed out of a flickering illusion and found myself even with a row of sauté skillets dangling from a deep shelf under one of the tables.

The killer took another step.

Glancing along the floor, I saw his shoes clearly. One string was completely undone and dragged off behind him. I fixated on it, but pulled myself together when he turned and walked back toward the sink. He ran more water. He also hissed in pain as he flung it into the wound.

Carefully unhitching a small, heavy pan, I slowly maneuvered my position until my firing line was unencumbered by the blocky shapes of the room. I came to a partial stand, flung the pan at the storm lamp, and hit it dead-on, smashing the globe and extinguishing the light. He spun about and shot a round at the wall, the darts falling harmlessly to the floor. Before I knew what was happening, he'd turned his aim toward me and pressed off a few more arrows, but in the darkness, he missed.

With my lycanthropic sight, nothing was hidden from me. I watched as he groped toward the pantry door, looking for a light switch. His hand felt around the outlet, but narrowly missed it. As he moved down the wall, I retrieved the blade from my pocket. I had picked up a chef's knife, one that was too big to toss with the expectation of hitting anything. I would have to get close to this man to go in for the kill.

Another delusion swamped me before I could do anything. I lay there, willing myself not to make a sound. It was hard because I was immersed in a new fragment, one that served only to confuse me.

I imagined Blackburn as being Gibson—handsome, intense, and caring. Try as I might, I couldn't release the picture, and I couldn't figure out why I would want to kill the very person who wanted to help me.

The figure turned toward me again with a snarl on his lips. In my demented state, he abruptly transformed into a black wolf whose golden eyes could pierce the dark. He glared at me.

A small shake of my head and I came back to myself. Blackburn was just a few steps from my hiding place, but he suddenly turned his back on me. I crawled toward him, and transferring my gaze to the floor, I noticed his shoestring again. Instead of staring at it like an idiot, though, it actually helped me to keep my thought patterns logical.

He was unaware that I was right beside him. With a huge effort to control the wolf, I roared, and balancing my weight just right, I plunged the knife into the man's thigh until it was buried to the hilt. Blood spurted over me like rain and, abruptly lost again to my lycanthropic delusions, I savagely twisted the blade.

He went down with a scream. He dropped the auto bow, but managed to hold onto the gun. I jumped on him and wrestled for the weapon, punching my weight against his battered thigh. It was enough to make him release the revolver. Just as he did, the lights came on and LaRue barked at me.

Ward cops fanned out to surround us. Blackburn put up a pitiful fight at this point, and at that very minute, I experienced the floating feeling that marks a deeper collapse into moon madness. I paused to cast off the dizziness and try to deny the toll it would take on my ability to think straight. As I did, I caught the expression on the killer's face. He stared up at me with such abject terror that I was sure he could see the true, supernatural nature of the beast who had just defeated him.

65

GIBSON ENTERED THE crime scene to take me back to his apartment after LaRue pulled me away from Blackburn. I kept tripping in and out, but I was so emotionally spent from trying to control the full moon stretch that for the rest of the evening I was disoriented and lethargic. I remember Gibson undressing me and then drawing a hot bath to rinse off the killer's blood. He tended to me in silence, spending time to shampoo my hair and massage my scalp, and in the process, making me realize that I had a clinker of a headache.

As dawn approached, I felt myself beginning to shrink back toward normality. My mind settled into its usual troubled thoughts, my bones cracked and popped and were left to ache, my vision turned blurry, and my hearing turned softer. My very being seemed to deflate as if my soul was depressurizing.

I fell into a deep, comfortable sleep once the bath was done. It was the next evening when I woke up in Gibson's apartment laboratory. He was sitting at the table sharing a bottle of homemade ale with LaRue. My partner was going on about the old Russian aristocracy and how he had once been lucky enough to see an actual diamond-encrusted Fabergé egg. The doctor was nodding politely, but his expression was glazed, so I did what I could do to get LaRue to shut up by stretching and yawning. The simple movement was enough to interrupt his one-sided conversation and he greeted me with a curt toss to his chin. Gibson squinted at me.

"Thirsty?" he asked.

I nodded and lay there in the bed like a queen while he

fetched me a mug of water. I polished off this tiny oasis and begged for more.

"You had a busy full moon," LaRue said. "And you're damned lucky you didn't get killed. Again." He took a swig of beer. "I told the good doctor, here, to lock you up next time. I suppose you forgot to tell him it was necessary in the first place, huh?"

I drank the rest of the water before answering. "I could have sworn I'd mentioned that."

Gibson grunted and reached for the empty cup. I swung my legs over the side of the bed, experiencing the familiar, gelatinous feeling as my body firmed into its old shape. The doctor steadied me by the elbow. "What happened with the collar, Andy?"

He took a tug from his bottle again and shook his head, catching dribbles of beer with the back of his hand. "Like we expected it would, Ty. Someone got to Jessica. They don't want information to get out about the problems in District Twenty-one. She won't press charges against Blackburn and we're to forget we ever heard of the plague."

"St. Ophelia hates us," I said. "Did they discount the arrest?"

"Yes, on the public record. Jack and Emily were released this morning, Jessica got all the old man's money, and the family units of those killed were given duty bonuses and letters of condolences. You and me? No financial remuneration of any kind."

"Not even any incentive credits?"

"Nothing. The watch commander did shake my hand, though."

"And Blackburn? What happened to him?"

"Ronald Orson Blackburn is listed in critical condition at a maximum security hospital after undergoing surgery to finish cutting off the leg you started to amputate last evening."

My stomach jackknifed and pushed its way up my esophagus. "Am I in big trouble with internal affairs?"

"No. Thanks to Gibson."

I turned my attention on him. "What did you do?"

"Called in some markers and pulled some strings. You owe me. Big time."

LaRue saved me from asking what the hell was going on. "You've been officially remanded to the specific care of Dr. Gibson for a period of two years," he said. "He's also supposed to oversee a program of psychiatric counseling and make regular reports on your progress."

I glanced at Gibson again. "I don't understand. I was just doing my job, however bloody it got."

He stared at me with a serious expression on his face. "The government got into it, Merrick. Counsel for the defendant wanted you locked away in a mental institution. Probably the same one where Blackburn will eventually go when they get around to pulling him out of society. They're serious about this plague information remaining a secret and they were afraid you wouldn't be stable enough to keep it as such. I could only do so much to make a deal."

I turned back to LaRue. "Is that true?"

He wouldn't return my gaze. Instead, he focused on the table. "Yes. You can even keep your class designation and your job if you play the game."

"That bad, huh?"

"You really bloodied the guy up, Ty. He almost died and he may still. Not that he shouldn't go down on this one mind you." Taking another sip, he added. "There's more."

Of course there was more. There always was when we were talking about the trouble my lycanthropy caused. "What, then?"

"Remember, Virgil Cree, the guy who was supposed to lay on his good luck for your tax break?"

I thought of the dollop of warm spit in the middle of my forehead. "Who could forget? What's with him?"

"His spell worked."

"What? How?"

"Your filing requirements now fall under an official PHO medical exemption status because of Gibson's influence."

"So, what's my tax break?" I asked.

LaRue smiled. "Henderson has been replaced."